THE TENTH VOTE

A STEIN & ASSOCIATES THRILLER

MARIAN K. RIEDY

WITH KIM SPERDUTO

Black Rose Writing | Texas

This is a work of fiction. Names, characters, businesses, places, events, and incidents are either the products of the author's imagination or used in a fictitious manner. Any resemblance to actual persons, living or dead, or actual events is purely coincidental.

ISBN: 978-1-68513-574-4
LIBRARY OF CONGRESS CONTROL NUMBER: 2024946548
PUBLISHED BY BLACK ROSE WRITING
www.blackrosewriting.com

Printed in the United States of America
Suggested Retail Price (SRP) $21.95

The Tenth Vote is printed in Sabon LT

*As a planet-friendly publisher, Black Rose Writing does its best to eliminate unnecessary waste to reduce paper usage and energy costs, while never compromising the reading experience. As a result, the final word count vs. page count may not meet common expectations.

PRAISE FOR
THE TENTH VOTE

"In *The Tenth Vote*, the intrepid lawyers at Stein & Associates throw away their law books and engage in a fast-paced battle of wits and nerves with hackers, blackmailers, and killers, with lives, fortunes, and the integrity of the Supreme Court on the line."
–Allen Rothman, Lawyer, Austin, TX

"*The Tenth Vote* is a highly original legal thriller featuring fascinating characters and creative plot twists from start to finish. In a page-turning race against time, the story takes the reader into the inner workings of one of our nation's most closely guarded institutions under attack from within and without."
–Dan Schorr, author of *Final Table*, National Indie Excellence Awards Winner for Literary Fiction

"*The Tenth Vote* pulls back the curtain for a peek at secret intrigues within the Supreme Court and the very real perils of being a Justice. The amateur sleuths who come to the rescue are regular attorneys who go far outside their comfort zone, risking their careers if not their lives. You'll love the unexpected twist at the end."
–Nan Shuker, Retired Judge, D.C. Superior Court

"*The Tenth Vote* rejects the simple "good guy, bad guy" approach and instead paints a picture of crime in real life, with an ever-expanding network of sleuths and suspects and blurred boundaries between the two. With twists until the last line, this legal thriller is realistic fiction at its finest."
–Susan Reslewic Keatley, Ph.D., Writer, Author, Scientist

To friends, without whom life would be a thin gruel, indeed.

Special thanks to Nan Shuker, retired D.C. Superior Court judge, for instructing us on the finer points of legal ethics; Christina Rebarchek for the cover design; and our families, for putting up with us.

THE TENTH VOTE

CHAPTER 1

Wednesday, Sept. 6, 8:15 p.m., Metropolitan Hospital
A distant siren wailed. Inside, only the ticking of the institutional black clock on the wall interrupted the silence.

The door from the waiting area outside swung open. A skinny young man in navy blue scrubs with a markedly pallid face stepped into the MRI procedure suite. He stopped at the entrance, scanning the room.

A glass booth the size of a minivan sat adjacent to the right wall. The door to the booth, the control center, hung open. Inside, two unoccupied swivel chairs faced a counter loaded with blinking computer terminals.

On the far wall, a line of closed doors hid the changing rooms. The space between the changing rooms and the control center stood empty, save for a hospital bed strewn with crumpled, dirty linens.

The siren blared, closer now.

One of the changing room doors opened. A woman in a wheelchair emerged, clad in a paper-thin, lime-green gown and paper booties.

The woman appeared to be in late middle age. The fluorescent lights in the ceiling deepened the laugh lines bracketing her full lips. Gray streaked her black hair, pulled into a ponytail hanging over the back seat of the wheelchair.

The shapeless gown hid the woman's torso, but her broad shoulders and upright posture reflected an athletic past. The still hands on the arms of her wheelchair were strong and heavily veined.

The woman wheeled herself across the room to the control center and peered inside. Sighing, she swiveled her chair to face the flat-screen TV sitting on a console against the wall.

A talking head from a news channel chattered soundlessly on the muted device. His captioned report floated across the bottom of the screen.

This morning, the Administration announced an expansion of the country's exclusive economic zone off the coast of Alaska based on revised measurements of the Outer Continental Shelf. The controversial move is expected to draw protests from other countries, including Russia and China, as the nations of the world jockey for access to the trillions of dollars of oil, gas, and rare earth metals under the Artic Sea. For more on this story, I'll turn now to a spokesman from....

The woman reached for the monitor lying beside the TV just as the man in blue scrubs appeared beside her wheelchair.

"Mrs. Gillman? Brenda? I'm your technologist. Last procedure of the day, thankfully. All set?"

The woman hesitated, then, nodding, dropped her outstretched hand.

"Let's roll," the tech said, moving behind her to grab the wheelchair handles.

She disengaged the brakes, a slight frown creasing her forehead.

The technician wheeled her around and hit the automatic door opener with his elbow. The doors to the procedure room swung open. The MRI magnets hummed faintly from within.

The tech ran through his prep. He helped her onto the sheeted table.

"Would you like to listen to music?" he asked, holding up a set of headphones.

"Yes, please. Classical."

She adjusted the headphones. Flat, tinny orchestral music sounded faintly in her ears.

The tech handed her the cord with the call button.

"Press this if you need anything," he instructed.

The tech engaged the mechanism at the foot of the table. With a decided clunk, the table rolled backward, sending the patient, headfirst, into the brightly lit interior of the scanner. Her view of the room telescoped into a flat half-moon rising over her green booties.

"The first scan will start now," the tech's voice sounded in her ears, "and will last ten minutes."

The familiar auditory extravaganza began, an irregular metallic tapping accompanied by the rhythmic chant of the spinning magnets, "bop, bop, bop, bop," like a robotic heart beating madly.

She breathed in deeply. As she exhaled, the tube went dark. With a click, as though a switch had been thrown, the music in her headphones stopped, although the otherworldly symphony of the MRI machine played on.

She pressed the call button. No response. She tried again.

"Hey," she called.

No answer.

The room beyond her booties disappeared into impenetrable gloom.

Her chest constricted. A scream bubbled in her throat.

She placed a hand on either side of the tube. She could not extend her arms far enough to get much purchase, but she flexed her biceps and pushed, straining against the dead weight of her useless legs.

She moved. Barely.

She paused, panting.

She raised her fists and pounded against the unforgiving walls penning her in.

The pale technician, slumped against the door outside the procedure room, straightened. He walked to the control center, his ghostly image reflected in the glass. Tilting his head, he looked into the unblinking eye of the CCTV camera mounted above him and nodded.

CHAPTER 2

Thursday, Sept. 7, 8:00 a.m., The Office

Miranda stepped out of the elevator to their fourth-floor office suite. She paused before entering. Black block letters, eight inches high, etched on the glass doors to the suite, announced its occupants: Aaron Stein & Associates, Attorneys at Law.

She had almost forgotten. Today was the fifth anniversary of Miranda's first day at the firm.

She smiled, remembering her clammy hands and roiling stomach the first time she walked in this door.

It all started with the phone call, catching her just before she left the office for the day.

"Miranda," she had warmed at the sound of Marlon's voice.

A graduate of her law school, Marlon White taught Miranda's trial advocacy class as adjunct faculty. He told her she had great promise as a trial attorney.

Miranda dreamed of being in front of a jury. The job market for new lawyers was tight when she graduated law school, though. She was lucky to find a job at all. Still, practicing commercial insurance defense in the D.C. branch of an Omaha-based firm was as far from a courtroom as she could get.

"Free for a drink after work?" Marlon had asked.

"Sure, love to," Miranda answered.

They met at a dive in Adams Morgan. The place reeked of stale grease and beer, but Marlon swore the bartender served the best martinis in town.

"You're looking good," Miranda said after they had air-kissed and sat at a rickety wooden table.

Marlon, whose idea of exercise was playing the piano, tended to fluctuate in weight. Slim-boned, of average height, Marlon's extra pounds showed. This evening, he was on the light end of his spectrum, and he did look spiffy, the light gray suit he was wearing complementing his dark eyes and hair.

Marlon preened, pulling open his suit coat with one hand to pat his flat tummy with the other. Then, he sobered.

"Aaron fired a senior associate this morning," he said. "Told him to pack his things and leave, on the spot."

"Wow. I feel bad for the guy."

"Yeah, well, he was kind of a jerk. I won't exactly miss him. But, anyway, the point is, he's left a ton of work to do and not enough of us to do it. We could really use you on board."

"Me?" Miranda spluttered through a mouthful of her drink.

She could not have been more surprised if Marlon had asked her to marry him. Which he would never dream of doing. She was the wrong sex. Besides, Marlon was besotted with his husband.

"Yeah, you. Right now, in fact. Like, tomorrow."

"But it's … it's…." Miranda stuttered.

"It's time for you to make a move is what it is. Look," Marlon reached over to pat her hand, "you're not exactly a risk taker. I get that, and I understand why. But you don't exactly love your job, do you?"

"Ha. That's an understatement. Every day is the same. I read through a mountain of boring documents, all pretty much identical, and figure out how we can deny coverage."

"If you don't make the change soon, it's going to be too late."

"I know, but I'm not sure this is right for me. Aaron's a tough boss. You've made that very clear. Plus, you guys are such a tight bunch."

"You'll be great, and you'll fit right in with the other guys. Promise. Think about it, anyway. I'll call you in the morning. The answer should be 'yes,' I'm telling you."

Miranda had tossed and turned all night.

Marlon's firm, Aaron Stein & Associates, practiced medical malpractice law. Many looked down on med mal lawyers as "ambulance chasers." Even insurance defense was higher up the food chain.

But Aaron's firm did not chase anybody. People came to them. Real people, with real problems Aaron helped fix. Miranda could say goodbye to her lonely office and the piles of exclusion clauses she read and reread every day.

Best of all, Miranda would be in a courtroom trying cases.

What could get better than that?

But was she good enough?

She took the leap and, happily, never looked back.

Miranda's attention was caught by movement inside the suite. The firm's receptionist, Beebe, appeared from the corridor leading off the foyer to the attorneys' offices.

Miranda shouldered open the heavy glass door. She greeted Beebe, who had taken her station behind the desk, just as Cassandra Robins emerged from the small conference room across from the reception desk. Cassandra's cherubic face, normally accompanied by a wide, cheerful smile, was stony.

"What's wrong?" Miranda stopped and asked her senior colleague. Marlon had been Aaron's first associate, hired right out of law school. Cassandra came next.

"Nothing, sugar," Cassandra answered, managing a tight smile. "Nothing really." She motioned for Miranda to follow her a few steps away from the conference room. "This Bolkonsky case is a bear, is all," Cassandra whispered.

Miranda glanced over Cassandra's shoulder and through the opened conference room door. Sonya Bolkonsky sat at the far side of the room, facing Miranda.

Although Sonya was seated, Miranda could tell she was a tall woman, buxom under her well-fitted, sage-colored jacket. Platinum blonde hair framing ice-blue eyes, an aquiline nose, and prominent cheekbones fell smoothly to her shoulders.

"We're in final prep for her deposition," Cassandra continued. "It's this afternoon."

"Ugh," Miranda responded, "I hate doing the client's depo. You win or you lose depending on how it goes. The other side is firing all guns, trying to show the client's a liar or a jerk. Or both. Meanwhile, all you can do is keep your mouth shut and pray the client remembers her prep."

"I know," Cassandra said, "not my favorite thing, either. A necessary evil, though."

"And you know what you're doing," Miranda replied, patting Cassandra's shoulder.

Cassandra nodded. "Yeah, I do. Sonya's not used to being told what to do, though. She's a tough one."

It was all tough for Cassandra. Not because she lacked the skills. Far from it.

Cassandra had gone to law school when it was still exceptional to see a black person, let alone a black woman. Cassandra still had to be twice as good as everybody else to pass muster, because somebody in the room, sometimes everybody in the room, assumed she was less than she was.

"It's Joe taking the depo, right?" Miranda asked.

Cassandra nodded.

"Don't worry, then. He'll be distracted by Sonya's boobs."

Cassandra hooted.

"Good luck," Miranda said, giving a little wave. She turned and headed down the corridor past the associates' offices.

Nobody else in yet? But then Miranda heard the unmistakable sounds of a ping-pong game in progress.

Miranda walked into the fluorescent-lit, office breakroom containing a full kitchen and, crammed into a corner, a ping-pong table. Marlon and their newest associate, Betsy Thornhill, whacked a ball back and forth.

They stopped when Miranda walked in.

"Hi, Miranda," Betsy called. "In early. Busy day?"

"Not really," Miranda answered. "In fact, I'm light for a week or so, which is great because Chad's birthday...."

"Miranda, call for you, line 7," Beebe's voice called over the office intercom. "It's from Metropolitan Hospital. The general counsel's office."

Miranda frowned. She looked at Marlon.

"We don't have any cases pending against Metropolitan, do we?" Miranda asked. "Why are they calling me?"

Marlon shrugged. "I assume they'll tell you."

A few minutes later, Miranda stood on the pavement outside their office building, waiting for her Uber driver. Counsel to the hospital wanted to talk to Miranda about Brenda— immediately, if possible. Brenda was fine, but she had been admitted the night before after an incident with an MRI procedure.

Miranda stared at her phone screen, mindlessly watching the cab icon turn onto 17th Street.

An incident? An MRI was a routine, noninvasive diagnostic test. Brenda had undergone a dozen of them, at least. What could have gone wrong?

CHAPTER 3

Thursday, Sept. 7, 8:15 a.m., The Office

"Who's Brenda," Betsy asked Marlon after Miranda charged out of the kitchen, "and what do you think happened at Metropolitan?"

"She was a client. Reaction to the contrast, probably."

Betsy looked at him blankly.

Betsy had fit in so smoothly that Marlon kept forgetting she was new to the firm. Her inexperience with med mal explained why she was not familiar with the basic medicine, bread-and-butter to Marlon.

"Actually, it could have been anything," he continued. "Stick around awhile. You'll see. Mix stubborn and irrational human beings with the complexities of modern medicine and, voilà, a recipe for disaster."

Marlon grabbed his paddle off the table. He ran his thumb down the soft groove worn into the paddle's wooden handle. "Finish the game?"

"Absolutely."

Marlon put a wicked spin on his serve. It bounced beyond Betsy's reach.

"Pitiful," Marlon taunted.

Betsy grinned. "We'll see who's pitiful."

Betsy won the next two points.

Marlon, frustrated, cursed under his breath. On another level, he was delighted. He finally had a worthy opponent in the office.

Marlon managed to win the game, to his relief. Betsy congratulated him.

"Next one's mine though," she teased.

Marlon snorted. "Dream on."

Marlon walked into the kitchen area and poured himself a cup of coffee. "Want one?" he asked, brandishing the pot.

Betsy wrinkled her nose. "The coffee's awful. So's the ping-pong table. What's with that?"

"The table was abandoned by previous tenants of the suite. Aaron never throws anything away. Enjoy it now. When it finally collapses, it won't be replaced. And the coffee," Marlon paused to take a sip, "is bad because it's cheap."

Betsy laughed. "By the way. I'm curious. What was Brenda's case about?"

"A car accident. We don't do many of those. But Brenda Gillman was famous. Is famous, I suppose. Aaron figured it would be good publicity for the firm to take her case. You haven't heard of her?"

Betsy shook her head.

"Brenda blazed out of Columbia University's journalism school like a comet. Landed an assignment with the Times of London right off the bat. She worked all over the world before settling in Russia. She rose to the top of the heap of foreign correspondents there. A celebrity journalist, really."

Betsy looked at him, an eyebrow cocked.

"You don't sound like you're exactly a fan of hers, though."

"Well…."

What did he think about Brenda? He did not suppose he had given it all that much thought, but something about Brenda rubbed him the wrong way.

"Oh, she's talented," he said, still trying to clarify his thoughts. "Successful. She's got guts, too, running around the world by herself, interviewing drug lords and mercenaries. But I think it's all more about Brenda than about the story."

"I don't suppose that's uncommon. Not only among journalists, either."

"No, of course not. We all look out for ourselves first. Brenda thinks she's better than that, though. Acts like it, anyway. I don't know, a saint in journalist's clothes, or something."

"Hmmm, well. Was it a bad accident?"

"Yes and no. Brenda was rear-ended. A minor collision, but her seat failed, collapsing backward. Brenda broke her neck."

Betsy shuddered. "How awful. Brenda survived, obviously, but in what shape?"

"She's a paraplegic. What they call 'high functioning.' Brenda can't walk and is in a wheelchair. She has full use of her shoulders, chest, and arms, though, thank goodness. She can drive and care for herself. She lives on her own."

"If the seat failed, you sued the car manufacturer, I presume."

"Yep. The first product liability case we ever took, and the last, Aaron decided. We're sticking with med mal. The doctors' lawyers fight hard, but the Gillman case was an all-out brawl. Think mixed martial arts."

"And I take it Miranda was lead attorney, since Metropolitan called her."

"Right. Miranda was technically second chair to Aaron, but she did all the work. Miranda poured her heart and soul into that case. She really cared about Brenda. Still does."

"Huh, that kind of surprises me. Miranda seems, well, maybe prickly's the right word?"

"Oh, nah, she's, well, heart of gold and all that."

"Okay, then."

"But you're right in a way. Miranda's an only child and fits the stereotype. Independent, stubbornly self-sufficient. But she was raised by a single mom. Miranda's father left when she was just a baby. So she's defensive and insecure in a lot of ways, too."

"I can empathize with that. The single parent, anyway."

"Don't worry. Miranda likes you just fine. She'll show it eventually."

That brought a smile.

"How'd the case turn out?" Betsy asked. "Brenda's, that is."

"Oh, it was a great outcome. The case was settled with the manufacturer paying a decent amount of money. A lot goes into Brenda's medical expenses, though. She'd have a lot more money if she'd been able to keep working."

"Well, thanks for sharing. Enjoy your cheap coffee."

Betsy turned and walked into the corridor, almost colliding with Jim, who was carrying two bankers' boxes stacked atop one another. Jim stopped abruptly to avoid running into Betsy. The top box slid sideways, threatening to topple onto the floor.

"Oops, sorry," Betsy said, grabbing to steady the errant box.

"No prob," Jim said. He hefted his load, shoulder muscles flexing under his T-shirt, and juggled the top box back into place.

"Wow, impressive," Betsy whistled. "I can barely manage one of those, and I'm no wimp."

"A runner, right?" Jim asked, eyeing Betsy's tall, wiry frame.

"Yep."

Jim snorted. "I'd look ridiculous with a runner's body. Like a...."

"Blonde, blue-eyed, six-foot-four-inch giraffe?" Marlon proposed.

Betsy chuckled.

"Exactly," Jim responded. "I'm going for another look. Let's call it...."

"The Hulk?" Marlon interrupted.

"Mr. America?" Betsy suggested.

Jim waggled his shoulders and fluttered his eyelashes. "Mr. Gay America, maybe," he crooned in a spot-on falsetto.

Betsy grinned. "Say," she cocked an eyebrow, "you've got the muscles for it, but why are you carting boxes, Jim? I thought you did the scheduling around here."

"I do," Jim answered, "plus what everyone else ignores, like cleaning up the file room. It's a mess in there. Takes forever to find anything."

"Well, thanks for all you do," Betsy said, smiling. Turning, she started down the corridor toward her office.

"Let me get rid of these, and I'll join you for coffee," Jim said.

Marlon was about to protest. He had almost finished his cup and should get to work.

Or not. Miranda had said her schedule was light and, unusually, Marlon's was, too. He had cleared the deck to prepare a big case for trial. The case was settled the Friday before, and his calendar had not yet filled with other matters.

Jim strode into the kitchen and poured himself a cup of coffee. Marlon refilled his, even though the pot already smelled more like sludge than coffee.

"I like Betsy," Jim said, taking a seat at the table. "And you didn't think she'd work out, did you?"

"I like her too," Marlon replied. "A lot, actually. But, no, I didn't. Did you know she's Ivy-league law and an MIT grad?"

Jim shook his head. "No. Why would I? Betsy doesn't go around boasting about her credentials. She's not that type."

"No, she doesn't, and I thought she would. Be a *prima donna,* that is. Turn up her nose at the grunt work and suck up to the boss, like the new associates do at the big firms to get a partner's attention."

"In which case, you guys would have frozen her out."

"Totally. But none of that happened. She's new at this, but she works hard and she's doing great work. Aaron barked at her, for no good reason, just like he does at the rest of us. We took her out for martinis and told her not to worry about it. No bite and all that."

"Hah, a martini drinker, too. She's in like Flynn. Speaking of new to this, why'd she come here, anyway? Why not one of the brand-name, corporate firms?"

"I asked her. She tried that first. She said it bored her, and she doesn't do bored."

Jim cackled. "My kind of girl."

Jim looked down at his cup of coffee and grimaced. "Enough of that."

A few minutes later, Marlon walked past the open door to Betsy's office. Betsy sat behind her desk with her phone in her hand. She looked up and caught his eye.

"Robert's back in town," she reported.

"Good. We'll have our bridge game tonight, then."

Marlon would not be socializing with Supreme Court Justice Robert Wells except that Wells was Betsy's godfather. The relationship between the two was far more than the title implied. Justice Wells essentially raised Betsy after her parents were sent to jail for life after a political protest gone wrong. A man had been killed.

Betsy nodded, but a frown creased her face.

"Robert traveled alone again," she said. "I worry about him. He always refuses a security detail."

"I thought that was common," Marlon responded. "That is, as powerful as the justices are, nobody pays them much attention. Except, of course, when they decide a big, controversial case. But there's nothing like that on the docket, is there?"

"No," Betsy conceded, "and you're right. I always worry, anyway. The justices usually fly under the radar. But think about it. That means there is a radar. Someone's always watching."

CHAPTER 4

Thursday, Sept. 7, 8:30 a.m., Metropolitan Hospital
Miranda got directions at the information desk, then took the elevator to the fourth floor. She walked into Brenda's room and stared at her friend.

Brenda lay motionless, all but her gowned shoulders covered by a sheet.

"Brenda?" Miranda whispered.

No response.

Except that she was paler than normal, Brenda looked like she always did. No sign of any physical injury, at least.

Miranda unbuttoned her jacket as the oppressive heat of the room caught up with her, as did the usual pungent hospital smell of antiseptic over a faint stench of urine.

Undecided whether to stay or go without knowing Brenda's status, Miranda was relieved when a woman in scrubs slipped in behind her.

"Good morning, Debbie," Miranda said, eyeing the woman's nametag. "I'm a friend of the patient. You must be her nurse."

Debbie, smiling, nodded.

"How's she doing?"

"Fine. She's sleeping off a mild sedative. She should be wake shortly."

"Thanks. I'll come see her again later."

Miranda returned to the first floor and headed toward the administrative suites. As she strode down the brightly lit corridor, she noticed, not for the first time, that the staff pictures garnishing the walls were almost all white men. A handful of darker faces and the occasional female signified welcome cracks in the glass ceiling.

She entered the office of the general counsel. At the receptionist's desk, Miranda announced her name. The woman behind the counter did not look up from her computer.

"I'm here to see one of the attorneys. A secretary called and asked me to come in. It's about Brenda Gillman."

That got the lady's attention.

"Oh, I'll check the schedule to see who you're meeting. But please have a seat while you wait. Can I get you anything?"

Miranda almost laughed. A med mal lawyer visiting hospital administration never received such a warm reception.

The receptionist made a call.

"Ms. Poller?" she said into the receiver. "Miranda Patel is here."

Ah, now Miranda understood.

Gretchen Poller was the assistant general counsel, second in command. Gretchen and Miranda went back a long way. Before Gretchen took a position at the hospital, she worked for a defense firm. Gretchen and Miranda had an amicable, if technically adversarial working relationship.

The gracious welcome, the choice of Gretchen to deliver the news. The hospital was buttering Miranda up, hoping to avoid a lawsuit.

Why would they be worried? Brenda looked fine, but was she?

Miranda's stomach clenched.

"Miranda," Gretchen bustled out from behind the reception desk, a faint whiff of citrusy perfume accompanying her. Petite, grey-haired, Gretchen was well turned out in a dark pants suit.

As she stood to greet Gretchen, Miranda glanced at herself in the mirrored column beside the chair she had vacated. The short, pencil skirt of her suit showcased the tanned length of her legs, and the pink cotton blouse peeking out from her jacket complemented Miranda's olive complexion, curly dark hair, and deep brown eyes.

Luckily, she had opted for more than business casual today. She looked as much like the confident professional as Gretchen did.

Gretchen grabbed Miranda's hand and shook it. "Good to see you again. Thanks for agreeing to meet on such short notice. Come on back."

"What happened?" Miranda fired off as soon as the women had taken seats across from each other at Gretchen's desk.

"Nothing, really," Gretchen soothed, "but Brenda was terribly upset."

"That doesn't make sense. Brenda doesn't get upset for no reason."

"Well, she did this time."

Miranda felt a spark of anger. Of course, that's what the hospital would say.

"Just the facts, please."

"Brenda was in for a routine MRI. She was in the scanner for," Gretchen glanced down at the yellow legal pad lying on her desk, "seven minutes. She activated the emergency call button. The tech stopped the magnets immediately and had Brenda out within seconds. Brenda was extremely agitated."

Seven minutes? Miranda had an MRI once and didn't much care for the experience. Still, it had not been all that bad, and Miranda had been in the tube for forty-five minutes.

On a reporting junket in Colombia, Brenda spent forty-eight hours alone in an unlit, underground bunker while two drug lords waged war overhead.

There was a mistake here.

"That's what the tech said? Brenda was in the scanner for only seven minutes? He, or she, could have been wrong on the time, I suppose."

"Not possible. The time is recorded automatically. And the tech was a male."

"Could there have been a technical glitch?" Miranda responded. "With the recording? An electrical failure, maybe?"

"No, nothing was amiss. We have backup generators, anyway."

"Something else must have alarmed Brenda. You don't suppose she could have had, well, a stroke or something while she was in there?"

Gretchen shook her head. "The tech called the hospitalist, who examined Brenda and found nothing wrong, except for her injured hands. Trying to get out, she told the doctor. Brenda was taken for x-rays. Nothing broken, luckily, but she was kept overnight for observation."

Miranda stared at Gretchen, trying to figure this out. Nothing out of the ordinary in the procedure, except Brenda freaked out for some reason. Other than that, Brenda was unhurt. So why….

"Why are you here?" Gretchen asked, as if reading Miranda's thoughts. "Because Brenda kept yelling that we'd screwed up big time and somebody was going to pay. You should calm her down, Miranda, because that did not happen."

Miranda retraced her steps back to the fourth floor, dreading the conversation with Brenda she was about to have.

"That's total crap," Brenda said through gritted teeth after Miranda replayed what Gretchen had said. "I was in there over an hour. They abandoned me, alone, in the pitch dark, deafened by a hell's chorus of banging magnets."

Miranda took a deep breath. "I'm sorry you were so scared. But you're just wrong on the time. It's all computerized, Brenda."

"Computers can…."

Brenda's mouth fell open. Then, she closed her eyes and brought a bandaged hand to her face.

"What is it?" Miranda asked, reaching over to touch Brenda's shoulder.

"I … I don't know. I'm not sure, but it's possible." Brenda laughed shakily. "You wouldn't believe me if I told you. I'm not sure I believe it myself. Take me home, Miranda. I need time to think."

CHAPTER 5

Thursday, Sept. 7, 11:30 a.m., The Office
Marlon walked out of the copy room, pausing at the unexpected sound of somebody playing darts.

Miranda was meeting with an expert witness uptown. Marlon had just seen Betsy in her office and Cassandra working with Sonya in the conference room. Beebe was far too dignified to play a pub game.

"Who's there?" Marlon called.

"It's me," Marlon heard the response coming from inside the kitchen.

Ronnie stepped into the corridor, snapping a mock salute.

"What in the world are you doing here? And why are you all dolled up?"

Ronnie habitually wore black jeans and a kelly-green polo shirt matching his eyes. With his curly auburn hair, button nose, and round cheeks, Ronnie looked like a mischievous leprechaun, if a middle-aged one. This morning, he wore a sober suit and tie.

"Hello to you, too," Ronnie said. "I'm working."

Marlon felt a grin creeping across his face. "For real?"

Ronnie nodded. He opened wide his arms, and Marlon stepped in for the hug.

Ronnie Sloan had single-handedly dragged them both out of the closet during their senior year of college. Their friendship had only strengthened with time. Still, it was a friendship only. Ronnie and he had, perhaps thankfully, never been attracted to each other.

Ronnie secured a plumb spot at one of the highest circulation newspapers in the United States right out of college. A brilliant journalist, he nonetheless descended the career ladder, one rung at a time, falling victim to his temper and the bottle.

Marlon lectured and cajoled but made no headway. Instead, he was relegated to pulling Ronnie out of brawls and driving him from the police booking station directly to a rehab center. More than once.

Had the tide miraculously turned?

A few minutes later, Marlon and Ronnie sat across from each other at the break room table. Marlon offered Ronnie coffee. Ronnie declined.

"Your coffee is undrinkable," Ronnie complained.

"I know, I know," Marlon said, nodding. "But tell me all about it. What's up?"

"You're going to the opera thing tomorrow night, right?"

It was a rhetorical question. Ronnie knew that Marlon, as a new member of the patron's circle, as the principal fundraising arm of the opera was called, could not be anywhere else but at the opera gala.

"Why do you ask?"

"Is it too late to get me in as your guest?"

"Not if I buy you a ticket, which I would, but since when do you have any interest in opera?"

"I have none. But there's someone I want to meet who will be there."

"Who?"

"What's with the third degree?" Ronnie asked, voice rising. "It's a simple favor. I'll pay for my own ticket."

Marlon said nothing, studying his old friend.

Marlon would do anything he could to help Ronnie turn his career around. For Ronnie to attend the gala, though, sounded like a bad idea. The guests at this event had donated a chunk of change to the opera. In appreciation, the food would be good, and the champagne would flow.

Marlon hated to admit it, even to himself, but he knew there was another reason for his reluctance. Every member of the patron's circle would attend, as well as a handful of opera stars and assorted city luminaries. Marlon did not want to be embarrassed in front of them.

Ronnie sighed. "I'll be a good boy, Marlon. I told you, I'm working."

Ronnie stood and retrieved a dart he had left lying on the table. He flung it toward the board on the wall.

"Bullseye," Ronnie crowed. "Let's see you do that, sucker!"

Marlon grinned. "Okay, okay, but only if you tell me about this person you want to meet."

"Igor Petrov's his name. I've been trying to talk to him for months. He's cagey, though. He won't say 'no' outright, but he keeps putting me off."

"Igor Petrov," Marlon responded. "Sounds Russian. Not like your usual sources with names like Bambino and Scarfo."

Ronnie had been a finalist for the Pulitzer Prize for his series on the Philadelphia mafia. He had been nominated twice for his stories on corruption in city government. Russia seemed outside Ronnie's reportorial bailiwick.

"Sort of. Petrov is an American of Russian descent. He's one of those Washington operatives. He has the ear of every Congressman in town, but nobody's sure how. Maybe because he knows everybody who counts in Moscow, too. Anyway, the word on the street is he might be CIA, or a double agent."

"When did you start tailing spooks?"

"A couple of years ago," Ronnie answered. "I was looking outside my regular turf for new ideas. I need a headline, you know."

Marlon nodded. He knew only too well.

"Anyway, I started poking into the hacking of the Democratic National Committee in 2016," Ronnie continued.

"Hasn't everything that could be written about that already been written?"

Ronnie shrugged. "Maybe not. Sources of mine, professional hackers, claim that the technical mastermind behind the DNC hacking was an American working in Russia. I have reason to believe the guy was a CIA mole."

"Wow. Talk about dangerous jobs."

"Yeah. Depending on which side gets suspicious, waterboarded in a country with no extradition treaty with the U.S. or dying from a dose of Novichok."

Marlon shuddered. "So not my cup of tea. But I'm still not seeing your headline. Didn't the press already accuse the CIA of being involved in the DNC hacking?"

"Yeah, denied by the Agency, of course, and the story died. I still have my suspicions."

If this had come from anyone else, Marlon would have chalked it off as conspiracy theory nonsense. Ronnie, though, was a hard-headed investigator. Even if under the gun, Ronnie would never go out on a limb for a story. He stuck to the truth.

"Okay, interesting," Marlon said, "but what's this Petrov guy got to do with the DNC hacking?"

"He's tied to the American, I think. Petrov may have intel on my guy."

"You really think you can get anything from a spy on a spy? Talk about blood from a turnip."

Ronnie just smiled. "I have my ways. People sworn to Omertà talked to me, you know."

"You've got a point."

"Anyway," Ronnie continued, "Petrov disappeared shortly after I discovered him. Must have been early in 2022. I lost interest for a while...."

"You went on a six-month bender," Marlon interrupted.

"Then, recently, I found him again," Ronnie continued, unperturbed. "Petrov founded a nonprofit, the Russian American Forum, to improve U.S. and Russian relations, supposedly. His website says Petrov will be attending the opera fundraiser. So he's back making the circuits among Washington's chattering class. That's you, buddy, and I'll fake being a member tomorrow night. Deal?"

They shook on it.

"Now," Ronnie stood, straightening his jacket, "let's get out of here and have a long, boozy lunch."

"Ha!" he hooted a second later. "You should have seen your face!"

Marlon flipped him the bird. "Tab's on you, jerk."

CHAPTER 6

Thursday, Sept. 7, 11:45 a.m., Ballston, Virginia

Fifteen minutes after leaving the office of the expert witness she had interviewed, Miranda squeezed her Toyota into a parking spot just past and across from Brenda's condo building.

The close-in suburb of Ballston buzzed with young professionals spilling out of the office buildings lining the streets, headed for lunch at one of the dozens of neighborhood cafes and restaurants. Miranda joined the heavy foot traffic and headed toward Brenda's.

Earlier that morning, after driving Brenda home from the hospital, Miranda promised Brenda that she would return to check on her around noon. Miranda had a meeting in Arlington, anyway, and it would be simple for her to stop by before heading back to town.

Miranda dialed the condo from the call box in the foyer. Brenda buzzed her into the building, and Miranda took the elevator to Brenda's floor.

"Coming," Brenda called at Miranda's knock.

Miranda, relieved, waited for Brenda to unlock the door. Brenda sounded back to normal. She had been brusque and uncommunicative that morning.

When they first met, Miranda asked Brenda about her plummy accent. Brenda claimed that she sounded like any run-of-the-mill Philadelphian by way of New York.

Miranda thought otherwise.

Brenda had been immersed in an international culture for decades. English was the *lingua franca* in that milieu, but an

English accented with the hues of dozens of other languages. Besides that, Brenda spoke Spanish fluently and could get by in Russian.

Brenda's polyglot life transformed her native inflections into an unidentifiable sultry tone with just a hint of aristocratic British.

Miranda knew she sounded like her mother who, like Miranda, had been born in the District of Columbia. They both spoke in flat, uninflected, plain vanilla American.

Brenda opened the door looking disheveled, the top button of her blouse undone and her hair uncombed.

"Sorry," she said, running her fingers through her hair. "Just woke up from a nap. Come on in."

Miranda followed Brenda down the short entry corridor into the living room which doubled as Brenda's office.

"I do not understand how you can work in this mess," Miranda complained, for the umpteenth time.

A massive desk against the far wall dominated the décor of the modest sized room. Atop the desk an open laptop crouched between mountains of haphazardly stacked documents. Books and magazines lapped against the legs of the desk, spilled out onto the hardwood floor from the overstuffed bookshelves flanking Brenda's workspace.

Miranda resisted the urge to straighten everything into neat piles.

Brenda laughed. "Just because you've been arranging the pencils on your desk in straight lines since kindergarten doesn't mean the rest of us think that way. What about Marlon?"

"His office is a pigpen."

"My point exactly. But he knows exactly where to find any document he needs. He's got a map in his mind. So do I."

Miranda grinned. Caught up in their light-hearted banter, she almost forgot why she was there. She reached down and grabbed a single sheet of xerox paper lying on the seat of the chair beside her.

Miranda scanned the lead of an article downloaded from an international news podcast she did not recognize.

Industry insiders confirm that on Tuesday, Gazrom Nepra, LLC, purchased a patented undersea seismic surveying technology from TRC Ventures, a Delaware company.

"Okay," Miranda said, holding up the article, "what's your map say this is?"

"It's about a land grab," Brenda answered.

"Huh?"

Brenda waved her off. "Nothing, probably. Just following up on something that caught my eye."

"Well, okay. You passed the test, anyway."

Brenda smiled crookedly. "Sit. Make yourself comfortable."

Miranda tossed the article onto the pile atop the overloaded desk and settled herself on the chair she had just cleared.

"I see you've taken the dressings off."

Brenda's hands had been swathed in giant beehives of blindingly white gauze at the hospital.

Brenda smiled. "Overkill. Those probably cost me five hundred dollars apiece, at hospital rates, anyway."

Miranda chuckled.

Brenda stretched out her hands. "Bruised, but not bloody."

"Thank goodness. Look, I've been thinking about what happened to you all morning. I think we should pursue this. I'm not talking about a lawsuit, but if the hospital screwed up, they at least owe you an apology. Besides, if it happens again, whatever it was, somebody might get hurt."

Brenda stared at her, an unreadable expression in her almond-shaped, dark-blue eyes.

"I wanted to talk to Marlon about it," Miranda continued, "but I didn't have time."

"So you do believe me," Brenda said, her voice neutral.

Miranda had wondered about that all morning, too. She was not about to tell Brenda, though.

Miranda knew full well that medical professionals made mistakes. They were human, after all. She also knew they did not like to admit their blunders. Well, nobody did, but doctors were notoriously defensive.

But where had there been room for human error in what happened last night? A computer recorded Brenda's time in the scanner.

Still, that had not been Brenda's first ride in an MRI machine. Plus, she was a tough cookie, and why would she lie?

Something did not add up.

"Of course," Miranda responded.

"I have to be sure, Miranda," Brenda continued. "You like to keep your head down and not make waves, you know."

There was some truth in what Brenda said, but not the whole truth.

"What are you talking about?" Miranda protested. "I just said we should push back on what the hospital claims."

"Oh, I know, and I appreciate that. But that's what you do. You're in your comfort zone fighting with hospitals."

Miranda, mildly offended, opened her mouth to protest.

"I'm not being critical," Brenda interrupted. "Besides, you're also good at keeping secrets. What I'm about to tell you must stay between us. I don't have enough information to point the finger yet, and I have to be sure. Damn sure."

Miranda, intrigued, sat up a little straighter.

"Do you remember, about a year ago, I told you I'd started working on something?" Brenda asked.

Miranda nodded.

She remembered the conversation well. Brenda had looked energized, purposeful, focused, in a way Miranda had never seen her before.

Miranda had embarrassed herself by asking if Brenda had gotten an assignment.

Of course, she had not. Nobody in the established press, or even from a scrappy, mom-and-pop news podcast would ever again trust material produced by Brenda.

She had been contacted by an anonymous source, Brenda had said. She was pursuing the lead, but progress was slow.

Miranda paid little attention at the time. Oh, she was thrilled that Brenda was engaged in something again, but the details seemed unimportant. The chance of Brenda publishing anything was too remote.

"And?" Miranda prompted.

"I've gotten traction, and I must have been noticed. I've come to the wrong person's attention. I think the MRI incident was a warning. Back off."

"A, a, what? A warning? You mean, you think you were trapped on purpose? But how? By whom?"

"The hospital was hacked. The timing of the scan was altered. I wasn't inside the tube seven minutes. It was over an hour, like I said, and I have a good idea who's responsible."

Miranda stared at her friend, trying to think of a response.

What Brenda proposed was not impossible. Anybody could be hacked, even the National Security Agency.

Still, it seemed a wildly improbable explanation for what happened. So why would the thought even occur to Brenda, unless hacking was otherwise on her mind?

"Oh," Miranda ventured, "does your investigation by chance have something to do with hacking?"

"Yes. A business suspects an outsider has access to confidential information. In one case, for example, the company was desperate to offload an asset only it knew was failing. A buyer shows up offering a fire sale price."

"A hacker?"

"That's what the business thinks. It calls in its data security provider to check. No evidence of a hack."

"An insider, then? Somebody inside the business is leaking info and selling it?"

Brenda shook her head. "No evidence of that either, and the company's confident in its people."

"Huh, a nice little puzzle, but why're you interested?"

"Because this happened more than once, and the suspicious transactions involved a shell company with ties to a Russian...."

Brenda stopped herself abruptly. "I've said too much."

"But wait a minute...."

Brenda cut off Miranda's protest.

"I wanted to justify your belief in me. For you to understand that I may have a tiger by the tail. But if I do ... I shouldn't have involved you at all. And stay away from the hospital, okay?"

CHAPTER 7

Thursday, Sept. 7, 12:50 p.m., Bethesda, Maryland
Miranda waited impatiently, turn light blinking, as a Mercedes SUV struggled to extricate its bulk from a parking space clearly labeled "compact cars." Her dashboard clock told her that she had ten minutes to spare, but she was still anxious about being on time.

The SUV popped free. Miranda slid into the space, less than a block from the new burger place Sully had suggested they try.

Miranda exhaled, then checked her texts, one each from Brenda and Marlon.

Thanks for stopping by. I'm good.

The jury was still out, as far as Miranda was concerned, on Brenda. That hacking was the explanation still seemed far-fetched, but something about the incident did not sit right. Brenda seemed back in control, though, so no need to worry right now.

Are you back in the office? Ronnie and I are just finishing lunch, but you could join us for dessert.

No, thanks, I'm in Bethesda, Miranda answered. *I'm lunching with Sully.*

She watched the bubbles dancing and waited for Marlon's response.

Ask Sully for his inside scoop on the 2016 DNC hacking, would you?

Marlon apparently sensed her confusion, for the bubbles danced again.

It's for Ronnie. He's working a story. More later.

Miranda shrugged. Whatever. She and Sully had other things to talk about first.

A few minutes later, Miranda spied Sully sitting at a high-top toward the rear of the restaurant, past the bar. She grinned. Sully's six-foot-four linebacker frame was hard to miss.

Sully stood as she approached and enveloped Miranda in his hug. They murmured greetings, then disengaged and sat.

"Has it been that long? I think I spot some grey," Miranda teased, knowing that one of Sully's few vanities was his thick, lustrous dark hair.

"No way," Sully responded, running his hand over his head. "Besides, that's mean. You're supposed to say how good I look."

Miranda stuck her tongue out at him and they both chuckled.

Miranda was so used to hiding her feelings for Sully that she did it by rote, even though she was long over her law school infatuation. She still thought of him as one of the handsomest men she'd ever met, though, with his high cheekbones and dark-brown eyes, up-tilted at the corners, that almost always held a smile.

"How are all your girls?" she asked, picturing Sully's lovely wife and two daughters, the girls both tall, athletic, and smart, just like their parents.

Sully ran through the latest on his family, the waiter interrupting to take their orders. Sully, in turn, asked Miranda what was going on with her, and they chatted casually while their food was served, and they ate.

"So how's work?" Miranda asked as she poured catsup over her french fries.

She did not expect a detailed answer.

Sully had never practiced law. He had taken his undergraduate degree in computer science to a position with the government. Unsaid between them was the understanding that he worked in the Central Intelligence Agency. From what he did say, Miranda knew Sully worked in cybersecurity.

"I've been seconded to the NSA," Sully responded.

Miranda raised her eyebrows. "Is that a promotion?"

"We'd call it a demotion," Sully responded, trying but failing to hide his smile. He shrugged. "They asked me in for advice on a project."

Miranda laughed. "Speaking of advice, can I pick your brain a minute?"

"Shoot."

"Okay, this is goofy, because I know what you do is way more sophisticated than this. But Aaron wants to upgrade the network security in the office. We already use one of those brands you see advertised all the time, but Aaron wants something more sophisticated. He asked me to ask you for a recommendation."

"Well, I'd be happy to help, but I'm no expert on corporate security. That's your friend's bread-and-butter, isn't it? Why not ask Chad?"

"Well," Miranda speared her last fry, "Aaron doesn't quite trust Chad yet. You know how Aaron is."

Sully raised an eyebrow. "Paranoid?"

Miranda giggled. "Totally."

Sully chuckled, then sobered.

"You know," he said, "Aaron's paranoid about everything, but he's right to be concerned about data security. It's crazy out there, I'm telling you." He shook his head. "Anyway, Firefly has a good reputation. Cerberus is big. I'll ask around the shop, too. I'll let you know what I hear."

"Thanks, Sully. I owe you one."

Sully beamed. "Great. Then you'll agree to cosponsor next year's alumni reunion with me."

Miranda groaned. "Can't say no, now, can I? Okay, tell me what I'm in for."

A few minutes later, standing on the sidewalk outside the restaurant, Miranda remembered Marlon's text.

"Have a couple more minutes?" she asked.

Sully wagged his head. "Walk me to my bike. It's around the corner. We can talk on the way."

"I know the Russians took credit for hacking the DNC in 2016, but did they really do it?"

Sully paused and raised an eyebrow, but then kept walking. "Talk about out of left field. Why are you asking?"

"Didn't you meet Marlon's friend, Ronnie Sloan, at one of Aaron's holiday parties?"

"Yeah, I remember him. The reporter. I liked the guy. He was funny and seemed a straight shooter."

"Right on both counts. Anyway, Ronnie still thinks it was the CIA. He's pursuing the story. Not that you'd tell me if he's right, but as a favor to Ronnie, I'm asking."

"His theory's wrong," Sully replied, "but Ronnie might be right to keep digging."

Miranda stopped in her tracks. "Really? Why?"

Sully had kept walking. Miranda trotted to catch up to him.

"I'm not telling you anything that's not public knowledge," Sully said over his shoulder. "Well, public if you dig hard enough."

"Okay, got it, go on."

"There was a shake-up in the Kremlin after the break-in at the DNC. One man had played a major role in recreating a Russian intelligence bureau after the Wall went down and the Soviet espionage network collapsed. This guy got booted."

"Is that an answer?"

"One explanation is that the break-in was not planned. Not by the Russians, that is. So the guy supposedly in charge had lost control. He was out."

Miranda shuddered. "Dead, I presume."

"Nah, he's alive and well. Living in Washington, D.C., actually."

"Huh, interesting," Miranda mumbled, "but I'm confused. I remember now that there was an official report from you guys. You confirmed the Russians as the hackers, didn't you?"

"The report was issued. Two separate hackers were identified, both supposedly affiliated with the Russian government. But there is a theory floating around that one of them was an independent player, with digital footprints that made them look Russian."

"Well, I'm glad for Ronnie. Maybe there is still a story out there."

"He should be careful. It's not a popular theory."

"Can you explain that?"

"No."

They had reached the bicycle stand. Sully bent down to unlock his bike, then backed it out of its stanchion.

"Finished with the first-degree, counselor?" Sully asked, smiling.

Miranda laughed, then gave Sully a hug. "Take care and say hi to the girls. Oh, and I forgot. Maybe Ronnie'd like to talk to him. What's his name? The Russian who's living in D.C.?"

"Nikolai Bolkonsky."

Before Miranda could collect her wits, Sully pedaled off. Miranda whipped out her phone and texted Marlon.

I'm headed back to the office. Tell Ronnie to stick around. I've got news for him.

CHAPTER 8

Thursday, Sept. 7, 5:30 p.m., Upper Northwest, D.C.
A line of cars parked bumper to bumper crowded the curb in front of Aunt Kitty's house. Cassandra found a place down the block and pulled in.

Peering into the rearview mirror, Cassandra fluffed her cap of salt-and-pepper curls. She grabbed her bag and the gift box with a blue ribbon tied around it and hustled out of the car.

She glanced down at her black suit. She wished she had had time to change into something more festive for Uncle Robbie's birthday party. Sonya's deposition had lasted far longer than Cassandra had expected, though, so here she was in her work clothes.

Cassandra walked up to the house and pushed open Kitty's front door, its glossy white like a cheerful summer cloud in the sky-blue color of the house.

"Your house stands out in this neighborhood like a sore thumb," Cassandra had admonished Kitty after the new paint job was completed.

Kitty had sniffed, waving away Cassandra's concerns. Cassandra supposed it was to Kitty's credit that she did not care what the neighbors thought. Her pastel house no doubt reminded Kitty of her youth in Nevis.

Cassandra squeezed her way through the hubbub in the living room to the steamy, crowded kitchen. Kitty and an assortment of female relatives were finalizing dinner preparations.

Cassandra caught the rich, smoky tomato smell of the barbecue. Her mouth watered.

Kitty bustled out of the fray around the stove. "Why you come dressed for a funeral, child?" she scolded.

Cassandra kissed Kitty's cheek. Thinner, now that Kitty had passed her eightieth birthday, but her beloved face remained unlined.

"Kitty, I invited our newest associate. I hope that's okay. You'll like her. Her name's Betsy. She's...."

"She's stirring the gravy," Kitty interrupted, pointing back over her shoulder.

Cassandra had missed her in the throng, but she now caught a glimpse of Betsy bent over the stove, chatting with the woman beside her who was polishing a crystal wine glass with a tea towel.

"You've met, I see," Cassandra said, smiling, "and already put her to work."

"Oh," Kitty waved dismissively, "Betsy and I are old friends. We both volunteer at Rachel's Kitchen."

Cassandra was not surprised that Betsy worked at a soup kitchen. It just seemed like something she would do. But Kitty?

Cassandra tutted. "You shouldn't be doing that anymore, Kitty. It's hard work. You're too...."

"Bite your tongue, girl," Kitty admonished.

Cassandra rolled her eyes but did as commanded.

Kitty turned back to oversee her kitchen.

Cassandra managed to open the refrigerator door a crack and retrieve a bottle of chardonnay. She poured herself a generous glass and steered back through the crowd.

The din had risen in the last few minutes. More guests had arrived, and those in attendance were loosening up from the day's work, getting into party mode. Cassandra smiled and waved, patted backs, and shook hands as she crossed the living room.

"Ma," she heard from behind. Cassandra turned and pulled her daughter, Mary, in for a hug. Cassandra stepped back, eyeing Mary's attire.

"Real nice," Cassandra said. "Where's my favorite son-in-law?"

Mary laughed. "Your only one, you mean. He's in Boston for a trial starting tomorrow. Remember? I told you last night."

"Oh, that's right. It slipped my mind."

Mary patted her arm. "I know, you've been busy. Anyway, he'll be back Saturday, and we'll come over with the kids."

"Sounds good," Cassandra responded. "Go say hi to everyone, sweetheart. I'll save a place for you at dinner."

Cassandra blew her daughter a kiss as Mary obediently walked off.

Cassandra spied Marlon in the solarium, sitting on the overstuffed, floral-patterned loveseat. Cassandra's cousin Linda sat across the room in the white wicker rocker.

"I think he's going to choose Morehouse," Linda was saying. "Oh, hi, Cassandra," she interrupted herself as Cassandra entered the room, lit in the fall evening by glowing table lamps.

After a few minutes of small talk, Linda excused herself to refill her glass.

Marlon patted the emptied cushion beside him. Cassandra settled into the loveseat.

"How'd Sonya's depo go?" Marlon asked. He speared an olive from his martini with the toothpick he held in his hand, popped it in his mouth, chewed, and swallowed.

Cassandra grimaced. She gulped the last of her wine and set the empty glass on the coffee table beside the loveseat.

"She blew it," Cassandra answered. "I don't know whether Aaron is going to kill me, Sonya, or both of us."

"It can't be that bad."

"It is that bad. You know this case rests on one fact. Did Doctor Patterson tell Sonya to push right before he delivered her son? Sonya says he did. If she's right, the doctor did the wrong thing. He should have ordered a c-section, stat, given the decelerations on the fetal heart monitor."

"Yeah, I know the medicine," Marlon interrupted. "Tell me about the depo."

"Well, Joe did his excruciating, minute-by-minute routine." Cassandra deepened her voice, mimicking the defense attorney's booming baritone. "'According to the record, at 8:19 a.m. you had a seven-minute contraction. What happened at 8:20?'"

Marlon shuddered. "Been there, done that."

"Anyway, I thought Sonya was imperturbable, but Joe got under her skin."

"And?"

"She shut down. Joe said, 'I need your verbal answer,' but Sonya just shook her head and said nothing."

"Oh, lord."

"Yeah. I took a break, of course, but Sonya wouldn't talk to me, either. I told Joe we'd have to end the deposition because Sonya felt ill. He didn't believe me, but what else could I do?"

Cassandra reached over for her wine glass, having forgotten it was empty. She sighed, puffing out her cheeks, and crossed her arms instead.

"Aaron shouldn't have agreed to represent this spoiled child," Cassandra said. "Sonya could buy a tropical island in the Pacific if she wanted, and an airplane or two to jet there. She couldn't be bothered, though, to do what she needed to for her child."

"Aaron was bedazzled by Sonya's father. Even Aaron couldn't resist the exotic aura of a Russian gazillionaire. I guess he's still got his money, anyway."

"What's that supposed to mean?"

"Turns out Nikolai was, well, deposed I guess is the word. Miranda had lunch with Sully today. Sully said Nikolai played some major role in Russian cybersecurity. He was kicked out by the Kremlin when the DNC was hacked back in 2016. The hacking was a mistake, supposedly."

Cassandra rubbed her forehead. "I can't think about Bolkonsky père right now. I'm too focused on his daughter."

Marlon reached over and patted Cassandra's knee. "I know you're upset with Sonya but let that go. Joe intimidated the President of the United States in a deposition. It's no wonder Sonya couldn't handle him. We'll fix this somehow."

"I hope so. And I hope you had a better afternoon than I did."

"It was lovely. Ronnie's in town. We had a late lunch."

"How's Ronnie doing?" Cassandra asked, knowing Marlon could read between the lines. She was asking whether Marlon's college roommate was still on the wagon, or not.

"He's doing well," Marlon responded. "We had a great time. Laughed ourselves silly. You know Ronnie when he's on a roll. And it turns out…."

A gust of hearty laughter from the living room swept into the solarium.

"Speaking of on a roll," Marlon, standing, grinned, "let's get in there and enjoy some of it."

Cassandra rose and stretched.

"I'm sorry I have to miss bridge tonight," she said, "but Aunt Kitty'd kill me if I left early. Make sure Betsy leaves when you do. You'll probably find her in the kitchen washing dishes. And say 'hi' to Justice Wells for me."

CHAPTER 9

Thursday, Sept. 7, 6:30 p.m., American University Campus
Ronnie grabbed the front passenger door handle. Marlon motioned for him to get in the back. Ronnie jumped in, and Marlon pulled away from the curb.

"How was your meeting?" Marlon asked, looking at Ronnie in the rearview mirror.

"Good. Why'd you stick me back here? And aren't you headed in the wrong direction?"

"I'm picking up Justice Wells. I told him it would be no problem because I'd be in the neighborhood, anyway."

"In the neighborhood? Isn't Kitty's halfway across town?"

"You gladly go out of your way for a Supreme Court Justice, dummy."

A few minutes later Marlon pulled in front of Justice Wells's home, a modest, two-story ranch in the Spring Valley neighborhood. He reached for the phone lying on the passenger seat and texted the Justice.

The black, lacquered front door swung open. A man in blue jeans, orange polo shirt, and baseball cap, carrying a canvas bag, emerged. A logo was emblazoned on the man's shirt, cap, and bag, but Marlon did not recognize the image.

Justice Wells walked out behind the man in jeans, pulling the front door closed behind him. Wells said a few words to the man who smiled, nodded, then walked off. Marlon noticed him climb into a white van parked a dozen yards down the street.

"Marlon, good evening," Justice Wells said as he climbed into Marlon's Volvo sedan. The Justice nodded toward Ronnie. "Do we have a substitute for bridge tonight?"

"Not me, luckily," Ronnie answered. "I haven't played bridge since college, and I was lousy then. I'm Marlon's houseguest for a couple of nights. I need to freshen up, then I'm leaving for an appointment. I won't be sitting around second-guessing your bidding."

Justice Wells chuckled.

"Ronnie Sloan, by the way."

Ronnie reached his hand over the seat.

"Robert Wells," murmured the Justice. The two shook hands as Marlon pulled onto Massachusetts Avenue, headed for home.

"I'm glad I didn't have to make you wait," Justice Wells said. "The computer tech finished just in time."

"Computer problems?" Marlon responded. "Always a pain in the neck."

"Yes, although I certainly can't complain about our IT service. That man today, for example, made two house calls just this week. Anyway, enough of that." He turned to the backseat and addressed Ronnie. "From out of town, then? What brings you to Washington?"

"Work," Ronnie replied. "I'm a journalist...."

Marlon tuned out the rest of his passengers' conversation.

Two hours later, Marlon sighed deeply, waiting impatiently for Miranda to play a card. Across the table, Justice Wells glanced up. With the slightest twitch of one of his bushy grey eyebrows, his partner made his wishes clear.

Marlon would have snapped at Miranda. Wells, as suited his temperament and his job, had more patience. As the Justice requested, Marlon kept his mouth shut.

Miranda finally played the ten of spades. Wells trumped it and took the hand. He tossed down a jack of diamonds, winning the game.

"Sorry, Betsy," Miranda said to her partner.

Betsy shrugged, gathering the cards to shuffle. "Nothing you could do," she said. "Not against Robert, anyway."

Justice Wells, smiling, nodded his agreement.

Marlon's lips quirked. Mercifully, Robert made no attempt at false modesty.

Justice Wells was a bridge master. He played in the rarified league occupied by Bill Gates and Warren Buffet. Marlon knew that Wells deigned to play with the Stein lawyers only because of Betsy.

Marlon had thought it odd, before he met Justice Wells, that the lifelong bachelor had taken on the task of raising Betsy. Once he got to know Wells, Marlon understood. The cerebral professor, a man of few words, Robert's austere demeanor belied a genial warmth, generosity, and a wicked sense of humor.

"Can I get anybody anything?" Marlon asked, holding up his half-empty martini glass.

As usual, Marlon was hosting. The foursome had gathered at his townhouse in Adams Morgan.

The others murmured that they were fine.

Betsy took the last hand. She conceded, when the game was over, that her opponents had had terrible cards.

"How about one more hand?" Marlon asked.

"Let's see," Robert glanced at the phone lying by his elbow. "Okay, I've got time for one more."

Robert dealt the cards, but he seemed distracted. Come to think about it, Wells had seemed unusually distant all evening.

Work, probably. But then Marlon remembered his conversation with Betsy that morning.

Marlon understood Betsy's concern for Robert's safety. After all, judges had been attacked and even killed because of decisions they made.

That level of emotion, though, usually accompanied a high-profile criminal case or a bitter domestic dispute over divorce, money, and child custody. The Supreme Court dealt more often with paper than with passion.

There were exceptions, to be sure. Protesters camped out on the lawn of one of the justices after a particularly contentious civil rights decision by the Court.

Money talked, too. In commercial cases, billions of dollars rested on the outcome of one decision, such as blocking or approving a merger. Enough was on the line to spawn retaliation by the loser, at least theoretically.

But Justice Wells did not attract controversy or enmity.

Yale-educated, Wells was a scholar and professor before becoming a well-respected judge. In a rare show of bipartisan unity, the Senate confirmed his nomination to the Court by a vote of ninety-nine to one. The hold out wanted to abolish the Court entirely.

Wells's expertise lay in arcane matters of international law like bilateral tax treaties. His decisions on the subject did not make headline news.

"Marlon?"

"Oh, sorry Betsy."

Marlon opened. Robert raised their bid. The others passed. Marlon, who opened the suit for the partnership, had to play the hand. Robert, as dummy, laid down his cards.

Marlon felt his face redden, a "tell" he hated but could not control. Robert had pushed the bidding far beyond where Marlon was comfortable. Marlon gritted his teeth and recalculated.

A few minutes later, the last card fell.

"Well done, Marlon," Robert called.

Marlon leaned back and blew out his cheeks. He hated to lose. He would have hated it even more to let Robert down.

"I need another drink," Marlon said. "Anybody else?"

His colleagues declined, citing the hour. Justice Wells said he had work waiting for him.

Betsy walked Robert to the front door. Marlon noticed that they stopped for a brief, whispered conversation in the foyer before Robert kissed Betsy on the check and walked out.

So ironic, Marlon thought, that his own father was also named Robert. Marlon wondered briefly where the old man was these days. Not that he cared. Marlon had severed ties with his father years ago, after the last fight over Marlon's "lifestyle choices," as the bastard put it.

"What happened to Brenda?" Marlon heard Betsy ask.

Betsy had left for a day in court before Miranda returned to explain her call from the hospital.

"Uh, I'm still not sure," Miranda responded.

Marlon frowned. "What's that supposed to mean? You said this morning nothing went wrong. Nothing could have gone wrong. Brenda just panicked during a routine MRI procedure."

"That's what I thought then...."

"Oh, no, Brenda's not asking you to look into a lawsuit, is she?" Marlon interrupted. "We're not wasting our time...."

"No, not at all," Miranda interrupted. "Brenda's not hurt, really, except her hands are bruised. That's not the problem."

Marlon shrugged. He did not believe he had gotten the whole story. He was not interested in any more of Brenda's drama, though, so long as the firm was not involved.

"I'm glad Brenda's okay," Betsy said, "but I'm not so sure about Robert."

"Why?" Marlon's chest tightened. "I thought he seemed off tonight. Is he ill? I know he saw his cardiologist last week."

Betsy shook her head. "That's not it. You know he gets threats, right?"

Marlon frowned. "I know judges are threatened, of course. I didn't think of Justice Wells as a likely target. He's too, well...."

"Too boring?" Betsy asked with a smile.

Marlon felt himself flushing. "No, not at all...."

"He usually brushes them off," Betsy interrupted. "All the justices get crackpot messages from time to time. Anyway, I could tell he was tense tonight. When I asked him why, he said he'd gotten a threatening email yesterday. He's worried about this one for some reason."

"Did he say why?" Marlon asked. "What's different about this one?"

"I don't know. Robert wouldn't tell me any specifics. I think I caught him off guard when I asked what was wrong. He regretted saying anything about it."

"What did this person threaten to do?" Marlon persisted.

Becky shook her head. "I told you, I don't know any more. But from prior threats, I'd guess various unpleasant things."

"If he's worried, Robert should call the authorities," Miranda chimed in.

"I know," Betsy replied, "but he won't. He's insistent. This stays in the family."

She caught Marlon's eye. He saw the admonition and nodded vigorously.

"Miranda?" Betsy asked.

"Oh, sure, of course. Scout's honor."

"Let's hope Robert's overreacting and it's only another wacko with an ax to grind," Betsy added.

After his guests had gone, Marlon returned to the kitchen to straighten up.

He stared out into the dark patio, trying not to think about "various unpleasant things."

Short, slight, gray-haired, seventy-four-year-old Robert could not defend himself against anybody.

Marlon suspected that Robert would try, though.

Marlon sensed a quiet, steely courage in Robert, a quality Marlon had always lacked. At least, that is what his father groused when Marlon would not even try to fight against the bullies at school.

Marlon sighed and turned out the lights in the kitchen. In the pale glow from the streetlights in the alley, he poured himself another finger of gin.

CHAPTER 10

Thursday, Sept. 7, 10:00 p.m., Adams Morgan
Marlon sat alone in his kitchen sipping his gin. He seemed to be doing a lot of that lately.

He picked up his glass and walked into the living room. Opening the bottom drawer of the credenza, he extracted a framed picture of his wedding day. Grinning broadly, they both looked so handsome in their matching blue blazers and grey dress pants.

When Marlon was young, he did not allow himself to imagine that a day like this could happen in his lifetime. Then, miraculously, it had.

Then, Allen left him.

Devastated, depressed, Marlon tried meditation. He could not focus. He went to yoga class. He hated yoga. He forced himself to take long walks, which gave him shin splints. He settled on martinis.

Marlon returned the photo to its resting place. He gulped a too-large mouthful of his drink, coughed, and returned to his kitchen.

Marlon's phone beeped. An unknown number. Something compelled Marlon to answer, anyway. A few minutes later, after gulping a tumbler of water, he backed his Volvo into the alley and started for the airport.

Thankfully, traffic on the access road was light. Only forty-five minutes after he left his townhouse, Marlon spied the graceful, concave swoop of Dulles Airport off to his left. The beauty of the building, a gift from its architect, Eero Saarinen, always lifted his spirits, but not tonight.

Ronnie had said little on the phone. He needed a ride from Dulles. Whenever Ronnie asked, Marlon responded.

But why not just grab an Uber?

Ronnie had not sounded drunk, and that was a relief. Something was wrong, though.

Marlon reached into his breast pocket, fingered a tablet from its wrapping, and popped another Tums.

He pulled into the cell phone lot. Marlon had no way to contact Ronnie, but they had arranged to meet here, and Ronnie would be on the lookout.

To Marlon's right, beyond the semidarkness of the lot, loomed the main terminal. Marlon peered that way, from which Ronnie should be coming.

Marlon startled at the rap on his window.

Ronnie, grinning, waved. Trotting around the front of the car, he tucked himself into the passenger seat beside Marlon.

"You idiot," Marlon said. "You scared me."

"Good to see you, too," Ronnie responded, blowing Marlon a kiss.

Ronnie had the beginnings of a black eye. His right cheek, badly bruised, was swollen, as was his upper lip. His worn, leather bomber jacket, his good luck charm, was ripped at the shoulder.

"Does the other guy look worse?" Marlon asked. He attempted a chuckle, but it came out more like a groan. "What happened?"

"Mugged in the men's room."

Ronnie flopped his head back against the seat and closed his eyes. "I'm okay," he murmured.

Marlon grasped Ronnie's bicep. "Are you?" Marlon asked.

"I'm fine," Ronnie grunted. "Stripped of everything I was carrying, but otherwise I'll live."

"That includes your phone, I take it," Marlon said. "That's why the number you called from was unfamiliar. You're lucky I answered, old chap."

"It was a security guard's," Ronnie explained. "I told him what happened, and he let me use his phone. I knew you'd answer. You'd feel my unique vibes through the handset."

Marlon glanced at Ronnie. His eyes were still closed, but he was smiling.

"Wait a second," Marlon replied. "When you said 'everything,' do you mean that literally?"

"Yep," Ronnie answered. "My phone and wallet, sure, but also my backpack with my laptop and notebooks. That, my friend, was the point. C'mon, let's get out of here."

Marlon started the car and pulled out of his parking space.

"Okay, tell me the rest of it," Marlon said. "You said you'd be home late tonight because you were meeting a source. At Dulles? Who was it? And why'd he beat you up?"

Ronnie sat up and rubbed his hands together. The adrenalin was kicking in again.

"Yeah. I'll call him Sergey. He's not the mugger. That was later. Sergey's on his flight back to Tbilisi, the capitol of Georgia, in case you don't know."

Marlon took his hand off the wheel and gave Ronnie the finger. Marlon had a mental map of the globe in his head, and Ronnie knew it.

"Sergey's a spy-for-hire, a mercenary spook," Ronnie continued. "Was, anyway, during the Cold War. He was loosely employed by the Soviets, the Americans, and sometimes both sides at the same time, gathering intelligence and disseminating lies."

"Ooh, I can imagine it," Marlon responded. "One of those men in black trench coats, nationality unknown. East German, Hungarian, Kazakh, whatever, shadowy figures skulking in foggy alleys in Berlin, Budapest, or Almaty, waiting for the unknown contact who responds with the right code phrase. Or a gunshot to the head."

"Yeah, and all of them at loose ends after the Wall came down. Russia and the United States were supposedly friends again. They didn't need spies anymore. Sergey had to acquire new skills to find a job. He had an aptitude for code breaking, anyway. He just switched to bits and bytes. He turned himself into a hacker."

"That was a while ago. There were hackers back then?"

"Whenever and wherever there's code, there's a hacker."

"Huh, well, anyway, it doesn't sound like a great addition to a resume."

Ronnie laughed. "In fact, it was. Sergey and a bunch of other drifters like him got jobs—good paying jobs—with an American company, he said, although a Russian shell corporation signed his paychecks."

"American?" Marlon asked, not sure he had heard that right.

"Yeah, the Americans like everyone else were in Russia trying to grab a piece of the action. You'd recognize the names of some of those Americans, the ones who succeeded, anyway."

The inside of Marlon's Volvo brightened. Marlon glanced into his rearview mirror. A dark SUV crowded his bumper. Marlon felt his heartbeat quicken.

The van swerved into the left lane and swept past, horn blaring.

"Road hog," Ronnie called.

Marlon glanced at his speedometer. He was going ten miles an hour below the speed limit. He had been too engrossed in Ronnie's story to pay attention to his driving.

No wonder the other driver had been annoyed.

Marlon was seeing bad guys everywhere. He was either getting paranoid, or his sight was just fine.

"Nah, my fault," Marlon said. "Go on. Wait a minute. What kind of business staffed itself with hackers?"

Ronnie shrugged. "Sergey said he spied on the boss's competition, at first. Sergey was cagey about it, for obvious reasons. As I understand it, though, they moved from industrial espionage into political espionage. More lucrative."

"Spying for whom?" Marlon asked.

"The highest bidder," Ronnie answered.

"This is all fascinating history," Marlon replied, "but why did that get you attacked?"

"Has to be because of the story," Ronnie answered. "Somebody noticed me and isn't happy about my snooping around."

"Hmmm."

"I'm really onto something big, Marlon. Sully says the DNC break-in wasn't CIA. I tend to trust him. He also says it might not have been the Russians. And I've got an American running a private hacking and espionage company in Russia. Plus, I've got a couple of new leads."

The excitement in Ronnie's voice told Marlon all he needed to know.

The attack, whether it came from the CIA, the Kremlin, or someone else entirely, would not discourage Ronnie. Instead, Ronnie would double down, and Marlon could not do a thing to stop him. All Marlon could do was pick up the pieces if the story blew up in Ronnie's face, which was literally what Marlon was starting to fear.

They drove in silence after that, both lost in their thoughts. They had turned onto Canal Road and crossed the D.C. line when Ronnie next spoke.

"Could you fix me something to eat when we get home? I'm starving."

Marlon was about to tell Ronnie that he could scramble his own damn eggs. When he looked over at his friend, though, Ronnie's head was laid back against the seat again. The only color in his drawn face came from the bruises.

First an ice bag for that eye, Marlon decided. Then, eggs and toast. Bacon too, if Ronnie stayed awake long enough.

CHAPTER 11

Friday, Sept. 8, 8:10 a.m., McLean, Virginia
Miranda cranked down the window of her Corolla. Reaching out, she pressed the call box on the pillar next to the ten-foot high, iron-barred gate to Chad's grounds.

"I'm here," she called when she heard the intercom engage.

"I'll be right out," Chad's voice replied.

The gates swung open. Miranda drove up the winding driveway leading to the house.

For Chad's birthday, Miranda had taken the day off from work. To celebrate, Chad suggested they attend the first session of a four-day, Olympic equestrienne trial in Fauquier County, Virginia's celebrated horse country.

"Really?" Miranda had exclaimed. "I figured you for a football guy, or maybe baseball."

After all, Chad's father was career military. Chad grew up on an Army base in Kansas.

True, Chad then attended the Massachusetts Institute of Technology. He now lived in a mansion overlooking the Potomac in McLean, Virginia, and drove a Tesla. Still, he had not seemed the horsey type to her.

Chad had smiled and shrugged a shoulder. "I never learned to ride," he had said, "but I got hooked on watching the ponies when I attended the Grand National in England years ago. Horses are such beautiful animals. I love their combination of grace and power—their elegance. I even love the warm, peaty smell of a horse."

Miranda had patted his arm. "Fine," she had said. He had laughed with her when she added that she was glad he preferred a trip to the countryside to a football game.

As she waited for Chad, Miranda idly admired the architectural wonder of his home. From the two-story, central core, dominated by floor-to-ceiling glass windows, two wings, also dominated by glass, sprang gracefully from the main part of the house.

Bright, witty, engaging, generous, Chad was the miracle partner Miranda had feared she would never find. Still, she knew Chad had a complicated and secretive history. While he seldom talked about himself at all, he never talked about his work, past or present.

Early in the relationship, Miranda asked Sully to check on Chad Blakely. "No issues," Sully had reported. Still, Miranda detected a faint note of reserve in his voice suggesting that Sully was holding something back.

Oh, well, Miranda had decided. Whatever it was had to be no big deal. Chad could not have built his lucrative consulting business if he had major skeletons in his closet.

She told herself that, anyway, because in all other respects Chad was a gem. He thought the same of her, it seemed. She had not had that feeling in such a long time.

Chad emerged from the house and walked to the Corolla. Leaning into her open window, he gave Miranda a kiss.

"A beautiful day and a beautiful lady," he said, beaming. "It doesn't get better than that!"

Miranda reached up and tousled Chad's silky blonde curls. He usually kept his hair closely cropped. He had evidently forgotten his monthly appointment at the barber shop. Buried in a job, probably.

"Happy birthday, sweetheart." She giggled. "Where'd you get that jacket?"

Chad wore a short, silky coat, elasticized at the wrists and waists like a bomber jacket, except it was bright pink. The puffy jacket atop Chad's long-legged, six-foot-two-inch frame reminded Miranda of a stork with a bundle of baby girl hanging from its beak.

"This?" Chad glanced down at his attire.

"Oh," Miranda had not noticed the logo of a horse clearing a jump stenciled on Chad's shoulder, "jockey silks?"

"Yep. A thank-you gift. I did some work for these guys." He pointed to the logo. "One of the oldest stables in Kentucky. Three-time Derby winner."

"Why would a stable need a cybersecurity consultant?"

"For the same reason everybody else does. To protect their data."

While Chad walked around the front of the car and got in, Miranda wondered what data a stable would have to protect, and from whom. Oh, well, Chad probably could not tell her, anyway. Client confidentiality, which she respected.

As Miranda drove off, Chad launched into a tale about his favorite birthday, "so far," he said, winking at her. Miranda decided to wait until later to ask him about hospitals.

Forty-five minutes later, they sat on a metal bleacher beside the jump on the far turn of the racecourse. They were surrounded by rolling green hills, crisscrossed with dense stands of oaks, stretching to the horizon. Miranda heard a voice from the loudspeaker at the stables, off to their left a quarter mile or so, but she could not make out the announcer's words.

The cold seat chilled Miranda's bottom. She shivered as a sharp breeze rose from the east. She snuggled into Chad's warm body, and he put his arm around her.

"Do you want my jacket?" Chad asked.

"No, thanks," Miranda replied, smiling. She would look even sillier in it than he did.

Miranda, about to ask Chad about the hospital directly, stopped herself. Brenda had been adamant. Her suspicions about what happened in the imaging center were to remain their secret. Chad would wonder why she was asking if Miranda raised the hacking issue pointblank. A bit of indirection would be a good idea.

Remembering their earlier conversation, Miranda saw an opening.

"You know," she began, "I was thinking about your stables. Your client, that is. It reminds me how pervasive hacking is. Even hospitals have been hacked. Ransomware attacks, usually, aren't they?"

Chad nodded. "Freeze the data and demand payment to unfreeze it. Simple. Effective."

"Simple? I would have thought...."

"Wait," Chad said, putting his hand on her knee and turning to his right.

Miranda looked too, hearing hoofbeats, muffled, but distinct, as if a mighty drummer a mile away were rhythmically pounding an enormous kettledrum.

"There he comes," Chad cried, rising to his feet. The handful of other spectators at this jump on the outer loop of the steeplechase also rose.

A gray dappled horse crested a rise at a full gallop. With each stride of its long, muscled legs, the animal hurled itself and its rider, barely visible behind the flowing mane, toward a five-foot, wooden barred gate. The beat of its hoofs blended into a dull roar as the stallion accelerated for the jump.

"My god, he's huge!" Miranda whispered.

The animal rose, effortlessly, the jockey crouched over its neck. They sailed over the jump with a foot to spare, landing gracefully. The horse galloped on without breaking stride, heading toward the next jump.

Chad glanced at the program he held in his hand. "One more entrant for this jump. Then, we'll go."

The last thoroughbred, this one a chestnut, cleared the jump as cleanly as had the first. The audience murmured its appreciation.

Miranda and Chad rose from the bleachers with the others.

"Shall we walk back to the stables?" Chad asked.

"Sure," Miranda replied, reaching to take Chad's hand. They strolled off after waving and smiling at the knot of people waiting for the shuttle bus back to the stables.

"Honey?" Miranda began. "Back to hacking hospitals?"

"Huh?"

"I thought it would be hard to do," Miranda persisted. "I presumed hospitals were more secure than other businesses. After all, they're required by law to protect confidential client information."

"HIPPA, sure. But that's an old statute. It was directed more toward paper than digital. Hospitals are notoriously open books. Different departments have their own software systems, for example. When they talk to each other, the connection isn't secure. The list of data security issues within hospitals is a long one."

"Could a hacker even manipulate individual patient information?"

"Sure. Not easy money like a ransomware attack, though. Blackmail is a possibility, I suppose."

"Or murder." Miranda shuddered. "Change the dosage of a prescribed drug with a keystroke and the patient dies."

"Well, that's more complicated. There are human checks in place to prevent that, like the nurse or PA administering the meds."

Human checks.

Miranda, imagining the scene in the MRI room when Brenda was trapped in the scanner, had an idea.

CHAPTER 12

Friday, Sept. 8, 10:00 a.m., The Office
Marlon hung up the phone, having spent forever going over the office mail with Aaron. It was a chore Marlon could not avoid, though. Aaron hated being away from the office for so long. He needed to feel connected somehow.

Marlon swiveled idly in Aaron's leather chair. Another round of medical tests next week would determine when Aaron could return to work. Marlon refused to consider the possibility that Aaron might never be back.

At least not today. Like Scarlett O'Hara, Marlon would put off thinking about troubling things until tomorrow.

Aaron's health problems. Ronnie's assault. It was no small matter that his bridge partner, the otherwise imperturbable Justice Wells, was worried about an unusual threat, either.

Something weird was going on with Miranda and Brenda, too. Maybe not so much troubling as annoying, but still. The associates did not usually keep secrets from each other.

Marlon inhaled deeply through his nose, a calming technique he learned in meditation class.

These were not his problems.

Ronnie had supped with mobsters. He knew to use a long spoon with bad guys. The authorities would find whoever was bothering Justice Wells, charge him, and that would be that. Miranda would humor Brenda but, ultimately, do the right thing.

Marlon relaxed. He decided he would leave early and primp for the opera gala.

"Marlon?"

He turned to see Cassandra striding into the office.

"Good morning. How was the rest of Kitty's party?"

"Nice," Cassandra, breathless, dropped into one of the chairs in front of Aaron's desk. She loosened the top button of her suit jacket, then looked down at herself.

"Is this a little tight?" she asked.

Marlon eyed Cassandra's considerable chest. "You look ravishing, my dear. All dressed up for Dr. Patterson's depo, I see."

Cassandra looked up and nodded. "And I've only got a minute. I need to get back to my notes. But I remembered you said something last night about Sonya's father. I wasn't paying much attention. What was it, again?"

"As I understand it, Nikolai was the Russian equivalent of our CIA Director. Something like that, anyway. He screwed up and got fired."

Cassandra huffed. "Fat chance. We're talking Russia. You screwup, you're dead. Nikolai's alive, so he's probably still spying for them."

Marlon shrugged. "Could be. Can't see that it matters to you." He grinned. "Keep your head down if there's crossfire, though."

Cassandra rolled her eyes. "Not to worry. I doubt I'll even meet Sonya's father. Why would I? Nikolai has nothing to do with the case. The only crossfire I'll be exposed to will be during this depo. Wish me luck."

Jim poked his head around the corner of the door as Cassandra walked out of it.

"I'm going to be out for an hour or so," Jim announced.

"Why, what's up?"

"Ronnie got a call. He's meeting somebody for breakfast. A source for that story he's working on, I take it. Anyway, Ronnie asked me to join them." Jim raised his arm and flexed his bicep. "Security."

"Ronnie?" Marlon echoed.

He had left Ronnie sleeping in the guest bedroom a couple of hours earlier. Marlon had not expected to hear anything from his friend before noon.

"You're the long spoon, then," Marlon muttered.

"Huh?"

Jim looked the part, but he had as much experience in brawling as Marlon did. Which was none.

Marlon tried to imagine sitting around twiddling his thumbs, waiting for another phone call like last night.

"I'm going with you. Where are we meeting?"

"The L&F."

"They serve food there?"

"Apparently," Jim answered. "Survival, I guess. Nobody dances anymore."

"Okay, let's get going. My car's downstairs."

Marlon plugged the address into his maps app. Back in the day, he could have gotten there with his eyes closed. Not anymore.

Deep in Southwest D.C., Marlon parked in a public lot. He and Jim crossed the street to the L&F, housed in a nondescript, windowless building crouched uneasily between two multi-storied condos, all glass and reflected light from the morning sun. Marlon paused in front of the unmarked door.

Back in the day, a line of young men dressed to the nines spilled out of this door, snaking down the block. The boys would strut in, eager to disco all night under the spinning strobe lights of the most popular gay bar in D.C.

Marlon could almost feel the heat and smell the sweat of the packed dance floor. He smiled, remembering.

Jim shouldered Marlon aside and pushed the door open. Marlon, squinting, followed Jim into the dimness inside. Smoking in public had been banned for years, but Marlon swore he smelled stale cigarette ashes.

To the right, behind the bar, stood a man, less than average height, in a blue-and-white striped button down, idly turning the pages of a newspaper. He was late middle age, Marlon surmised, given the man's bald pate surrounded by closely cropped gray hair. Still, his stomach was flat, and he stood erect, shoulders back, graceful, as though he had once been a dancer.

The bartender looked up, caught Marlon's eye, and nodded a greeting. Then, he returned to his newspaper.

Marlon and Jim walked into the club proper. In front of them, on what used to be the dance floor, a handful of couples occupied a dozen or so high-top tables. At the rear of the room Ronnie sat facing them.

A frown crossed Ronnie's face. Then, he waved.

"I'm not sure I needed an army," Ronnie quipped as Marlon and Jim approached. "You may scare him off."

"We're not that scary," Marlon replied, hoisting himself onto a stool as Jim slid onto his.

"True enough. If he asks, I'll make something up. Anyway, I'll do the talking. You guys stay mum."

"Who is this guy?" Jim asked.

"I don't know. He'd heard I'd been asking around about the connection between a CIA agent and the DNC break-in. He wants to talk."

"Does this 'he' person have a name?" Jim asked.

"I presume he'll tell us. Soon, I'm guessing," Ronnie said, staring over Marlon's shoulder.

Marlon turned to see a man in a dark suit, white shirt, and shiny black shoes standing beside the bar. The man scanned the room, shot his cuffs, and headed directly for their table.

Ronnie held out his hand to the stranger. "Ronnie Sloan."

At this range, Marlon could detect the solid frame under the close-fitting suit. Cropped blonde hair, probably in his forties, an intelligent face with a high forehead and narrow nose. He shook Ronnie's hand, then reached into the pocket of his jacket. Pulling out a wallet, he flipped it open to reveal his identification card.

Apollo Satrazemis. Central Intelligence Agency.

Apollo's gaze swept around the table.

"My friends," Ronnie replied. "Problem with that?"

Apollo shook his head.

"Let's not beat around the bush," Apollo began, staring at Ronnie. "It appears we're looking for the same person."

Ronnie cocked an eyebrow. "Could be. Who's your guy?"

"Tony Blunt's the name," Apollo answered. "One of ours. Was, anyway. He's disappeared, and we want him back. You see, some folks think Tony was turned. Doing the Kremlin's bidding, that is. If you track him down, we need to know. Am I clear?"

Ronnie had that stubborn look on his face Marlon knew all too well. Marlon prayed Ronnie would not say something stupid, like "in your dreams, buddy."

Instead, to Marlon's relief, Ronnie smiled at Apollo, leaned in, and opened his eyes wide, a portrait of friendly cooperation.

"Can you give me some backstory on that?" Ronnie asked mildly.

Apollo grimaced, glaring at Ronnie. Apollo may not have been fooled, but he took his chances, anyway, complying with Ronnie's request.

"Yeah," Apollo responded. "Way back. After the Wall came down, we flooded Russia with agents. Everybody knew about it, including the Russians. A few folks on both sides bought the dream that we'd become best buds." Apollo chuckled dryly. "Didn't quite turn out that way."

A waiter appeared beside Marlon's elbow. A short, scrawny, red-headed, pimply teenager. "Menus?" he asked, sounding as though he would be surprised if they asked for one.

"Just coffee," Ronnie replied, waving the waiter away.

"Anyway," Apollo continued, "some hinky shit happened before the doors slammed shut again. All the wires got crossed. Our people got involved in commercial stuff, both sides got too cozy with the other, then nobody knew who to trust. A rotten fruit salad."

Apollo paused, staring off into space.

"I'm with you so far," Ronnie prompted.

"Soon after the Wall fell, we placed an agent high up in Russian intelligence," Apollo's voice had hardened. "A computer superstar. Could have made a fortune coding in Silicon Valley. Anyway, Tony Blunt's the name, liaised between his contact and American industry. We were even selling high tech software and equipment to the Russians if you can believe it. Obsolete stuff for us, but still."

"This is classified, I take it," Ronnie said, "and you're an 'unidentified source.'"

Apollo ignored him. "Tony pulled the plug in early 2017. He wanted out. He claimed a faction in the Kremlin wanted his head. We extracted him. Then he came up with this hairbrained idea that the Russians were not behind the hacking of the DNC in 2016."

"He blamed the CIA?" Ronnie asked.

Apollo shook his head, a disgusted look on his face. "No, but he might as well have. Our cybersecurity experts said it was the Russians. The Russians said it was the Russians, for god's sake. But Tony's theory, which must have been leaked, created doubt. That's when those stories accusing the CIA of a cover-up started circulating."

"You didn't need to rough me up before you told me this," Ronnie said.

"Wasn't us," Apollo said, pushing himself up from the table. "Tony's made a lot of people unhappy. Could have been any of them."

"What's next, Ronnie?" Jim asked after the agent slipped out of the club.

"Breakfast," Ronnie answered. "I'm starved. Did anybody see where that kid with the menus went?"

As if summoned like a genie from a bottle, the scrawny redhead appeared again at Marlon's shoulder.

"Excuse me, sir," he said. "I'm afraid we have…."

Marlon turned as a raised voice behind him interrupted the lad. The bartender stood at the entrance to the club with his nattily striped back to Marlon. Arms raised, he gripped the frame of the door with both hands.

Marlon glimpsed two men outside the door, look-alikes in black leather jackets, balaclavas obscuring their faces. Both were a foot taller and fifty pounds heavier than the proprietor.

"We have a problem," the waiter continued, beckoning toward the back of the club. "Those men don't belong here. You need to get out. Quickly."

CHAPTER 13

Friday, Sept. 8, Noon., McLean, Virginia

Miranda had wanted to treat Chad at one of the nicer restaurants downtown after the steeplechase. He had too much work to take the time, he said.

So Miranda made a reservation for lunch at Divan, a Middle Eastern restaurant in McLean.

"Perfect," Chad had said, on the drive back from the country, when she told him their destination. "Close to home and," he glanced down at his pink silk jacket and blue jeans, "I don't have to change. The host at Marcel's would have a heart attack if I walked in like this."

Miranda giggled.

"Besides, the cuisine suits me better," Chad concluded.

Miranda kept promising herself to give vegetarianism a try. Chad had converted years ago. She did like her steak, though.

They arrived at Divan on time. The hostess, clad in a multi-colored kaftan, seated them side by side at a banquette on the wall, facing the expansive dining room. A waiter in black smock and pants appeared promptly to distribute tumblers and offer menus.

They ordered an array of appetizers to share. Their food arrived promptly. Miranda leaned in and sniffed, detecting saffron, turmeric, and cayenne.

"Yum, I'm starved," she said.

Chad, nodding vigorously, was already spooning rice off a steaming pile onto his plate.

When they had finished, and the waiter arrived to clear the table, both ordered Turkish coffee.

Across the room, a man, dining alone, stood and buttoned his suit jacket as though preparing to leave. He glanced their way, then frowned slightly, cocking his head.

"Huh," Chad said beside her, "what a coincidence. That's Jeremy Ross. He's a client. I work with his tech people, of course, but I've met the boss a couple of times."

From the coldness in Chad's voice, Miranda could tell that he had not enjoyed those meetings, which surprised her.

With rare exceptions, Chad lived inside his own head, solving convoluted technical problems, oblivious to the personalities around him. Something about Jeremy, something nasty, apparently, had penetrated Chad's self-contained serenity.

Miranda was about to ask Chad about it when Jeremy, still looking at them, smiled, then started wending his way through the tables toward them.

Maybe Miranda had misread Chad's reaction.

"Nice of him to stop by to see the hired help," she said, playfully poking Chad in the waist.

"You might have heard of him," Chad continued, ignoring her jibe. "He owns Cerberus Solutions. Cybersecurity, and a big player internationally. It's hard to know how big because the company is privately owned. But I've seen Cerberus products in a lot of my clients' networks."

"I've heard of the company. My friend Sully mentioned it. The owner's name sounds vaguely...."

The pieces came together. Jeremy Ross. Brenda's nemesis.

Because of that, Miranda was supposed to dislike Jeremy, she supposed. That was their fight, though, not Miranda's, and it had happened years ago.

Still, Miranda felt slightly disloyal. She told herself not to be silly. A chance encounter meant nothing.

Jeremy reached their table and extended his hand to Chad. "Blakely, isn't it?"

"Yes," Chad replied, rising from the table to shake. "Chad Blakely. And this is my, uh, friend, Miranda."

Jeremy stood several inches below Chad's six feet. Jeremy was slender, almost skeletal, and slightly stooped. He wore a gray suit matching the color of his hair, swept back from a high forehead. With grey eyes, pale complexion, and regular features, Jeremy looked like an accountant who worked for an obscure government agency.

But then she noticed that Jeremy's watch was Phillipe Patek. His cuff links sported diamonds. The suit was not so much gray as a rich silver, and it fit Jeremy perfectly. Designer, surely, and bespoke, probably.

A big player, indeed.

"Nice to meet you," Miranda said, reaching toward Jeremy, whose hand felt cool and papery.

"The pleasure is mine," Jeremy responded in a pleasant tenor, smiling slightly. "Miranda?"

"Patel," Miranda said, answering the question in Jeremy's voice.

If Jeremy was confused, he did not show it. Most people were. Miranda had an olive complexion, but it would be a stretch to place her as from the Indian subcontinent.

"My grandparents emigrated from Italy," Miranda went on. "They shortened their surname, Pescatelli, to what they thought was a more Americanized version. They came from a village deep in the Italian boot and didn't know their new moniker was a common South Asian name."

She was babbling. Why would Jeremy Ross care where Miranda got her name?

Jeremy chuckled appreciatively, though, which made Miranda feel better.

"What brings you to McLean?" Chad asked.

"A meeting at Langley," Jeremy replied.

How interesting. The Cerberus data security system must be good if the CIA used it. Or maybe Jeremy and the Agency consulted on cybersecurity?

Either way, Miranda was impressed.

The waiter brought their coffee.

"I had some concerns about a report you submitted to my internal security team," Jeremy said. "Now that I've got you in person, do you mind if I ask a few questions?"

Chad touched her shoulder. "Miranda?"

She looked at him, understood, and approved of his consideration. Chad was asking for her permission.

"Of course, Jeremy, please do." Miranda indicated their steaming cups. "Join us?"

Jeremy, smiling, nodded. Chad asked the waiter to bring another cup while Jeremy sat down across from them.

A technical discussion ensued. Miranda listened with half an ear, wondering how Jeremy got into cybersecurity.

Chad, she knew, started down that road because he was a math whiz in school. Jeremy did not seem nerdy enough to have gone that route. Perhaps Jeremy inherited money and bought an already-lucrative business. That would explain Chad's distaste for the man.

"What do you do, Miranda?" Jeremy asked, surprising her out of her thoughts.

"I'm an attorney," Miranda answered. "Med mal's my specialty."

She got a slight frown and pursed lips from Jeremy, the usual response. Most people took a dim view of med mal lawyers.

She should probably let it go. But she had the usual urge to justify herself.

"We have the most fascinating clients," Miranda continued. "My colleague, Marlon, settled a case for a retired Admiral. Boy, did he have interesting stories about his career."

Jeremy tilted his head slightly. At least he was listening.

"I've represented a Metropolitan opera star. And then there's Brenda Gillman."

Miranda could not believe she had said that name. What was she thinking? Because Brenda had popped into her mind earlier, probably. But still....

"The famous correspondent, you know," Chad piped in, trying to be helpful. Miranda could have kicked him.

"I know who she is," Jeremy snapped.

Chad looked surprised at the vehemence of Jeremy's reaction. Miranda would explain later.

Jeremy straightened slightly. "Such a shame about her accident," he said mildly. "It ended her career, I understand."

Was Jeremy being sarcastic? After all, he had to know Brenda was forced out of her job long before she was rendered a paraplegic.

No, his last words had almost sounded like a question, as though he was asking Miranda whether Brenda was working again, or not.

Maybe Jeremy felt guilty?

Miranda saw no reason to avoid the truth. It would not betray Brenda's confidence to tell Jeremy the bare facts.

"You'll be glad to learn that Brenda is working again," Miranda said. "Investigating a story, that is."

Miranda stopped herself abruptly.

Jeremy did not look glad at all.

His eyes bored into hers. The gray irises had all but disappeared, leaving enormous black pupils floating in pools of colorless ice. Jeremy had not moved, but he seemed to have coiled himself, like a snake, prepared to strike.

Miranda, shivering, closed her eyes. The thought occurred to her that Jeremy did not get to his position in life by being warm and fuzzy.

"I was afraid of that," Jeremy said coldly. "She's making a mistake."

Miranda frowned, confused. "What....?"

"Brenda can't be trusted, you know," Jeremy interrupted her, "to get the facts right."

Say something, Miranda scolded herself. Defend your friend. But she could not get that image of Jeremy as a malevolent serpent out of her head.

Across the table from her, the real Jeremy murmured something to Chad, then turned to her and nodded.

"Nice to meet you," Jeremy said mildly. He shot his cuffs. "I'm off to Dulles. Thanks for the coffee."

With that, Jeremy rose and strode out of the restaurant.

CHAPTER 14

Friday, Sept. 8, 1:00 p.m., McLean, Virginia

"What was that all about?" Chad asked, eyes on Jeremy's retreating back.

"He's sure not feeling guilty," Miranda mused. "Angry, I'd say, although he got control of his temper fast enough."

"Jeremy? Angry at Brenda? Why?"

"She defamed him. Well, according to Jeremy. He sued her for it. About four years ago now."

"Defamed him how?"

"Brenda published a story suggesting that Jeremy's business was built on lies. Businesses, that is. He owned several. I don't remember if Cerberus was on the list. Anyway, Brenda also claimed Jeremy was too cozy with the Russians. Too cozy as in not just selling them stuff, like all big companies do, but in undermining American national interests."

"Sounds like the ordinary dirt reporters throw at the wall to see what sticks," Chad replied, flicking a hand. "Hardly worth a lawsuit."

"Well, maybe, but Brenda wasn't just any reporter, you know. She was well known, and Russia was her beat. The lawsuit was in the news. I'm surprised you didn't see it."

Chad shrugged. "I might have and didn't pay any attention. Anyway, who won?"

"Nobody. The case ended in a hung jury."

"More coffee?"

Miranda looked up at the waiter at her elbow, then glanced at Chad.

"I'm good," Chad answered her silent question.

"Me too, then," Miranda said. "Just the check, please."

The waiter wandered off. Miranda kept thinking about her strange conversation with Jeremy.

"You know," she said, "I sort of agree with you that Jeremy's suing Brenda was overkill. I don't know why his publicists couldn't have air-brushed it away. Makes me think there was something personal behind it all."

"Did you ask Brenda?"

"Nah. It would embarrass her if it was true because Brenda sure hates and despises Jeremy now. I don't talk to her about the defamation case, either. I read most of the trial transcripts, though."

"Morbid curiosity?" Chad was smiling, though, and his remark did not sting.

"No, work. As Brenda's attorney, I had to know if any damaging character evidence came out in the defamation trial. The gunslinging lawyers for the car company we sued would have used it against us in our case."

"And? Was there any?"

Miranda squared her shoulders, uncomfortable, as always, with what she had found.

"Brenda's fellow reporters testified that she had a reputation for shooting first and nailing down her sources later."

Chad shrugged. "Is that so terrible?"

"Not when the sources come through, I guess. This time, Brenda's didn't. Meaning there were none or Brenda was protecting their identity. At trial, Brenda was all alone. It was her word against Jeremy's, and the parade of other witnesses his side called to testify to the sterling quality of his business."

Chad eyed her a minute. "Brenda against the conglomerate, yet there was still a mistrial. The jury must have believed there was some truth to her story."

"That's not exactly what a mistrial means here. Do you want the technical explanation?"

"Sure," Chad said, sinking back into the cushions of the banquette.

Miranda laughed. "It won't take that long. Anyway, in an ordinary defamation suit, truth is a complete defense. If what was said or, in this case, published, is true, it's not legal defamation, no matter how damaging the statement was."

"Proving my point," Chad offered.

"Hold on, I'm not done. Jeremy is what's called a 'public figure.' So, according to the law, he had to prove Brenda knew her story was false. I'm simplifying a bit, but that's the basic idea. Brenda testified that she believed she wrote the truth. That's what the jury hung its hat on. Her state of mind."

"Hmmm," Chad squinted an eye, "interesting. Brenda must have been one heck of a credible witness. Still, the outcome hung on a slender thread, yet Jeremy didn't try again. When there's a mistrial, the lawsuit can be refiled, right?"

"Yep. And, no, Jeremy did not file another suit."

"If he was so sure of himself, why not go back for another round?"

"There are lots of reasons a plaintiff won't sue again after a mistrial," Miranda replied. "For one thing, a lawsuit is expensive and time consuming."

"The expense wouldn't have phased Jeremy," Chad noted.

"True, but there's still the time factor. Jeremy would have had to testify again. Or maybe Jeremy's team decided it wasn't worth stirring up the press again with another big public fight. Another reason is that Jeremy got what he wanted the first time around."

"Meaning?"

"Brenda's reputation was shattered," Miranda replied. "Her sources clammed up. She lost her job."

Miranda felt the frisson of fear she always did when she dwelled on what happened to Brenda. One wrong step and the world fell apart.

"There's another possibility," Chad said. "Jeremy didn't bring the case again because he feared he'd lose. Brenda's story was all true."

"You don't like him either, do you? I would've thought that you'd admire Jeremy. He's a tech guy. One of you, and good at it, from what you've told me about Cerberus."

"Oh, he's wealthy, I'll give him that. I wouldn't trust Jeremy as far as I could throw him, though. You see," Chad wagged his head back and forth, "there seems to be more to the company than the Cerberus product. I probably shouldn't repeat water cooler gossip, but since it's you who's asking."

He raised her hand and kissed her wrist.

Miranda felt herself flushing.

"Divisions within Jeremy's company are working on super-sensitive stuff. People fly into town, show up at corporate headquarters in Reston, then disappear again. Coders, probably. Anyway, none of the regular employees knows exactly what's going on inside."

"Hmm, working for the CIA, maybe."

"Could be, although...."

The waiter appeared at their table holding an iPad to collect payment. Miranda stuck her credit card in the slot and scribbled her signature.

"You don't have to pay, you know," Chad protested.

"Of course, I do. It's your birthday."

Chad grinned and pretended to bow.

Miranda kissed him, giving it all she had.

"You took the whole day off, right?" Chad asked when she released him, his voice husky.

"Yeah, but you said you had to work this afternoon."

"It'll wait," Chad said, scooting himself off the side of the banquette. "Let's go home."

Miranda shimmied out from behind the table, catching the tablecloth on her knee and knocking over their coffee cups. As Miranda stood up, Chad grabbed her hand, and they fast-walked out of Divan's.

CHAPTER 15

Friday, Sept. 8, 2:30 p.m., The Office

Q:You admit there were signs of distress on the fetal heart monitor, correct?

A:Yes.

Q: The proper procedure at that point would have been to order a stat c-section, correct?

A:Yes.

Q:And it would have been a medical error to tell Sonya to push, isn't that right?

A:Yes, and that is why I could *not* have told Sonya to push. I would never do that.

Q:But you don't remember the delivery, correct?

A: I don't. That was six years ago, and I've delivered a lot of babies since then.

Cassandra shifted her gaze from the witness across from her, Dr. Patterson, to stare at the cityscape outside the windows of the conference room. That last exchange about summed up the four hours of the deposition. Cassandra scored a few points, but so did the doctor.

At the far end of the conference room table, the court reporter cleared his throat, punctuating the heavy silence. Cassandra dragged her attention back to the people waiting for her to say something.

"A moment, please," she said. She put on her reading glasses and bent over the legal pad in front of her.

The tension in the air seeped from the room like the air from a punctured balloon. Joe, Dr. Patterson's lawyer, leaned back in his chair. His client followed suit.

It was clear to all that the deposition had concluded with Cassandra's last question. The review of her notes before dismissing the witness was *pro forma*.

A few minutes later, after a brief, whispered consultation with Sonya, Cassandra rose. She thanked Dr. Patterson and the court reporter, who began packing his equipment.

"I'll be in touch about the expert witness lists," Cassandra said to Joe, who had also gotten to his feet.

Joe nodded. He touched Dr. Patterson's shoulder and gestured toward the door leading out of the conference room.

"Have a good weekend, everyone," Joe called over his shoulder as he and his client walked out.

Cassandra shrugged out of her suit jacket and draped it on the empty chair to her left. She tugged her chair out from the table so that it faced Sonya directly and plopped heavily into it.

"I did my best, Sonya, but I have to be up front with you," Cassandra began. "Dr. Patterson was very convincing. You heard him. What do you think?"

"He lies," Sonya responded, voice flat, uninflected, face averted.

Oh, that's really going to convince the jury, Cassandra stopped herself from saying.

Sonya had not made eye contact with Dr. Patterson, either, although Cassandra had urged her to face him directly. Instead, Sonya had sat, motionless, hands in her lap, eyes downcast, for the entire deposition.

It occurred to Cassandra that she may have overlooked something about Sonya. She thought back over their interactions, cross-checking in her mind what the medical options could be.

Maybe Sonya was not a haughty Russian princess who looked down on her because Cassandra was not rich and not white. Maybe it was something else altogether.

Cassandra decided to test her theory.

Cassandra was a hugger. Sonya had always maintained her distance, though, and Cassandra respected that. Now, Cassandra slowly reached over and put her arm around Sonya's shoulder. Sonya flinched.

Her best lay person's diagnosis, based on this and other observations, was that Sonya was on the autism spectrum.

Cassandra did not care two hoots whether Sonya was autistic. Besides, Sonya's atypical traits were minor, and she seemed to be doing just fine.

Cassandra did care about how Sonya would come off in front of a jury, particularly in this "he said, she said" case.

The jurors in ethnically diverse Washington, D.C., a city accustomed to world citizens in its midst, could easily empathize with a Russian woman, even if they detested her government's endless wars. But if she could not look them in the eye?

Cassandra sighed. "Dr. Patterson will come off as a good, sincere person, who does a service to the world by delivering babies. And you're...."

"An icy Russian bitch," Sonya interrupted, but the corners of her lips tilted up.

Cassandra's mouth crooked, tentatively, not certain she was reading Sonya right. Then, Sonya looked Cassandra in the eye and grinned. My goodness, Sonya was beautiful when she smiled.

Cassandra relaxed, for the first time that afternoon. "Look," she began, "predictions are risky. But, in my experience, when it's a doctor against a former patient in a lawsuit, the odds favor the doctor unless he comes across as a total jerk. I don't see that happening here. That's all I was trying to say."

"I understand," Sonya replied. She rolled her shoulders.

Sonya had been tight as a drum all day, too, Cassandra realized, even more so than other clients.

Sonya looked directly at Cassandra again, all humor gone from her sculpted face.

"Do you believe me?" Sonya asked, eyes riveted on Cassandra's.

Cassandra's thoughts flashed back to her conversation with Marlon at Aunt Kitty's the night before. Cassandra had bad-mouthed Sonya, accusing Sonya of failing in her duty to her child.

Cassandra had jumped to the conclusion that Sonya clammed up during her deposition because of pride. That had not been it, at all.

She mentally kicked herself.

"I do," Cassandra answered solemnly.

Sonya's gaze shifted slightly, then returned to Cassandra. Sonya's features softened, and she nodded. Cassandra had been tested and passed.

"There is a witness," Sonya said, "who would swear I am telling the truth."

Cassandra cocked her head. A witness to what? If this had anything to do with the case Cassandra should have known about it long ago.

Her confusion must have shown on her face.

"To my son's birth," Sonya continued.

Cassandra straightened herself in her chair. "What are you talking about? Who?"

"My husband, Josef, was in the delivery room. Briefly, because he arrived late. Everyone was rushing around by then, and Josef had found a pair of scrubs. I doubt anyone noticed he wasn't on the medical staff. But he knows what happened."

"And why did I not know this until now?" Cassandra asked, exasperated.

The complications ran through her mind. The deadline for deposing fact witnesses had passed. Joe and the judge would complain about this late entrant. She would look like a fool for not knowing the whereabouts of the husband.

A faint flush rose on Sonya's pale face. "It's complicated," she said, her accent deepening. "My father sent Josef away. Josef cannot return."

"Who does your father think he is?" Cassandra asked rhetorically.

She was about to add "a spy king" but stopped herself. She took a deep breath.

"We're not going to lose this case because of some drama going on in your family. Talk to Nikolai. Josef must come back."

"You talk to my father," Sonya replied, angry or frustrated, Cassandra could not tell. This was the first time she had heard emotion in Sonya's voice. "This lawsuit is all father's idea, anyway. I didn't want to have anything to do with it."

Cassandra wondered why but decided not to go there right now. She did not want to provoke Sonya further.

"Deal," Cassandra shot back. She could handle this. She could take on the oligarch. Spy. Whatever. "Give me his number. I'll call him right now."

"It would be best if you met him first," Sonya replied. "Break the ice, before you, ah...."

"Tell him what to do?"

Sonya actually giggled. "Father's at home. I will introduce you. Are you willing?"

Cassandra had pretended nonchalance when talking to Marlon earlier, when he warned her about avoiding Nikolai, who might be trouble. In fact, she did not take lightly the possibility of being caught in crossfire.

When she was a child, they lived, briefly, in a rough neighborhood. A friend of hers, a teenage boy, was killed coming home from school, the innocent victim of a gang fight.

Get a grip. She was meeting with a client's father. That would be that.

She nodded at Sonya. "Let's go."

CHAPTER 16

Friday, Sept. 8, 3:15 p.m., Ritz-Carlton Hotel, Georgetown
Cassandra watched the floors tick by as the elevator ascended to Nikolai's penthouse suite. Sonya, standing beside her, said nothing until their car rocked to a stop.

"I'm not staying," Sonya said. "I told him what you want to talk about. It's best if you do it without me here."

Cassandra nodded her agreement. Sonya spoke of her husband with affection, yet Nikolai had banished Josef to parts unknown. It would be wise to keep the emotions of this family disagreement out of it and stick with the facts.

Cassandra needed Josef as a witness.

Sonya stepped out of the elevator, Cassandra behind her. They stood in a long, carpeted corridor with only two doors, one at either end. Sonya turned to the left, and Cassandra followed.

As they approached the door to Nikolai's suite, it swung open. Two men in navy blue suits complete with white shirts and ties, one with a briefcase in his hand, stepped out. Behind them a taller, bulkier man dressed all in black loomed in the doorframe.

"Looks like we're interrupting a party," Cassandra quipped.

Cassandra glanced at Sonya, whose expressions Cassandra was learning to read. Sonya was not amused.

"Bah," she huffed. "Another stupid interrogation."

"What?"

"Ladies," one of the suits greeted them, touching his forehead with his index finger as he and his companion walked by.

Cassandra smiled and nodded at the familiar deep twang of rural Virginia.

Cassandra understood. A pair of white men in suits, Americans, an interrogation, and an ex-Russian spy.

Maybe not so ex.

A different man had taken the place of the butler, or more likely bodyguard, Cassandra realized, in the doorway to the suite. With a slight bow, he spoke.

"Good afternoon," he said in a heavy accent.

The man's baritone voice suited his stature, broad across the chest and shoulders. Cassandra had to look up into his arresting blue eyes, so like Sonya's. His were framed by thick, surprisingly long black lashes. His face was craggy, but with high cheekbones, full lips, and square jaw, undeniably attractive.

Cassandra felt herself flushing. She nodded in response.

"Sonya texted me that you were coming. It's a pleasure to meet you. Please come in."

With a curt nod, Nikolai dismissed the bodyguard. The man turned and lumbered back into the suite, disappearing from view.

In a few minutes, Cassandra and the Bolkonskys were seated in the sunken sitting area of the living room. Sonya, after hugging her father, had curled herself close to Nikolai on a silvery, overstuffed sofa. Cassandra sat across from them in a chair matching the sofa.

"Can I get you anything to drink?" Nikolai asked.

Cassandra murmured her thanks but declined.

Nikolai's grammar was flawless, she noticed, but he spoke as though English was a bit of a stretch. She also noticed that Nikolai's expensive designer suit, wrinkled in the wrong places, needed a trip to the dry cleaner.

He had clawed his way up from the bottom if she had to guess. Way up. Cassandra could not help but admire him for that, although she did not want to think about what he might have done to get there.

"Pardon us," Nikolai said with a slight wave. He and Sonya then chatted in Russian for a few minutes, Nikolai seeming to ask questions and Sonya answering.

With a kiss on Nikolai's cheek, Sonya rose and bade them goodbye.

Nikolai sat back. Stretching his arms out against the back of the sofa, he crossed his ankles.

Cassandra felt the contrast with her stiff posture. She allowed herself to relax.

She should probably get right to Josef, but curiosity got the better of her.

"It looks like our arrival broke up a meeting. Sorry about that."

Nikolai responded first with a word containing mostly consonants, a Russian oath, no doubt.

"The FBI, the CIA, the SEC, or any of your other alphabet agencies call on me frequently. That I must at least pretend to cooperate is humiliating."

His voice had dropped to a low growl.

"I have no choice. I could be deported on some pretext at any time, leaving Sonya and my grandson on their own here. I can't have that."

Cassandra wondered how close he would get to the truth if she asked him. Well, why not try?

"Why does the CIA, or any of the others, uh, call on you, as you put it?"

Nikolai's lips quirked. "I thought a lawyer never asked a question she didn't know the answer to."

Cassandra laughed at the unexpected humor.

"I'm a businessman," he continued, "pure and simple. With hard work and good luck, I survived as my country crashed and burned. I did well. For that, you people call me an oligarch, shorthand for a despicable person."

Despicable was not the word that came to Cassandra's mind as she stared at Nikolai. His otherworldly blue eyes bewitched and disturbed her. So, too, did the sheer physical presence of this man.

She was about to prompt him for more when a bell chimed.

"Ah, room service," Nikolai got to his feet. "It took them long enough."

Cassandra watched Nikolai deal with the delivery, thinking she had best turn to the reason she was here. She decided to begin by exploring how invested Nikolai was in Sonya's case. If he cared enough, he should be willing to forgive and forget whatever had turned him against Josef, at least for the duration of the case.

Nikolai set a serving tray on the table between them. Cassandra leaned forward and inhaled the mouth-watering aromas that wafted from the food, pungent vinegar prominent among them.

"Please," Nikolai motioned toward the array of small plates on the tray, "try my Russian peasant food."

The handful of dishes and the modesty of the servings, not to mention the simplicity of the food, surprised Cassandra. She had imagined an oligarch would overindulge on mountains of rich food.

A few minutes later, Cassandra's mouth was full of heavy rye bread and pickle.

"Delicious," she mumbled. "The Russian version of soul food."

Nikolai laughed, a warm rumble that made Cassandra's face flush again.

"You're so right," Nikolai said. "Sonya teases me for my plebeian tastes in food, but I'll take this over a croissant and sugary jam any day."

"Speaking of your daughter, she told me she didn't want to sue the doctor. You encouraged her to do so. I wonder why?"

Nikolai cocked an eyebrow.

"Don't get me wrong," Cassandra said in response. "I am honored that you chose my firm to represent Sonya. But she doesn't need money to give her son all he needs to live a life as close to normal as possible. That's the reason most people sue for malpractice. What's your reason?"

Nikolai paused. From the look on his face, Cassandra surmised that he was struggling to find words.

"Too often in the rest of the world," Nikolai began, "the wealthy and powerful trample on everyone else with impunity. In America, everyone must answer in court for the wrongs that they do."

Cassandra almost laughed. She could imagine one of her grandchildren reciting something like Nikolai's little speech in a grade school civics class. He sounded so sincere, though.

"I'm not naïve enough to think that justice in America is always blind," Nikolai continued. "Still, most often it comes close. I believe in that system."

Cassandra's hogwash meter had not budged an inch. She did not want to believe that Nikolai was too good at dissembling for her to detect it. There was another possibility. Sully was wrong about him.

"Sonya is an American citizen. So in response to the wrong that was done to her in America, we turned to American justice."

Cassandra detected her opening.

"To get that justice, we need Josef," Cassandra replied.

Nikolai's face turned to stone.

"We do not speak of him," Nikolai growled.

Cassandra, startled, sat back. She felt a flash of fear, imagining the bodyguard springing out from wherever he was hovering and throwing her out of the suite.

She had been blinded by Nikolai's attractiveness. He was no more than a brute.

Angry at herself and at him, she snapped back.

"You don't tell me how to manage Sonya's case. We will talk of Josef because we must."

Nikolai heaved a great sigh.

"I apologize," he said. "I should not have spoken to you like that."

He raised his eyebrows in a question.

"Okay, apology accepted," Cassandra huffed, but mollified.

"Thank you. You must understand, though, that Josef is a bad person. I did not approve of Sonya's infatuation with him, but only because I thought Josef a spoiled, ne'er-do-well. Sonya was in love, or thought she was, and I gave in. I hoped Josef would settle down when his son was born. He didn't."

"I know it's so hard for parents of cerebral palsy children. Josef would not have been the only father struggling with that kind of life."

Nikolai snorted. "Josef didn't have anything to do with his son. Sonya bore that burden alone. They were living here, in Georgetown, in the house I bought them. When I came to help Sonya, I realized Josef had to go. I sent him away. He won't be coming back."

"Can I talk to Josef, though?" Cassandra asked. "If it turns out he is a good witness, I can arrange to take the testimony via videoconference."

Nikolai shook his head. "It's no use. The doctor's lawyers would interrogate Josef. That won't happen. The family would be disgraced."

Cassandra sat up straight and brushed the crumbs from her dinner off her skirt. "Well, Josef will be questioned, sure," she said. "But he won't exactly be 'waterboarded.' Besides, you underestimate me. I've had more than one witness with skeletons in the closet. I know how to keep them there."

Nikolai smiled.

"To the contrary, ma chérie," he said, "I estimate you very highly. I will seriously consider your request, for Sonya's sake, and my grandson."

Cassandra was on the verge of pushing him when she had a better idea. Flies with honey, and all that. Plus, it would not be unpleasant to spend more time with Nikolai.

"I have tickets to a fundraising event for the opera this evening. Would you like to come with me?"

Nikolai's smile broadened. Oh, my. Dimples.

"It would be a pleasure, but can I bring a guest?"

Cassandra's good mood evaporated.

"My bodyguard, that is."

And returned.

They made their plans. Cassandra left for the office.

CHAPTER 17

Friday, Sept. 8, 3:50 p.m., Metropolitan Hospital
Miranda walked into the hospital cafeteria. She bypassed the service line and headed toward the dining area. With any luck, her target, "Andy," would be having a bite before his shift started at 4:00 p.m.

The idea she had that morning at the steeplechase was the farthest thing from her mind an hour ago. Instead, she was luxuriating in the shower with Chad after their postprandial dalliance.

Chad had shooed her out the door promptly after, though, begging work. She understood. Miranda had done the same to Chad on occasion.

Driving back into town, Miranda thought again about Brenda's MRI.

A technician rolled Brenda into the MRI scanner. He rolled her out. The computer recorded the time between those two events as seven minutes. According to Gretchen, the hospital's lawyer, the tech confirmed this version of events. If the data was accurate, the tech was telling the truth.

But then Chad told her how easy it would be to hack the hospital's data.

Assuming the data was manipulated, as Brenda proposed, and she was in the tube for over an hour, the tech had to know.

In other words, the tech had been manipulated, too—as in paid or blackmailed maybe—by whoever Brenda was investigating.

When she met Gretchen yesterday, Miranda had not considered asking for the tech's name. What was the point?

Too late now, though. Miranda would not rouse Gretchen's suspicions by going back to ask her.

Miranda did know the man's first name. "Andy," according to his nametag, which Brenda remembered. Brenda also described Andy's appearance.

When she had gotten to the hospital a few minutes ago, Miranda went directly to the imaging center and asked at the check-in desk if her friend Andy was on shift that afternoon. The nice lady confirmed that he was.

Miranda scanned the dining room, which was emptying fast. Two men sitting at tables in opposite corners fit Brenda's description of a young, pasty-faced man with a mop of dark brown hair. Miranda took her chances on the one to her right.

She approached and peered at his name tag. Bingo.

"Andy?"

He looked up, his pie-shaped, doughy white face perched precariously atop a skinny neck and thin shoulders.

She smiled broadly and slipped into the seat across from him.

"I'm Miranda," she said. "Nice to meet you."

"Do I know you?" Andy asked in a heavily accented voice.

Up close, Miranda detected a whiff of alcohol on Andy's breath. And he was starting a shift? On the verge of accusing him, she stopped herself. Not her problem.

"No," Miranda answered. "Let me introduce myself. I'm a reporter. Er, working for a reporter, that is."

Maybe this ploy she had concocted was a bad idea, but it was too late to back out now.

"I'm working on a story about what it's really like to work in hospitals," Miranda continued. "Kind of a *Grey's Anatomy* thing, but with less sex and more of the crazy medical stuff. I heard one of your patients was stuck in an MRI tube for an hour. Talk about crazy!"

Could she possibly sound sincere? Miranda put on an exaggerated grin, trying to disguise her doubt, and her intense curiosity about what Andy was going to say.

Of course, he would deny it, even if Brenda was telling the truth. Would Miranda be able to detect the lie?

Andy's eyes rounded. "Did she send you?" he barked, his inky black eyes boring into hers.

"The patient, you mean? No."

Andy must have heard the truth in her voice. "Then why are you here?" he responded, sounding less angry and defensive than curious.

"I told you, I'm a reporter. I'm here for the facts. Your side of the story, let's say."

Andy studied her. Miranda shifted in her chair.

"Completely anonymous, of course," she continued. "If this makes it into the story at all, nobody would be able to link you or your hospital to any of it."

Andy looked at her steadily. "If not the patient, who told you about me?"

"Uh, I was interviewing another employee about something else. She mentioned you in connection with the MRI thing. I didn't catch her name, though."

Her words did not sound plausible, even to herself. Still, something seemed to convince Andy that Miranda was on the up-and-up.

"I guess it's okay," he said, "but I only have a few minutes."

"No problem," Miranda said briskly. She reached for the notebook she had tucked into her briefcase.

"I need a cup of coffee before I start my shift," Andy said, starting to rise.

"No, sit, I'll get it," Miranda said, waving him down. She fished her wallet out of her briefcase, rose, and trotted toward the coffee urns at the end of the serving line.

It took no more than a minute, but when she turned back to their table, Andy had disappeared.

CHAPTER 18

Friday, Sept. 8, 5:00 p.m., The Office

Marlon, sitting at Aaron's desk, fidgeted. The only thing worse in life than losing was being ignored.

Where was everybody?

Ronnie's whereabouts, Marlon knew, and disapproved.

Marlon had tried to make Ronnie see reason on the drive back from their meeting with Apollo.

"Why not stop now?" he'd said. "You wanted the CIA to be behind the DNC break-in. That was your big story. It seems clear now that you were wrong."

"I didn't want anything," Ronnie countered, "except the truth."

"Who cares anymore? Whatever happened is water under the bridge. Way under the bridge."

Ronnie had looked at him as if he were crazy.

"This, from a history major?"

"So, fine, keep digging. You'll find another CIA agent who'll haul you in for questioning. After that, you'll bump into those other ruffians anxious to rough you up again. Or worse."

"I'm not worried about the CIA. I'm a reporter. Not the one I used to be, but people still know who I am. People who count. The Agency's not about to disappear me."

"And those other guys? The big ones?"

Ronnie had squinted his eyes. "They make things even more interesting. Maybe Tony did change sides, and the Russians don't want anybody to find him."

"You included."

Ronnie had slapped him on the shoulder. "No worries. I have known knowns and known unknowns. So long as I don't have unknown unknowns...."

"Now that," Jim had interrupted from the back seat, "is giving me a headache."

When they got back to the office, Ronnie took off, promising to be back in time to dress for the gala. Jim left for a doctor's appointment.

Marlon had fiddled with a brief and eaten a takeout sandwich for lunch. He waited around, expecting a debrief from Cassandra after her depo finished. Instead, she disappeared without telling him where she was going.

Miranda was supposed to be back early in the afternoon, but she was AWOL, too.

He remembered he had planned on going home early to relax before the opera gala. That did not sound appealing right now, either. His townhouse would be as silent as the office.

Miranda, her hair tousled, burst into Aaron's office, cheering him considerably.

"I need to talk to you guys," Miranda said, shedding her jacket as she spoke. "Where's Cassandra?"

"I don't know. I'm afraid the depo didn't go well and she's off drowning her sorrows. She'd better not get so blotto that she forgets about the gala. I bought her two tickets."

"Okay, well, you'll have to do," Miranda plopped herself into one of the chairs arrayed in a semicircle in front of Aaron's desk.

"What do I have to do?" Marlon asked, ignoring Miranda's slight, which he knew was unintended.

"For starters, consider what I say attorney-client privileged."

"What do you mean, 'consider it' privileged? Is it, or isn't it?"

In the eyes of the law, the lawyers in the firm were as one. Miranda could freely tell Marlon confidential information disclosed by a client because all of them were equally bound by the attorney-client privilege to keep the secret.

Only communications with a client were protected, though, and not everything even a client revealed was privileged.

Miranda shifted in her chair. "Er, sort of. Not exactly. It's a former client."

Marlon tilted his head back and rolled his eyes at the ceiling. Miranda was dying to tell him something she had promised not to disclose to anyone. So she was trying to drag the info under the umbrella of privilege.

"Okay," he said, purposefully vague.

"Brenda's working on a story. She thinks her investigation caught someone's attention, and that someone is not happy about it."

"What's it about? The story, that is."

"Something about hacking and stealing inside information. Anyway, Brenda thinks she was purposefully trapped in the MRI scanner to scare her into dropping the story."

"But she couldn't have been trapped."

"Unless somebody monkeyed with the records."

"Monkeyed with?"

"As in hacked."

"Oh lord. Brenda's got hacking on the brain."

"Hold on. I figured the tech had to be involved if Brenda's story was true. So I went to the hospital to try to talk to him."

Miranda replayed her "interview" with Andy.

Marlon felt his face flushing. Miranda should not have been playing games with hospital personnel. If anybody found out, she, and the firm, by extension, would look like they were harassing staff for no reason, a blot on the lawyers' reputation.

"Brenda put you up to this, didn't she?" he asked. "She wants to find fault with the hospital somehow."

"No! She specifically told me not to do anything. And I'm not supposed to tell anybody else about what happened. You're different, of course."

"If she's not after a lawsuit, what is she after? I mean, you don't believe her crazy theories, do you?"

Miranda's face fell.

Crap, he had not meant to hurt her feelings.

"Well, if not me, who?" Miranda mumbled.

He got it.

Against all odds, Miranda and Brenda had become friends. Brenda, the glittering, swashbuckling, award-winning investigative reporter, and Miranda, the ambulance chaser who never crossed a street against a red light and, by force of lifelong habit, pinched pennies.

True, they had met after Brenda's series of misfortunes. But Brenda had pulled herself together remarkably well, even Marlon had to admit. Brenda was still an icon despite all she had been through.

So, against all odds, Miranda had to believe Brenda.

Marlon sighed audibly. He would have to tread delicately.

"Okay, let's start over," he said.

Miranda straightened in her chair. "Okay, I'm telling you, there was something off about Andy. He got really spooked when I asked him about his patient freaking out in the MRI. Doesn't his abrupt disappearance mean he's guilty as charged?"

"He got cold feet about an interview with a reporter and went to work," Marlon proposed, leaning back into Aaron's high-backed chair.

"No. I considered that. I went to the imaging center after Andy left me in the cafeteria. I told the check-in clerk that I needed to see him briefly with an urgent message from his mother."

Marlon groaned. "That's a lame story."

Miranda ignored him. "Andy did not show up for his shift."

Marlon shrugged. "Maybe he got sick on bad cafeteria food. If this Andy was really a hired gun, he would have quit right after he pulled the trigger, so to speak."

Miranda paused. "But wouldn't that have looked suspicious? I think he'd stay around, wait a decent amount of time, then quit. My showing up told him it was time to split."

Marlon stared at her, trying to figure out what to say next. "It's such a stretch, don't you see? Isn't it far more likely….?"

"Brenda had no reason to lie to me," Miranda interrupted.

Miranda did have a point. Why would Brenda concoct such a wild story?

"I think I have it," Marlon said. "Brenda freaked out in the MRI. That embarrassed her. She's supposed to be so tough. Coincidentally, she's working on a story. She realizes she *could* have been trapped to throw her off her investigation. So, voilà, that *did* happen. It's all in her head, though."

"Hmmm, maybe."

"She probably believes it herself," Marlon forged on.

Marlon stopped himself from verbalizing his next thought. It would suit Brenda's healthy sense of self-importance to think her investigation attracted somebody's attention.

"But what if she's really in danger? What if it was a threat?"

"Seriously, threat by MRI attack?"

Miranda chuckled. Good. He was making progress.

"If this were for real, Brenda would have gotten a nasty email," Marlon continued. "Or somebody like Andy pushes her out of her wheelchair when she's alone, wheeling herself down a sidewalk."

"That's the normal stuff, I agree. But there's something really threatening about being buried, alone and helpless, half-naked in a hospital gown, while a band of maniacal drummers pound on your head."

"True," Marlon admitted. "Except for the gown, sounds like something from the Middle Ages, or *Game of Thrones*."

"Or Russian. Andy had a Russian accent now that I think about it. Russians attack in weird ways, you know. Poison, nerve gas."

"The so-called fall off a hotel balcony."

That set them both off.

"It's not really funny," Miranda managed when they stopped laughing.

"No, it's not."

"And this thing with Brenda isn't, either. Do … do you think I should call the police?"

"I thought we agreed Brenda isn't really in danger."

"I know it's unlikely, but if somebody really did hack the hospital to trap Brenda in that tube, he's one scary guy."

Marlon shook his head. "Stay out of it. She's crying wolf, Miranda."

"But there was a wolf, you know. In that fairy tale. The kid really did see a wolf. The problem was nobody believed him. Until it was too late."

CHAPTER 19

Friday, Sept. 8, 5:10 p.m., The Office

Cassandra grabbed her phone. She had mistakenly left it on the conference room table before she left the office with Sonya after the depo.

She would have to hurry to get ready, having wasted time on this detour. Ordinarily, she would linger over her makeup and arrive late to the gala, but Cassandra had a feeling Nikolai would be there when the doors opened.

"Yeah, so how's that going to help?" Cassandra heard Marlon ask. "If there is a wolf, who is it? You have no idea."

Wolf? She would have thought Marlon was talking about a video game, or something, but he sounded frustrated and edgy.

"Heh, guys," Cassandra called to Marlon and Miranda from the doorway of Aaron's office. "What're you talking about? And why are you both still here?"

Marlon waved her in. "Oh, good, you didn't drown in gin."

"Huh?"

"Where've you been, anyway?" Marlon continued.

Cassandra hesitated.

Cassandra had done nothing but bad mouth the Bolkonskys. It would take too much time to explain why she had changed her mind about them both.

Besides, Marlon would only chide her for acting like a naïve teenager, being overly impressed by customized room service at the Ritz.

"Working," she answered. "I may be able to salvage Sonya's case, after all."

She told them about Sonya's husband, Josef, but not about his banishment by Nikolai.

"I met with Nikolai to see about contacting Josef. Josef's in Russia right now. I think. Anyway, we didn't have time to wrap things up, so I invited Nikolai to the gala."

Marlon pursed his lips but held his tongue. Cassandra had purposefully played the trump card. Work.

Relieved, Cassandra remembered why she had delayed heading home.

"Why are you two talking about a wolf?"

"While you've been occupied with your Bolkonskys," Marlon swiveled and pointed his index finger at Miranda, "she's had her own problem client to deal with."

Miranda explained about Brenda, Cassandra struggling to focus. Miranda was upset. Cassandra wanted to be supportive, but she was also in a hurry to leave.

"Oh, wait," Cassandra snapped to attention. "That's the wolf you were just talking about? Whoever supposedly trapped Brenda in an MRI scanner?"

Miranda nodded.

The image of the Big Bad Wolf from the children's book of fairy tales that her daughter had so loved popped into Cassandra's mind. The cartoonist had drawn the wolf with an enormous pink bow atop its head which always made Mary giggle.

"What's so funny?" Miranda demanded, scowling.

"Uh, well, I'd think there'd be easier ways to stop her," Cassandra managed, chiding herself as she wiped the smile off her face. "Brenda, that is, from pursuing her story."

"That's what I said," Marlon added. "And even if, and that's a big if, you believed everything Brenda says, we can't tell anybody. Can't do anything, either, because Brenda clammed up and won't say who she suspects."

"Why not?" Cassandra asked, directing her question to Miranda.

"Brenda said she's not sure enough to say anything. Not yet."

"If she's not worried enough to do anything about it, you should stop worrying, too," Cassandra replied, relieved that the problem was solved, for now, at least.

"I agree," Marlon added. "And I have to say it's a good thing Brenda's being more careful about accusing people this time."

Cassandra was about to ask Marlon what he meant when Betsy appeared at the door to Aaron's office, briefcase in hand.

"How was court, Betsy?" Marlon asked. "Took you longer than I thought it would."

"Fine," Betsy answered. "The judge granted the extension to my deadline. I stopped on the way back to give Robert his ticket. I'm taking Bella to the vet at 6:00 p.m., which means I'll be late to the gala."

"Uh, me, too, unless I get out of here," Cassandra said, turning and heading for the door.

"Did you find anything else out about the threat?" Marlon asked.

Cassandra stopped abruptly and spun around. "The what?"

"I mentioned it last night," Betsy replied, "at our bridge game. The second threat came today. Somebody wants something from Robert and is threatening consequences if he doesn't get it."

"What's the guy want?" Cassandra asked.

"Money," Miranda pronounced. "Isn't that usually what a blackmailer wants?"

Betsy shook her head. "Not money. He wouldn't tell me specifically what it is. But Robert said the demand only makes sense if the blackmailer has access to confidential information. Something only a Court insider should know."

Cassandra thought about that. "Judges are privy to all kinds of confidential business information submitted under seal by parties. Valuable information. Trade secrets, financial information...."

"Or maybe," Marlon proposed, "maybe it's not business at all, but something personal?"

"Or political," Cassandra mused. "Remember when somebody at the Court leaked the draft opinion overturning *Roe v. Wade*? Pundits speculated that the point was to sway public opinion in favor of the decision. The blackmailer could be demanding that Justice Wells leak a draft, for some reason."

"Whatever it is, Wells will ignore him," Marlon said. "There's no way Robert would give in."

"He won't give in, but he can't ignore it," Cassandra said. "I mean, it's probably an empty threat, but Wells can't take any chances."

"I agree."

They all turned at Ronnie's voice.

"You heard?" Betsy demanded.

Ronnie held up both hands in mock surrender. "Don't shoot, Betsy. It's just me."

"Nobody's supposed to know about this," Betsy said, her voice trembling, "except me. I shouldn't even have told these guys, but I trust them."

"You can trust me, too, Betsy. I know all about protecting sources." Ronnie mimicked zipping his lips. "Mum's the word."

Betsy looked at Marlon, who nodded. Cassandra agreed with Marlon. Ronnie was family.

"Robert regrets telling even me," Betsy continued. "He let it slip last night when I asked him why he was tense. Then today, I told him he owed me more. I needed to know how worried I should be."

"And?" Cassandra asked.

"Robert said I shouldn't be concerned," Betsy answered. "He's worried about a possible leak at Court, but not what the blackmailer will do."

"Better safe than sorry," Ronnie grumbled. "I don't understand why Wells wouldn't at least alert the U.S. Marshalls."

"I don't understand either," Betsy responded, "but it's not my decision. Or yours."

Ronnie was about to say something more, but Betsy held up a warning hand.

Betsy was conflicted, too, Cassandra could tell, but Ronnie's suggestion was no solution.

"Is there anything else we can do?" Cassandra asked. "Should do?"

"Go to the gala," Betsy said. Her lips quirked. "That's what Robert said. Business as usual."

"There is," Marlon said, "nothing usual about our business these days. But let's pretend otherwise, at least for this evening. Let's go, everybody."

CHAPTER 20

Friday, Sept. 8, 6:30 p.m., The Embassy
Marlon parked at the valet stand. He swung out of the Volvo as Ronnie emerged from the passenger seat. Marlon handed his keys to the attendant, then accompanied Ronnie toward the security gate.

Marlon peered at his friend.

"You could use a new tux."

Ronnie stopped and glared at him.

"I do not. I look good in this one. Better than good. Handsome, sophisticated, mysterious, bold. In fact ..."

Ronnie stuck out his chest, put one hand on his waist, and languidly extended the other.

"Call me Bond. James Bond."

Marlon, chuckling, pushed Ronnie playfully in the chest.

"Like every other man in a tux, you look like a penguin. And on you, a porky penguin."

Ronnie responded with a hearty Bronx cheer. Laughing, they walked through the scanner and into the embassy.

The gala organizers had been delighted to secure this elegant, spacious venue for the event, courtesy of a new NATO member anxious to secure most-favored nation status with its host country. Offering the public spaces of the embassy to a prominent Washington cultural institution would not hurt its cause.

Under the glass-domed atrium, the auditorium of the embassy was sparsely populated. Waiters glided here and there, and the handful of other early arrivals clustered around the food stations.

When the five-hundred guests they were expecting showed up, the place would be hopping.

"I'm going to get a soda and wander around," Ronnie said. "I'll see you later."

Marlon grabbed a flute of champagne from off the tray of a passing waiter. Sipping, he scanned the room.

On the far side, Marlon spotted Justice Wells, the picture of propriety in his well-fitted tux and dazzling white shirt punctuated by a conservative black cummerbund. The Justice appeared to be listening intently to the man in front of him, who was facing away from Marlon. That big, square head looked familiar, though.

Even across the one-hundred-yard auditorium, Marlon heard the high-pitched laugh. Stuart Hersch, whose long-winded closing arguments in court put the jury to sleep and drew yawns from even the starchiest of judges. Lord, Stuart would blather on forever and bore the Justice to death.

Marlon half-trotted over and put his hand on Stuart's shoulder.

"Stuart, I'm surprised to see you here," Marlon said. "I wouldn't have taken you for an opera fan."

Stuart showed a mouthful of blocky white teeth.

"Er, yeah, well...."

"Could I have a word with the Justice, please?" Marlon asked as he used his grip on Stuart to guide him firmly off and away.

"He's insufferable," Marlon groused after Stuart was roughly out of earshot. "His depositions go on for hours. He asked my client what kind of toothpaste she used, for god's sake."

"He's young, Marlon. That's all that's wrong with him."

Marlon took a sip of his champagne, struggling to find something more to say. The only things Marlon could think of right now was that threat and the Justice's odd response to it. But to speak of that was verboten.

"Uh, Betsy shouldn't have left you to fend off Court groupies unaided. But I get it. Pets come first, even before beloved godfathers."

Justice Wells, smiling, nodded. His expression changed, then he peered closely at Marlon. Marlon could not quite read the expression in his eyes, but Wells appeared deep in thought. About what? Surely not pets.

"We've an interesting docket this month. Feelings on the bench are running high."

This seemed an odd time and place to be discussing pending Supreme Court cases, but Marlon did his best to play along.

"Oh, uh, is that so?"

"We're jockeying for position, but keeping our cards close to our vest. On one case, I responded to the Chief's opening with a Michael's cue to keep things interesting."

Marlon, baffled, cocked his head.

How the justices lined up on one side or the other of a decision was a sensitive, internal matter. Why was Wells talking about it now, at a public event? And why to Marlon, of all people? And what did Michael's cue, an obscure bridge bidding convention, have to do with any of this?

Marlon was not about to challenge Wells on any of this, though.

"Uh, risky," Marlon hazarded. "The bid, that is."

"It's a useful bid to remember...."

"Robert," an unknown voice interrupted the Justice. A slight, older man had appeared at Robert's shoulder. "Nice to see you."

Justice Wells shifted his position and reached out his hand. "Good evening. Jeremy, this is Marlon White. Marlon, Jeremy Ross."

Marlon and Jeremy murmured their greetings and shook hands.

"Betsy attended law school with Jeremy's daughter," the Justice explained to Marlon.

"And my daughter clerked for the Chief Justice," Jeremy chipped in, "with whom I've become good friends. And we've met," he dipped his chin toward Robert, "at various Court functions."

"To square the circle here," Wells smiled, "Marlon and Betsy work at the same firm."

Marlon's mind had been elsewhere, puzzling over Wells's weird reference to bridge, but now it clicked. The firm. Jeremy Ross. Brenda.

That defamation suit was a shame for both, in a way. Water over the dam, though, and not Marlon's problem.

"Ah," Jeremy replied, "you're lucky to have Betsy. Wonderful girl, and so bright."

Oh, man, that was smarmy. Buttering up to Justice Wells.

Marlon took another good look at Jeremy, who was staring straight at Marlon. Jeremy had the oddest eyes, pale grey irises, almost white, unnaturally large black pupils.

Marlon stifled an involuntary shudder. He owed Jeremy a response.

"Yeah, Betsy's great," Marlon muttered.

"Where's your daughter working now?" Justice Wells asked Jeremy. "I can't recall."

Marlon did not need to know. Time to move on.

"Nice to meet you, Jeremy. Enjoy the evening, gentlemen."

With a wave, Marlon started to move on when a young man in a brown suit rushed up to him. The guy looked vaguely familiar, but Marlon could not place him.

"Marlon," the man beamed, "just who I was looking for. Remember me? Pete Kowski. We met at that seminar last week. I'm just out of law school. Is Aaron hiring?"

Marlon listened with half an ear as the recent graduate extolled his virtues, angling for a job.

Over Pete's shoulder, Marlon noticed Jeremy putting his hand on Wells's arm and stepping closer to the Justice. Wells looked uncomfortable but did not draw back.

"I don't see your security this evening," Marlon barely overheard Jeremy, voice pitched low. "Didn't the Chief order the justices to be accompanied by a Marshall on public occasions?"

It seemed an odd question. Why would he be asking about Robert's personal security? But then, hadn't Miranda said Jeremy owned a cybersecurity company? Did that explain it, somehow?

"It's a recommendation," Justice Wells's voice responded in his normal tone. "The Chief does not order us."

"Well...."

"Unless the Marshalls are aware of a specific reason for concern," Justice Wells continued. "Only then is it mandatory."

"That's a ... understandable," Jeremy responded.

Marlon's thoughts veered from his confusion about Jeremy when an idea struck him. Marlon would tell Betsy what he had overheard. With the Chief's recommendation, maybe she could convince Robert to engage the Marshalls more often, which would be a relief to her.

Marlon murmured something semi-encouraging to the job seeker, then set off to find a more entertaining conversation. He spied Cassandra sashaying toward the terrace in a marvelous, floor-length, cream-colored gown. Cassandra could always make him laugh. Marlon started toward her.

But then, Cassandra took the arm of the big man beside her, her guest, presumably. She turned to him and, with her face in profile, Marlon saw her beaming smile.

Cassandra had told Marlon that inviting Nikolai to the gala was all for work. Yeah, right. If Cassandra was going to be socializing with Bolkonsky, Marlon needed more intel on the man.

CHAPTER 21

Friday, Sept. 8, 6:45 p.m., The Embassy Terrace
Cassandra and Nikolai stepped out onto the starlit terrace, enclosed by whispering green walls of the old-growth trees in the neighborhood. One other couple stood, heads together, to their left. Otherwise, the terrace was for them alone, if she did not count the burly bodyguard hulking just outside the door to the embassy proper.

A bodyguard was no big deal. Half the people in town had one, it seemed. They tended to look alike. Fit, men mostly, wearing suits and that curly plastic mic cord coming out of their ear.

Nikolai's bodyguard had nothing coming out of his ear, but menace oozed from his pores. Blocky, with bulging arms and an enormous chest encased in a black shirt buttoned up to his chin, hawk nose and close-set eyes, the man glided like a jungle cat when he moved.

Cassandra caught a whiff of Nikolai's cologne, woodsy and piney, as if Nikolai had just emerged from the encircling forest.

The night was young. Cassandra had a handsome man on her arm for the first time in months. She would get to Josef, she promised herself, but not just now.

"Tell me about yourself, Nikolai. About your past, that is."

She felt Nikolai stiffen. "No. What's past is past. Leave it alone."

He glanced at her. Cassandra tried but apparently failed to hide how she felt about his rebuff.

"Why do you want to know?" Nikolai asked, the coldness mostly gone from his voice.

Maybe she should just drop it. Get on to her real business with Nikolai and talk about Josef.

No, Cassandra was not quite ready to give up. She was not about to show her hand, either, until she had a better idea of her man.

"Uh, it may be important to the case," she said. "Tell me about Sonya when she was growing up. Tell me about your family."

Nikolai cocked an eyebrow but nodded. He had accepted her explanation, or was pretending to, at least.

Or maybe his reticence was an old habit, and he was as interested in her as she was in him.

Stop overthinking it and go with the flow, Cassandra told herself.

Nikolai dipped his head toward the balustrade on the far side of the terrace, and they started toward it.

"Sonya's mother, Antonina, and I were both students at Moscow State University. We married a month after we met. Times were hard. The economy crumbled during the Yeltsin years."

"That was during the '90s, right?" Cassandra asked. "Things weren't so great for me then, either."

"Hah," Nikolai responded. "You have no idea. You may have tightened your belts, but we had no belts. Antonina and I wanted children, but we put it off. We could barely feed ourselves, let alone a family."

An image passed through Cassandra's mind. Her daughter, Mary, must have been five at the time. Mary wailed inconsolably because she only had a peanut butter and jelly sandwich in her lunchbox that morning.

Again, Mom? The cool kids have sandwiches from the deli, wrapped like presents in white paper.

But Cassandra stayed quiet. She had a feeling Nikolai and his wife had been through worse. Much worse.

Their stroll had taken them across the terrace. Cassandra turned to lean her backside against the balustrade, facing Nikolai, who stood in front of her.

"I was born in a poor village and was lucky to get a place in the university," Nikolai continued. "My family had no connections. Before the Wall fell, I would have stayed a nobody. With the disintegration of the Soviet regime, everybody had a chance. I managed to get a low-level position in the diplomatic corps."

Cassandra eyed her companion. Despite the elegant veneer his wealth gave him, and his inherent charisma, Nikolai had rough edges, unvarnished by society or pretense. He also exuded physical strength and energy. She had a hard time imagining him sipping tea in an embassy reception room.

"I was posted to the former Soviet, now Russian Embassy in Washington, which was a bit of a joke since I spoke almost no English. I learned it on the job. Anyway, Sonya was born nine months after we moved to D.C."

"How long were you here? In D.C., that is?"

"Until Sonya was three. I had decided I was at a dead end as a diplomat. I took my family back to Russia. I worked hard and got lucky. We had money for the first time in our lives. Then, Antonina died. Breast cancer. Sonya was only seven."

"I'm so sorry," Cassandra murmured. "Sonya told me you never married again. Did you ever consider it?"

"Never," Nikolai answered. "Antonina was … special, in a way I haven't and don't expect to see again."

Cassandra mentally shrugged off her unexpected disappointment. She was hardly ready to marry anybody, let alone this man.

"And Sonya?" Cassandra began. "When did you know she had … issues?"

"Asperger's, you mean?"

He had confirmed her suspicions. She nodded.

Nikolai sighed. "Far too late, I'm afraid. First, I thought it was grief for losing her mother. Then, I was away from home so much. I engaged a series of nyanyas, nannies, that is, but Sonya hated them. I fired one and tried another. I realized, too late, that it was Sonya, not the nannies."

"Not too late," Cassandra replied. "Sonya seems just fine. You should be proud. I know how hard it is to be responsible for a child on your own. I raised my daughter, Mary, after her father left us."

Nikolai raised his eyebrows in a question.

"I married my high school sweetheart shortly after graduation. Mary was born soon after. Lean years and my husband's increasing unhappiness followed. He decamped for Seattle. He's still in our lives, though, because he does love our daughter. He has his own family now, as well. I never remarried."

"We're not so different then, you and I," Nikolai remarked.

Cassandra was about to retort that she was not worth a billion dollars nor had drinking buddies in the Kremlin. Discretion prevailed, but he seemed to read her mind, anyway.

"You Americans think we're alike. You lump all successful Russians into this caricature called an 'oligarch.' We're all ruthless and corrupt. Our wealth came from doing deals with the Devil. As I said, I'm only a businessman, Cassandra, no more and no less, except I had to make my way in a world with no rules."

His little speech had gotten her back up.

"First, I'm not 'all Americans,'" she spat out the words. "Second, you have no idea what it really means to labor against a stereotype. 'No rules' is one thing. Try playing the game when the other side has designed the rules, so they win, you lose."

He had the grace to flush. "I'm sorry. I spoke thoughtlessly. Please forgive me."

She gave him a curt nod. She was still affronted, but her anger was waning.

"May we start over," Nikolai continued, "from before I mentioned oligarchs?"

She could not help but smile.

"When I returned to Russia from Washington," he began, "I found chaos. It was like your Wild West. My country swarmed with hungry men from all over the world, many Americans, anxious to steal our wealth in natural resources. I fought for what was rightfully mine."

"Puleese," Cassandra chided, "get off your soap box. You got rich."

Nikolai frowned. "It's not the money I care about."

"What is it, then? What do you care about? Other than Sonya, of course."

"Well, I...."

They both looked up at a burst of laughter. A cluster of fellow partygoers poured onto the terrace. Nikolai's bodyguard had moved from his post beside the door and was moving quickly toward them.

"Party pooper," Cassandra teased, inclining her head toward the approaching bodyguard.

Nikolai did not smile at her lame joke. Instead, he motioned for her to stay put. Nikolai turned, intercepted the bodyguard, and they spoke briefly.

Nikolai retraced his steps. "I must greet another guest. Shall we go in?"

Perfectly polite, but his easygoing warmth had vanished. Was it something she said?

Cassandra hoped she had not blown her chances with Nikolai. Then, she remembered her witness. She might have lost him on that front, too.

CHAPTER 22

Friday, Sept. 8, 7:00 p.m., The Embassy

Miranda was wondering whether she should go check on Chad when Marlon walked up and kissed her on the cheek. He eyed her gown.

She had splurged on a beaded black dress, low-necked, drop-waisted, with a hemline just above the knee.

"Well?" she asked. "Am I too old for the flapper look?"

Marlon waggled his eyebrows. "You look scrumptious, darling," he said.

"Thanks," Miranda said, relieved. Chad had raved, but of course he had to. "Congratulations, by the way, on a good crowd."

"It should be. We all worked our butts off selling tickets. We need to raise a ton of money for the opera to make up for the hit we took during the pandemic."

Miranda nodded. "Speaking of money, would you buy me a drink? I left my purse in the car, counting on Chad to cover my bar bill."

"Isn't Chad here? I thought he was your date for tonight."

"He is, but he's not feeling well. Something he ate, he thinks. He's in the men's room, and I have a feeling he'll be in there a while."

"Ugh."

"Yeah, poor boy. So one drink for me, and then I'm guessing Chad will want to go home."

"Bummer. The night's still young!"

"Yeah, well, I don't mind. I'm okay with an early evening."

"All that fresh air this morning and sleuthing in the afternoon," Marlon teased.

It was what came between in Chad's bedroom that really did her in, but Marlon did not need to hear about that.

"That drink?" she proposed instead.

Despite a flock of circling waiters, a knot of people surrounded the bar. They would have to wait their turn.

Jeremy Ross emerged from the crowd holding a plate of steaming pasta, orzo with scampi from the look of it.

"Hello again," Jeremy said, nodding at Marlon. "Oh, and Miranda. You two know each other?"

Miranda, surprised, was about to ask about that "again," when Marlon answered Jeremy's question.

"We're at the same firm. We both work with Betsy."

"Ah, how nice," Jeremy replied absently. "Oh, and Robert tells me you're one of the organizers of this, Marlon. Nice work. Great for the opera."

Jeremy smiled and moved on.

"You've met Jeremy before?" Miranda asked.

Marlon explained. "And you?"

"We bumped into him at lunch today. Turns out he's one of Chad's clients."

"What'd you think of him?"

Miranda shrugged. "Seemed nice enough. Except when I mentioned Brenda."

"Why would you do that?"

Miranda, embarrassed at her own behavior, avoided the truth, that she had been trying to impress Jeremy with her celebrity clients.

"Uh, Brenda's name popped up," she said.

Marlon raised an eyebrow but did not push it.

"Are you going to tell her?" he asked instead. "Brenda, that is."

"I already did. Just now. She and I were talking. I spotted Jeremy and mentioned that incident to her."

"Brenda's here, too?"

"You worked your butt off, remember? Brenda's email must have been on your list. You invited her, she came. Anyway, yeah. I was surprised, given her rough week, but she said she hoped to meet somebody here."

"Sounds like Ronnie."

"Yeah, exactly. She's trying to interview some corporate bigwig, about a recent sale of a company asset."

Marlon stared at her. "Is this that hacking thing she's working on?"

Miranda understood his cryptic comment. "I think so. She's not saying much about that."

"Brenda wasn't scared away, then."

Miranda pushed aside the feeling of disquiet that thought gave her. She was tired, Chad was sick, and all Miranda wanted to do was get them home and go to bed.

"You know," she replied, "I've changed my mind about that drink. I'll go make sure Chad's okay. Enjoy the rest of the evening, Marlon."

She blew him a kiss and went to find the restrooms.

Chad emerged, white-faced, before she could screw up the nerve to walk into the men's room. Miranda hooked her arm through his.

"Are you okay?"

Chad nodded. "Better now, but I'm not up for staying. I'll call an Uber."

"No way. I'm coming with you. Come on, let's get my car."

They wended their way out of the embassy. At the valet stand, Miranda fished her ticket out of her bag and handed it to the uniformed attendant. He turned and scanned the fobs and keys hanging on a peg board.

"Hmm, I'm not seeing it," the young man said. "Hang on a minute."

Miranda huffed. "Of all times for a screwup. Do you need to sit down while we wait, honey?"

"No, I'm fine," Chad responded, but he propped himself up against a planter box and closed his eyes, hands clutched to his abdomen.

Miranda looked up and spied the attendant down the sidewalk, at the corner of the embassy building, talking to another man, also in uniform. The second guy reached into his pants pocket, retrieved something, and handed it to the attendant.

The attendant trotted back toward them, holding a fob in the air.

"Got it," he said. "The new guy grabbed the wrong one. We'll have your car in a sec."

The attendant called for a driver. A few minutes later, Miranda's Toyota blasted up to the valet stand. The driver hopped out and, smiling, handed Miranda her fob.

"Great dress," he said.

Miranda, smiling, handed him the twenty she had gotten from Chad. A generous tip, but the delay had not been his fault. Besides, he had good taste in clothes.

The night air seemed to have revived Chad considerably, and they chatted comfortably as they headed toward McLean.

"I saw Brenda but didn't get a chance to talk to her," Chad said. "Did you?"

"Yeah, and I told her about our encounter with Jeremy today. She didn't seem to mind. She asked me what I thought of him."

"And?"

"I was noncommittal, but she said it wouldn't offend her if I admitted liking the guy. 'He can be quite charming,' she said. That's when she spilled the beans."

"About what?"

"Her affair with Jeremy."

"Ah. You were right, then. You suspected something personal about Jeremy's grudge against her."

"Yep. Anyway, the affair was years ago. They met in Russia. Jeremy was trying the commodities market there. He lost his shirt. Brenda said he didn't have the cojones for the vicious competition. Not as big as those of the Russians, anyway."

Chad chuckled.

Miranda braked as the light at Arizona and Macarthur Boulevard turned red. The pedal felt sticky. The car was probably overdue for service.

"Brenda broke it off," she continued. "Jeremy was amoral and unprincipled. He's loathed her ever since, as much for bruising his ego as anything else. That's why he filed that lawsuit, not because the story was false, Brenda said."

The light turned. Miranda crossed Macarthur onto the steep and windy descent to Canal Road.

She could see that the first s-curve was clear. But the line of blinking taillights beyond showed traffic backed up at the turn onto Canal.

The Toyota picked up speed. Miranda tapped the brakes. Nothing happened.

A wave of adrenalin hit like a hammer. Hot, skin prickling, Miranda's ears roared.

"Chad!" she yelled, eyes glued to the road, hands clamped to the wheel.

"Hit the brake, Miranda."

"I am!" Miranda cried, pumping the pedal. Nothing happened.

At forty miles an hour, the Toyota rounded the last stretch of the curve, a stopped car twenty yards ahead. Miranda braced herself against the steering wheel for the collision.

Then, she realized what else she was seeing. The cul-de-sac she had passed hundreds of times without really noticing it branched steeply up to the right.

She cranked the wheel. They shot off Arizona, rapidly losing speed. The road leveled at the top of the hill, and the car stopped completely as it bumped gently into a railroad tie marking the end of the pavement.

Blinking back tears, Miranda loosened her death grip on the steering wheel. Chad reached over and gently brushed her cheek with his finger.

"You okay?"

"Yeah," Miranda managed.

"The brakes go out?"

"I guess."

She laid her head back on the neck rest, listening to her heart pound. Opening her eyes, she turned to Chad. Her gaze caught on the fob nestled in the cup holder on the console.

"Chad?"

"Hmm?"

"Does this car's braking system have a software component?"

"Oh, sure, the newer ones all do."

"I'm guessing that means it could be hacked, right? To mess with the brakes?

"You guessed right."

"Can you hack a car with a fob?"

"Yes. Why are you asking right now? You sure you're okay?"

Weary, Miranda closed her eyes again, picturing the scene.

The new guy, pocketing her fob.

CHAPTER 23

Friday, Sept. 8, 7:20 p.m., The Embassy
Nikolai loosened up slightly once they were back in the auditorium. At least he squired her gamely around the crowd with a hand on her elbow.

Cassandra introduced Nikolai to Marlon, who was polite but said little, and Betsy, who, it turned out, spoke a little Russian. After her other friends wandered off, Cassandra looked for Miranda and Chad. She did not see them, though, which was not surprising given the crowd.

Cassandra excused herself to powder her nose. Staring at herself in the mirror, she mused at how easy it was to forget who Nikolai was and simply enjoy his company.

But what was he?

Only a businessman, as he claimed, suffering indignities and loneliness to take care of his family, as only a good man would. Or disgraced, stripped of his power and authority, exiled from his homeland? Perhaps a Russian spy.

Life was not so simple. Nikolai could be all these things.

Cassandra was sure she had met spies before. They abounded in Washington.

Should it be different because Nikolai was Russian? Or because she hoped to see more of him? That would be a first for her. A spy boyfriend.

She grinned, sheepishly, at her reflection. Boyfriend? They had not even had a real date.

Cassandra stuffed her makeup into her bag, reminded that she had to find another opportunity to be alone with Nikolai to talk about Josef.

Back in the auditorium, Nikolai was not where she had left him. Cassandra wandered around, murmuring greetings to strangers. When a familiar blond head appeared above the crowd, Cassandra maneuvered her way to Jim, whom she found chatting with Marlon.

"Hi, guys," Cassandra said.

Marlon tipped his champagne flute by way of greeting.

"Have you seen Nikolai?"

"Uh," Marlon pointed his thumb, "back there by the main bar, a few minutes ago, anyway."

Cassandra found Nikolai where indicated, in conversation with another man, also in a tux, also Russian, by the looks of him. Of average build, Nikolai's companion looked slender next to Nikolai's bulk.

Behind Nikolai hovered his bodyguard, whose twin stood to the right of Nikolai's acquaintance.

Cassandra was about to join the group when the two men in evening attire fell into a wide-armed hug. Something about the stiffness in Nikolai's shoulders told Cassandra that the embrace was not from affection, but a formality only.

Nikolai disengaged himself, spun on his heel, and caught himself just before bumping into her.

Cassandra's smile faltered. Nikolai's heavy body loomed over her. His beautiful blue eyes, darkened to the ominous gray of a gathering thunderstorm, stared sightlessly out of a frozen, angry face.

She felt, for the first time, in the company of a Russian gangster.

"I, uh, should we...."

He straightened, moving slightly away from her.

"Let's go, shall we?" Nikolai said, his voice tight. He cleared his throat and gave her a thin smile. "We still have our lawsuit to discuss, do we not?"

She agreed to his proposal. They would conclude the evening with a stroll to enjoy the lovely evening air. Nikolai called his driver. A stretch limo arrived. Nikolai invited Cassandra into the passenger seat with him. The bodyguard crammed himself into the seat beside the driver.

On the drive to the park, Nikolai said little. But his expression softened. He joked about the headache he would have in the morning. He should have had his usual vodka instead of champagne.

Cassandra wondered what had so infuriated Nikolai. She held her tongue for now.

Ten minutes after they left the embassy, they strolled down the promenade of the Georgetown Waterfront Park, the bodyguard trailing behind. The dense traffic over Key Bridge in the mid-distance created a lighted arc over the darkly gleaming Potomac.

Cassandra spotted an empty bench beside the promenade.

"Let's sit, shall we?" she asked.

They made themselves comfortable. For a few moments, they sat silently, watching the river flow by.

"About Josef," Cassandra began.

Nikolai sighed and stretched his legs out in front of him.

"I do not like to air my family's deepest secrets, even to the family lawyer. But you are persistent."

Cassandra smiled to herself.

Cassandra's shoulder was not quite touching Nikolai's. Still, she sensed him stiffening. His left hand, which had been resting on his knee, clenched into a fist.

"You cannot trust Josef. Besides, he can't testify. I had to send him away."

That sounded ominous. To where? Siberia?

"Josef beat my daughter," Nikolai continued.

Cassandra's chest tightened with anger. Her stomach churned. Siberia was too good for Josef. Anyone who abused her daughter, Mary, would get worse than that.

"Why, then," she said, as she forced herself to put that thought behind her, "did Sonya even tell me about Josef? She spoke of him with affection, too."

"This must be the lawyer in you," Nikolai responded. "The woman knows these incompatible things can both be true. Sonya did love Josef. Still loves him, I suppose. She could not accept the facts."

Yes, she did know about the complexities of love. Cassandra could almost imagine Nikolai's anguish when he broke Sonya's heart. She reached over and placed her hand on Nikolai's thigh.

Nikolai shifted toward her. He extended his arm and laid it on the back of the bench, behind Cassandra. Cassandra felt herself relax in the warmth of his embrace.

"Well," Cassandra broke their silence, "I'll have to work with what I've got. I've tried some hard cases. I can do it again."

"Thank you," Nikolai replied. "One day, perhaps, I can return the favor. I should thank you for the invitation to the gala, too. I enjoyed myself. It was nice meeting your friends."

"And, uh, you had a friend there too, I take it? That man, the other Russian I mean, who…."

"Anatoly," Nikolai interrupted. "Anatoly Guschev. He's no friend to me."

Cassandra saw that bear hug in her mind's eye.

"He didn't look like an enemy either," she replied.

Nikolai sighed heavily.

"I despise Anatoly, but he's Russian. A brother. I know what to expect from him. I like Americans, but you're unpredictable. You jump around like a cat on hot asphalt."

He had a teasing note in his voice, but Cassandra heard the underlying sincerity. She did not protest, because Nikolai had a point.

"I do business with Anatoly because I must. A necessary evil."

"Why do you despise him?"

"Anatoly is of the newest generation of oligarchs. We call them the *siloviki*. They care about nothing but power. Their own. Which means they will do anything to maintain their ties with the Kremlin, including supporting its vicious wars. Bah."

Nikolai's phone inside his jacket pocket beeped. Nikolai reached for it.

Out of the corner of her eye, Cassandra spotted motion behind the bench on which they sat.

Cassandra spun her head around to get a better look. It took a second for her brain to catch up to the image.

A man coming toward them at a full run from the direction of M Street. Carrying a handgun.

"Nikolai!" she screamed, turning toward him.

A metallic bark rang out behind her. Her ears registered a gunshot just as the heavy weight of a body slammed into her, knocking her off the bench. She cried out as she fell toward the stony promenade. Her head landed on Nikolai's cradling arm.

Before Cassandra had time to catch her breath, Nikolai was helping her to her feet. He simultaneously snapped something in Russian to the bodyguard, also with a gun in his hand, who had appeared behind them.

Nikolai hustled her up the incline from the river to the waiting limo, parked on M Street. Nikolai opened the back door. Cassandra jumped in with Nikolai right behind her.

Cassandra sat back, panting.

"Are you hurt?" Nikolai asked, leaning in, hand on her shoulder.

Cassandra was on the verge of telling him how she really felt. Frightened, yes, and angry, as much at herself as anything, for being stupid enough to walk alone in the dark with a man with violence in his past.

He looked so concerned, though, and deeply unhappy.

Cassandra forced her breathing to slow. She exhaled, puffing out her cheeks.

"I'm fine. You, though," she poked him in the chest with her index finger, "need a new bodyguard."

Nikolai grunted. "He's better at close quarters. Anyway," he shrugged one shoulder, "there was no real danger. If they want me dead, I'm dead. That," he nodded back toward the park, "was only a reminder."

"Who's 'they?'"

"My brothers," Nikolai made it sound like a swear word, "who don't trust me."

And why is that, Cassandra wondered, but said nothing.

CHAPTER 24

Friday, Sept. 8, 7:45 p.m., The Embassy

"Smile!" the photographer called.

Marlon dutifully obliged.

He turned to the woman beside him, six feet tall, curves bursting out of a crimson satin gown, his companion in the publicity photo.

"We can't thank you enough for gracing our company this evening, Anna."

"It was my pleasure," she purred in a warm contralto. She air-kissed Marlon on the cheek and moved on.

"Who's the babe?" asked the diminutive brunette at his shoulder, swathed in a black shawl.

"Kay, hi, nice to see you. That's Anna Kubatova. She's the hottest thing at the Met this season."

"Gorgeous, too," Kay said. "Russian, I take it?"

"Yes, but why...."

"The guy she's with. The one manhandling her. He's Russian too."

Marlon followed Kay's gaze. Indeed, the man with shiny black hair swept off a broad forehead, an inch or so shorter than Anna, had one hand planted on her waist, the other on Anna's shoulder.

"Russians all over the place tonight," Marlon mused. "I saw that man with Nikolai earlier."

Kay raised an eyebrow.

"Nikolai Bolkonsky," Marlon answered her question. "We're representing his daughter."

Kay raised the other eyebrow. "Wow," she deadpanned.

"Yeah, the oligarch."

"I suppose it doesn't matter to Aaron," Kay responded, "as long as it's a good case."

"Isn't that the way it's supposed to be?" Marlon asked, slightly offended on Aaron's behalf. "Equal in the eyes of the law, and all that."

Kay rolled her eyes.

Kay, a good friend of Miranda's, worked at the State Department in a high-level political capacity, the lengthy title of which Marlon could never remember. Kay would have the scoop on Nikolai if she was willing to share.

"Is he a spy?" Marlon hazarded. "Nikolai, that is."

"I doubt it," Kay responded. "He fell out of favor with the Kremlin a few years ago. Still," she shrugged, "you never know if someone's a spy until you know."

"Ugh," Marlon teased, putting his hands over his ears. "State gobbledygook."

"I'm just saying."

"He had something to do with Russian espionage, though? Before he came to the States?"

"Nikolai supplied the money, or lots of it, anyway," Kay responded. "He knew how to do business with the West, too. He arranged for the import of technology they needed. Found the people to run it, too, like programmers and coders."

"Sounds more like a regular businessman."

"I wouldn't go that far," Kay said dryly.

"And the other guy? The one mauling Anna?"

"Anatoly Guschev. He's an oligarch, too. He's on the sanctioned list. You know, I presume, what I mean by that?"

Marlon stopped himself from rolling his eyes. Kay could be a supercilious pain in the neck when she was talking about her work. She seemed to think the world would fall apart if the State Department did not keep its eyes on it.

"Of course. Those oligarchs on the list had their assets frozen and, uh, I think could be arrested in certain countries."

Marlon realized he did not know as much about it as he thought he did.

Kay, satisfied, smiled. "It's complicated. Anyway, a lot of people think Anatoly was unfairly caught in a net cast too wide. That he's a very successful businessman, but that's all. I've met him."

She switched her gaze over his shoulder, looking at Anatoly.

"He's smart," she commented. "Speaks French. Fluently. Cultured."

Marlon glanced back at Anatoly and Anna. "Not all the time."

Kay smirked. "Indeed. Heh, I can't find Miranda. Have you seen her?"

"She and Chad left early. He wasn't feeling well."

Kay nodded, gave a little wave, and started off.

"Heh," Marlon called. "Is Nikolai on the sanctioned list?"

"No." Kay shrugged. "Slipped through the noose somehow."

Kay turned and left.

"Marlon," a buxom, grey-haired woman trilled beside him. "Have you eaten anything yet? Come join us."

Marlon enjoyed a plate of thinly sliced, rare flank steak topped with béarnaise sauce while he and three of his new friends on the patron's circle congratulated themselves for a job well done.

"It's been a pleasure," Marlon said to the ladies as he set his plate on a passing waiter's tray. "See you at the board meeting Tuesday."

Marlon scanned the auditorium for another conversational partner. The crowd was diminishing, and Marlon noticed Joe across the room, near its entrance.

Might as well make nice. From the way it was going, Marlon might have to make overtures to Joe about settling Sonya's case, sooner rather than later.

Marlon wended his way over to Joe who, Marlon could now see, was talking with Jeremy Ross. Of course, Marlon remembered. Joe represented Jeremy in his defamation case against Brenda.

As his lawyer, Joe should know Jeremy well. Maybe Joe knew something about Jeremy that would explain the strange conversation between Justice Wells and Jeremy about security.

By the time Marlon got to him, Joe stood alone, sipping from a tumbler of cloudy brown liquid.

"Heh, Joe," Marlon slapped the defense lawyer's shoulder. "Nice of you to make the time to come support the opera."

"Yes, well," Joe smiled, "I'm a fan, you know."

"I met your friend, Jeremy, tonight," Marlon began.

"Ah, client, you mean. Was, that is."

"Just what business is he in? I heard cybersecurity, but is there more to it?"

"Jeremy's core business is Cerberus, but he also does a lot of consulting. Very lucrative consulting. You see, in implementing the security end, he gets to know his client's business inside and out. That knowledge is quite valuable."

"I suppose so," Marlon muttered, but he was still thinking about what Jeremy asked Justice Wells. "Does one of Jeremy's companies provide personal protective services?"

"Not that I know of." Joe cleared his throat and shifted his feet. "But, then again, it's been several years since I represented Jeremy. I have nothing to do with him anymore."

A coldness had crept into Joe's voice.

"You don't much care for him, I take it?" Marlon ventured. "Did he stiff you on fees, or something?"

"Nah, nothing like that." Joe shrugged. "I probably shouldn't say anything. He was a client. Let's just say the staff didn't like him. Margie said she felt like she should hide her purse when he came into the office."

Marlon grinned, thinking of the handful of Aaron's clients about whom their staff felt similarly. In the end, those had not been Marlon's favorite clients, either.

"They're always the first to know," Marlon proposed.

"Yeah, well," Joe smiled crookedly, "that was for your ears only, Marlon. Anyway, I should get going. See you around."

Joe had not been talking only about his staff. Joe had no love lost for Jeremy, either.

Jeremy had apparently been a difficult client. In what way, Marlon wondered?

Thinking about Jeremy and his lawsuit inevitably led Marlon to Brenda. Brenda had been a model client of Aaron's. Jim and Beebe loved her.

Maybe Marlon was wrong about Brenda.

A commotion behind him interrupted Marlon's musings. He turned. The guests nearest him jostled together, then parted as a man stumbled through. Marlon caught a glimpse of his face just as he stumbled, falling face first onto the marble floor. Ronnie.

Drunk again.

Marlon closed his eyes at the familiar sinking feeling in his chest. Disappointment. Sadness. Resignation.

He had not seen Ronnie since they arrived. Marlon wondered fleetingly with whom Ronnie had been drinking.

When Marlon looked again, Jim had emerged from the crowd. Dropping to one knee, he snaked an arm around Ronnie's neck, lifting his head off the floor.

Jim looked up at Marlon. "I'll get Ronnie home. You enjoy your party."

Marlon mouthed a "thank you." Then, he turned and walked away.

A few minutes later, Marlon had another full flute of champagne in his hand. He took a sip and felt his good mood return.

With any luck, Ronnie had only stumbled off the wagon, and he would get right back on again. And other than that, they'd raised a boatload of money for the opera, and everyone had fun.

Marlon raised his glass in a toast to a delightful evening.

CHAPTER 25

Saturday, Sept. 9, 7:30 a.m., The Office

Marlon unlocked the door to the office suite. The fluorescent lights were already on overhead. Seventies disco music blared from somewhere inside. Marlon smelled coffee.

He smiled. Jim was here and on time despite complaining about it all day yesterday.

Nobody was thrilled that the monthly case review was always scheduled for the crack of dawn on a Saturday morning. If they did not get started early, though, they would be in the office all day, an even worse prospect.

Today, everybody was running late. None of the associates' office lights were on except for Marlon's.

"How's Ronnie today?" Jim called from the door to Marlon's office.

"Up and about, surprisingly. Well, I guess not such a surprise. He said he didn't have anything to drink last night."

"You believe him?"

"I believe he wasn't drunk. I've seen the aftermath too many times. Ronnie's too clear- headed to be hung over."

"Then what happened to him? He was barely conscious when I hauled him off the floor."

Marlon shrugged. "Maybe one drink was too much for him after being sober for so long? I don't know. Ronnie says he doesn't remember much about the evening. When I left, he said he was going for a run. Maybe it'll clear his head."

"Hmm, well, as long as he's okay. You going to help me get the files into the conference room?"

Marlon grumbled but got up from his desk to lend a hand.

They ran into Betsy in the corridor.

"At least one of you people knows how to keep time," Marlon joked.

"I can't stay though," Betsy replied, clutching her phone. "I'd just walked in when I got a text alert from Robert's home security system. Somebody entered the house without disarming it. I called Robert, but he didn't answer."

"Doesn't the system alert the police, too?" Marlon asked, sure that the cops must already be on the way.

"No," Betsy's frustration was evident in her voice, "because Robert has accidentally set off the alarm so many times. He didn't want to keep bothering the police for no good reason."

"If it happens all the time," Jim shrugged, "try calling the Justice again later. We've got a ton of work to do here."

They had not yet told Jim about the threat.

Betsy looked at Marlon. She was keeping it together, probably because she was trying to convince herself that this was another false alarm.

But the timing looked bad.

"I'm going too," Marlon blurted. "We all will."

"What?" Jim spluttered. "Have you lost your marbles? Just call the police and ask them to run by for a security check."

Wells had been adamant. Do not call the authorities about the threat. This alarm might be unrelated, but Marlon did not want to risk disobeying Wells.

"No police," Marlon replied firmly. "Come on, let's get going."

"Thanks, guys," Betsy said, managing a wan smile.

"I'll tell you about it on the way," Marlon said, grabbing Jim's arm and hustling the two of them out behind Betsy.

Betsy wasted no time driving them to Justice Wells's house in Spring Valley. On the way, Marlon told Jim about the threats made to Justice Wells. He also texted Miranda and Cassandra that the three of them were on an urgent errand and would be back in the office asap.

From the front, the house looked intact. No broken windows, and the glossy black front door was closed.

Betsy pulled up to the curb, opened her car door, and stepped out. "Robert should be home," she mused, peering at the house. "I see his car in the garage. It's too early for him to be down at the shops. So why isn't he answering his phone?"

She started toward the house. Marlon and Jim piled out of the car and followed her.

Betsy grabbed the front doorknob and pulled on it. The door toppled forward. Jim reached up and caught the door just before it fell onto Betsy.

"The hinge," Jim nodded toward the jamb as he shouldered the door upright. "Wrenched out."

"Oh, lord," Marlon breathed, stomach clenching. "Someone *did* break in."

Betsy stepped into the vestibule, Marlon right behind her. Marlon realized what she was going to do a second before she called out.

He bolted forward, clamping his hand around Betsy's mouth. Luckily, only a stifled "Ro" escaped.

"Sshhh," Marlon hissed. "The burglar could still be here!"

Betsy's eyes widened. She nodded. Marlon dropped his hand.

"If he *was* here, I think he's gone now," Jim whispered. "He had to have heard me banging that door around."

"What if you're wrong?" Marlon hissed. "What if he's up there," he gestured toward the second floor, "with a gun?"

Marlon put a hand on Betsy's shoulder. "I don't think we have a choice, now. We get out of here and call the cops."

Betsy stared at him. Marlon could see the indecision in her eyes. Then, she shook her head.

"We're going in. Robert could be hurt, tied up and gagged somewhere in there, while we stand around talking. Follow me."

"No," Jim commanded. "You follow me."

The three of them, Jim in the lead, trotted through the dining room and kitchen, then circled back to the front of the house. As they entered the living room, Marlon could not help but notice the spare furnishings, a cane-backed rocking chair beside a standing reading light and a simple wooden settee.

Only the riot of color and light in the small, framed oil painting above the mantle relieved the severity. A real Monet if Marlon was any judge. Marlon almost smiled. One of Robert's few indulgences.

Jim bounded up the stairs, Betsy and Marlon right behind. After a quick pass through the room to the left, Robert's bedroom, the three of them ran into the only other room in the house, Robert's home office.

"Oh, lord," Betsy croaked.

The intruder had axed the roll-top desk that sat against the far wall, cleaving it down the middle. Before he destroyed the desk, the guy had pulled out all the drawers, emptied their contents onto the floor, then smashed the drawers, for good measure.

The thief toppled the bookcase and kicked the thick legal tomes that fell out of it across the room. He had apparently stomped through the manilla folders, legal pads, slip opinions, and notebooks strewn across the floor, for he left the occasional dusty footprint on the papers.

What riveted Marlon's eye, though, was the twelve-inch knife stabbed into the frame of one of the pictures hanging on the wall. The haft, handprints grooved into its black matte surface, underscored the latent violence of the steel shaft.

Before leaving his calling card, the assailant used it to slice through the center of the picture, leaving the reclining figure of one of Matisse's nude, blue women chopped in half.

Betsy dropped her head into her hands. Marlon knew what she had to be thinking. The thief had taken Robert.

Marlon glanced at Jim, whose pinched, white face reflected Marlon's own frozen uncertainty. What now?

Footsteps from below. Marlon's pulse raced.

"Get behind me, guys," Jim hissed, moving toward the office doorway.

"Who's here?" Wells's voice sounded more annoyed than alarmed.

"Robert!" Betsy cried. She bolted toward the door just as her godfather stepped into his office. Betsy grabbed Wells in a hug.

Wells gently disengaged himself as he glanced around the room. Marlon noticed Wells's gaze light on the Matisse. The corners of Wells's mouth drooped.

"This one's real too, isn't it?" Marlon asked.

Justice Wells nodded. "Sadly so."

Wells lowered himself onto one of the wing-back chairs on either side of the window. "A bit of a mess, isn't it?"

"Are you okay, sir?" Jim asked.

"Yes, I'm fine. I couldn't sleep. I went out for a walk."

"Are you calling the police, or am I?" Marlon asked.

"Neither. The only thing to report is a routine break-in. Nobody was hurt. The police have better things go do."

"Robert, there's no need to pretend this is 'routine,'" Betsy responded. "I told these guys about the threat, as you surely assumed I would."

Justice Wells nodded. "I thought you might."

"So you'll call?" Marlon asked. "After all, this," he gestured around the study, "isn't this the work of the blackmailer? And proof that he means business?"

"Yes, to the last two questions," the Justice responded, "but I'm not calling the police."

"Robert," Betsy said, steel in her voice, "don't be foolish." She pointed to the knife. "What's next?"

Robert raised his arms, palms out. "Calm down, everyone."

Betsy, sighing heavily, plopped onto the chair across from Robert. Jim leaned back against the wall next to the study door, and Marlon managed to hitch his backside onto a corner of the ruined desk.

"Betsy," the Justice said, "please don't worry. As I told you, this blackmailer wants something from me, and I must be alive and well to accomplish it. He won't hurt me."

An idea popped into Marlon's head. What was something only a judge could give?

"Your vote," Marlon blurted. "He's telling you how to decide a case."

Justice Wells squared his jaw. "Almost worse. He demands that I change the opinion I already submitted."

"Can you do that?" Betsy asked. "I mean," she flushed, "not that I think you would."

"Of course, I wouldn't," the Justice replied gruffly, "although it is feasible. It is not uncommon for the justices to submit revisions until the decision is finalized. For this case, that will be Monday, when the ruling of the Court is announced."

"This would be more than a revision," Betsy said. "Wouldn't it raise eyebrows if you switched sides suddenly?"

"It would be unusual, to say the least. But, as I said, I have no intention of doing that."

"If the blackmailer wants you to *change* your opinion," Betsy murmured, "that means he doesn't like the version you submitted. Which means he has access to it, which shouldn't be possible, unless…."

"Oh!" Jim sounded horrified. "The blackmailer's somebody at Court!"

"No," Justice Wells said firmly. "Not possible. But I do think an insider leaked my opinion to the blackmailer."

"That's about as bad," Jim sputtered.

Marlon barely heard him. He had been distracted by another thought.

"Not an insider," he proposed. "An outsider. A hacker. The Court could have been hacked."

The Justice shook his head. "I considered that possibility. I spoke to the Chief and requested a security check after I received the first threat. I didn't tell him why, nor did he ask. Anyway, there was no evidence of tampering."

"Okay, well, back to the leak," Marlon said. "Who has access to the opinions before they're made public? Any idea which of those folks could have done it?"

The Justice closed his eyes. "I know a person at the Court with secrets to hide and, therefore, vulnerable to duress," he said with a deep sadness in his voice. Reopening his eyes, Wells peered at Jim. "Pressure from the blackmailer, that is."

"Gabe," Betsy murmured. "Oh, dear." She kneaded her forehead vigorously with both hands. "This is all too much. You must tell the Chief everything. And call the Marshalls. Now."

A muscle in Justice Well's cheek twitched.

"If I report these threats, I will be expected to recuse myself. Refrain from participating in the case, in other words," he added, again directing his explanation to Jim.

"But why?" Jim asked.

"Because if I remained on the case, my decision would always be suspect. People would think I bowed to the pressure of the threats, whichever way I voted."

"What 'people?' Who would know?" Jim persisted.

"Well, everybody who knew about the threats. That would start with the Chief, then the Marshalls, then the FBI, presumably. The word would get out. It's hard to keep a secret in this town."

Betsy jumped up from her chair. She stepped directly in front of Justice Wells. Leaning down, she looked him squarely in the face.

"You have been threatened with physical violence," she said. "You need protection. You report the situation to the Marshalls, then recuse yourself." She threw her hands in the air. "What am I missing here?"

The Justice narrowed his eyes. "If I recuse, the blackmailer gets the outcome he wants, you see."

"But I don't see," Jim protested.

Wells sighed, closed his eyes, and pinched the bridge of his nose.

Marlon understood. Wells had been patient, but he had more pressing matters to deal with than explaining the intricacies of legal procedure to Jim.

Marlon waved his hand, catching Jim's eye. "Later," Marlon mouthed.

"Look," Betsy said, "I know you'd hate for the blackmailer to get his way. But it wouldn't be *your* fault."

"Not my fault, but my failure. I'd have given in."

"So?" Betsy tried again. "One sin does not a sinner make. You've fairly decided thousands of cases. This one case will make little difference in the world. Or is there something special about this one?"

"All cases are special, or at least should be considered so. That's judicial integrity. I won't dishonor mine."

"But if you don't recuse and you don't change your vote, what happens on Monday? The Court's opinion goes public. The blackmailer knows you've refused his demand. What then?"

Betsy's voice quavered to a halt. She cleared her throat.

"Is your judicial integrity worth dying for?"

Justice Wells leaned over and patted Betsy's knee. "You don't need to ask," he said gently. "You know me better than that."

Then, he straightened and squared his jaw. "Yes. My answer is 'yes.'"

CHAPTER 26

Saturday, Sept. 9, 8:15 a.m., Spring Valley Neighborhood
Justice Wells raised his hands, palms out. "Let's not get overly dramatic. The odds are the blackmailer will disappear after Monday. What would be the point of bothering me further?"

Marlon did not agree on those odds, but he saw no reason to voice the thought. All of them were probably thinking the same thing.

Wells rose from his chair. "Thank you for coming, but I have work to do." He gestured toward the stairway, a clear invitation for them to leave.

"Can we help you clean this mess up first?" Jim asked.

Justice Wells smiled. "I appreciate the offer, but no. All I need now is a legal pad and pen. I'll see to the rest of it another time."

A few minutes later, Wells escorted them out the front door.

The others started toward the car, but Marlon stopped. This did not feel right. No police, okay, but there were other options.

"What about a private security guard?" Marlon blurted as the thought struck him.

Wells shook his head. "No need. Our criminal has made his point." He turned away.

Marlon joined the other two in Betsy's car. She sat silently, staring out the windshield.

"Explain that recusal thing, Marlon," Jim called from the back seat. "Wells needs protection. He'll get that in spades if he calls the authorities. He won't, though, because then he has to recuse. What's the big deal about that?"

"Well," Marlon twisted around to face Jim, "I'm presuming here, but this is the only thing that makes sense to me. On this case, the other justices are split, 4-4. That means Wells is the deciding vote."

"I'm with you so far," Jim responded.

"Concentrate, because from here it gets a little technical. The Supreme Court is reviewing a decision by a lower court. If the vote at Court is a tie, that decision is effectively approved. The blackmailer apparently likes that lower court opinion, but Wells voted to reverse it. If Wells recuses, or doesn't vote at all, we're back to a tie. The blackmailer gets what he wants."

"Oh," Jim's face cleared, "I see. Recusal would be the same as if Wells went ahead and changed the opinion he already submitted, right?"

Marlon nodded. "The only thing I can't figure out is this. How could the blackmailer know all this? About the tie vote, that is. Nobody is supposed to."

Jim sighed audibly. "What now? Back to the office? Or does somebody have a better idea?"

"I do," Betsy answered. "It's a long shot, but we've got to try something." She glanced at Marlon. "Right?"

Marlon gritted his teeth. A lifetime of walking the other way to avoid the bigots and the bullies screamed "wrong."

But he was aware of a credible threat to a Supreme Court Justice who was also a mentor, a role model, a friend. Marlon closed his eyes, seeing that knife and the severed figure of the nude.

Betsy grabbed her phone and started scrolling. "Ah, here's the address. We're going to Capitol Hill. Well, I'm going. You guys don't have to."

"We're going with you," Marlon said firmly. "But why Capitol Hill?"

Betsy looked in her rearview mirror and pulled away from the curb. "To confront Gabe. To find out who's threatening him, and Robert."

Marlon frowned. "Wanna explain?"

"Gabe Stills is the Court clerk," Betsy answered. "Has been for decades. When Robert mentioned secrets and duress, Gabe came immediately to mind."

"Why him? And would the clerk have access to Robert's opinion?"

"I doubt it," Betsy responded, "but Gabe probably knew how Robert voted in the opinion he submitted. Robert respects Gabe's knowledge of the law and consults with him frequently. Those two are close. I know Gabe quite well, too. He's a dear man, but," she shrugged, "he's gay, you see."

Marlon flinched. No, he must have heard that wrong.

"Surely you don't think...." Marlon's words stumbled to a halt.

"Oh," Betsy glanced over at him, "of course not. I don't believe a gay or any non-hetero person is *per se* more vulnerable to blackmail."

"What do you mean, then?" Marlon asked. "Why do you think differently about Gabe?'"

"It was before my time," Betsy replied, "but you might remember when the government wouldn't hire gays."

"Oh, yeah," Jim said from the back seat. "I was told by friends to not even apply."

"It was official policy, too, wasn't it?" Marlon added.

Betsy nodded. "Directives from the CIA counseled against granting a security clearance to a job applicant who was gay. Gays were supposedly unstable, for one thing, and subject to blackmail and other undue influence. So what did gay applicants do?"

Marlon shrugged. "Lie, or not get the job."

"Precisely," Betsy said. "Gabe lied."

"But that was a long time ago," Marlon protested.

"A security clearance doesn't last forever," Betsy said. "Gabe had to reapply. He kept lying."

Marlon shook his head. "But why? Attitudes changed, thank goodness."

"Gabe started out in the closet because he had to," Betsy answered. "He got used to it. He built a life with nobody knowing the truth. He feared what would happen when they did."

Marlon stared at the Capitol building looming ahead of them on Pennsylvania Avenue. He knew people who had made the same choice that Gabe did. To be "outed" was their worst nightmare.

"If Gabe has protected himself this long," Marlon proposed, "he'll deny everything."

"He's a better man than that. Gabe would never have breached Robert's trust to save himself. No, he feared for the reputation of his beloved Court. He would not want it known that the Court had harbored a dishonest man for all those years."

"Fine, but where does that get you? For a different reason, maybe, but Gabe still won't talk."

"I'll try to convince Gabe," Betsy replied, "that the only way to save his Court now is to come clean. Tell the authorities. Who blackmailed him? That's a crime and enough to put that person behind bars."

"And nothing ever comes out about the demand on Robert," Marlon said, thinking aloud. "Gabe probably doesn't know. The blackmailer wouldn't tell Gabe why he wanted Wells's opinion. The blackmailer will keep his mouth shut. Why would he confess to an even greater crime?"

Marlon felt a grin creeping across his face. Problem solved, game over.

They drove the rest of the way in silence.

Betsy turned onto G Street. A police car, lights flashing, and an ambulance were double-parked in front of a modest, one-story bungalow in what otherwise looked like a quiet, residential neighborhood.

A knot of people huddled on the sidewalk across the street from the police, staring at the commotion.

Betsy pulled up to the curb. "Wait here," she said.

She trotted over to the onlookers and engaged them in conversation. Betsy's back was to Marlon, but he could tell when her shoulders slumped that the news was not good.

Betsy walked back to the car, climbed into the driver's seat, and dropped her ashen face into her cupped hands.

"He's dead. Gabe's dead. He was found in his garage, in his car. The car was idling, and the garage door was closed. Asphyxiated, apparently."

CHAPTER 27

Saturday, Sept. 9, 8:40 a.m., Capitol Hill
Marlon cursed under his breath.

They were back to square one. Gabe had been their one and only link to the blackmailer.

"Poor Gabe," Betsy's voice quavered.

Marlon felt a wave of shame. He had been thinking of Gabe as a means to an end, not as a troubled individual who had been horribly victimized.

"Guilt," Jim said from the back seat, "is a terrible thing."

Betsy turned her head. "It's not that," she murmured.

"He couldn't bear the guilt," Jim continued, "of giving in to the blackmailer. Of throwing Justice Wells under the bus. Gabe killed himself."

Betsy shook her head. "Gabe was a devout Catholic. Suicide is a mortal sin. He would never have done that."

"Besides," Marlon muttered, "why now? The timing can't be a coincidence. The blackmailer upped his game with that break-in. He's got to be careful to cover his tracks. So, he killed Gabe."

"Murder?" Jim sounded horrified.

Jim's voicing the word gave Marlon an idea.

"Robert will change his mind now," Marlon said. "A smashed desk is one thing, but murder?"

Betsy turned and looked at him. She nodded, but her expression was still grim.

"Let us hope."

She picked up her phone and called Wells.

"I'm in the car with Marlon and Jim," Betsy said when Wells answered, "and I'm putting you on speaker."

Listening to Betsy explain about Gabe, Marlon expected a tongue-lashing from Wells to follow. In going to Gabe's house, they had disobeyed Wells's order to keep what they knew about the threats to themselves.

Wells did not rebuke them, but he did say that Gabe's death should be a stern lesson. Stay out of it.

Although Wells was shocked and saddened about Gabe, his death had not changed his mind.

"It's my neck," Wells said, "and I get to decide what to do with it."

"What now?" Betsy asked woodenly after Wells disconnected the call.

An unexpected wave of anger struck Marlon.

Justice Wells, acting like Marlon's father. Always so sure of himself, heedless of others' feelings.

Stubborn old coot. But for Betsy, Marlon would be tempted to wash his hands of the whole thing.

"Let's go back to the office," he said, "and regroup."

Twenty minutes later, Marlon unlocked the door to the office suite. The three of them silently filed in.

"Hello?" called Cassandra's voice.

She stepped out of the conference room, a Kindle dangling from her hand.

"What was your big emergency?" she groused. "A bagel run? And where's Miranda? I'd have left a while ago except," she raised her Kindle, "I had a juicy best-seller to read while I waited. We're so late starting the damn case review."

Marlon had almost stopped listening, but Cassandra's last words caught his attention.

"The case," he said. "That's the other link."

"The link to what?" Cassandra asked.

"Whoever is threatening Justice Wells. The guy's demanding that Wells change his vote on a case. That case is the link to the blackmailer. The murderer, that is."

"Murderer?" Cassandra spluttered, her Kindle dropping to the floor with a thud.

Marlon explained about the break-in, their trip to Capitol Hill, and Gabe's death.

"Somebody badly wants to win that case," Betsy concluded for him, "and is making sure he does. Somehow, he got to Gabe. Gabe leaks the decision Robert submitted. Our bad guy realizes he's going to lose unless he forces Robert to change his vote."

"So, he threatened Robert, then got rid of the informer, Gabe?" Cassandra said.

"Looks like it," Betsy answered.

Cassandra shook her index finger. "I told you guys last night Wells should take any threat seriously. Surely, he is now. He's in protective custody, right?"

"No," Betsy said. "Robert won't cave to the blackmailer. Telling the authorities would end up doing just that."

Betsy explained the reasoning behind Robert's decision.

"And you agree with him?" Cassandra's disbelief could not be more evident.

Betsy stuck her chin in the air. "It doesn't matter whether I agree or disagree. He's made his decision. He's doing what he thinks is best for the Court."

"There's brave and there's stupid," Cassandra muttered.

Betsy's face flushed bright red.

"Cassandra," Marlon admonished, holding up a warning hand to keep those two stubborn women from each other's throats.

Cassandra sighed. "Sorry, honey, but, well, I admire the man's courage, I really do. Your loyalty, as well. But this just doesn't feel right. There must be another way."

Her face cleared. "I've got an idea. Don't we, as lawyers and officers of the court, have an ethical obligation to report to somebody, the Chief, I guess, if we know of a good reason a justice should recuse? Robert couldn't fault us for doing our duty, I don't think."

"I considered that," Marlon responded. "We talked about it on the way here." He glanced at Betsy. "But it won't work. We'd have to tell somebody if we knew Wells was being bribed, or otherwise being dishonest. That's not happening here. So, it's Wells's call, and only his call."

Cassandra blew out her lips. "Okay, I tried. So, we just wait around until somebody else gets killed?"

Betsy blanched.

"Nobody's going to get killed," Marlon said, "but we're not slapping Robert in the face, either. Which is exactly what we'd be doing if we went behind his back and reported all this just because we're scared. Come on," he shooed them toward the conference room, "I've got an idea."

The attorneys took seats at the conference room table while Jim shoved the boxes of case files off to the side.

"The blackmailer needs to be stopped," Marlon began, "without involving Robert. If Gabe were alive, his testimony alone could have put the blackmailer behind bars. Now, it's Gabe's death that may do that, because the blackmailer may have left some evidence of the murder."

"But nobody's going to look for that evidence, even if it exists," Betsy protested. "It'll be too easy to rule it a suicide. Asphyxiated in your own car, in your own garage? Come on. It's classic."

"Unless something else points to possible foul play," Marlon persisted. "What if the Court is deciding a case involving a death row prisoner? Or, better yet, a Mafia don? And then the clerk of the Court ends up dead? Isn't that enough to raise suspicions?"

Cassandra looked skeptical; Jim intrigued.

"It works," Jim said. "I can see it."

He leaned in and dropped his voice an octave.

"Don Corleone, whispering to his consigliere, 'we gotta win this. Do whatever it takes.'"

"It's not funny," Betsy complained, but she was almost smiling as the others chuckled.

"'He who laughs, lasts,' right?" Jim responded.

Marlon agreed, although he had a feeling that tempers would continue to flare. He was going to have to do his best to keep a handle on his own.

"It would be a lot smarter just to get the case name from Justice Wells," Cassandra objected. "Obviously, he knows which one it is."

Marlon, stung, on the verge of snapping at her, stopped himself.

"I thought of that, of course, Cassandra, but ...."

"Robert won't tell us," Betsy interrupted. "He's a smart guy. He'll know exactly what we're up to, and he told us in no uncertain terms to stay out of it."

"You could try calling the Court," Cassandra persisted. "Ask which opinion Wells submitted."

Marlon shook his head. "One, it's Saturday. Nobody would answer our call. Two, why would anybody there tell us? We're not supposed to know that kind of thing in advance. Three, what if Wells submitted an opinion in more than one pending case? I could think of more reasons your idea won't work if you give me a minute."

Cassandra shrugged. "Okay, let's see if we can find anything on the docket that screams bad guy."

"We'll divide up the cases on the docket," Marlon answered, "and start by crossing off any in which the parties are cuddly nonprofits."

To Marlon's satisfaction, everybody laughed again.

Jim left to get food.

A half hour later, Marlon closed his eyes and pumped his fist. His theory had paid off.

"Listen to this, people," he said. "At issue here is the confiscation of a yacht. An island-sized yacht. The U.S. government seized it during a round of sanctions imposed against Russian oligarchs supporting the Kremlin. The company owning the yacht sued the government, challenging the legality of the seizure."

"And you think the company wants its yacht back that bad?" Betsy sounded dubious. "Bad enough to threaten a justice of the Supreme Court?"

Marlon shrugged. "An oligarch must own the company. That's why they seized the yacht. And those oligarchs would do about anything to get their way, from what I understand."

"It's plausible," Betsy replied, "but I'm not sure this advances the ball game. We don't know which oligarch owns the company. How many oligarchs are there, anyway? The FBI can't chase them all down."

"Ah, but we have a clue," Marlon said, "as to which oligarch owns this big boat. You see, the name of the yacht just happens to be *Sonya*."

CHAPTER 28

Saturday, Sept. 9, 9:40 a.m., The Office
Marlon stared at her, as if asking for a response. Cassandra could not think of anything to say.

She could not think at all, frozen in a cold fury at Nikolai. How could she have been so gullible? She had almost believed there was such a thing as a good oligarch.

"We can't know it's Nikolai," she dimly heard Betsy say, "only from the name of the yacht."

"I agree, we can't be sure," Marlon replied, "but I think it's enough to raise eyebrows. Besides, Nikolai just strikes me as the kind of violent, lowlife who would be enraged if the U.S. government took his stupid boat."

The "stupid boat" jarred Cassandra's brain back to life. He might not be a perfect man, but Nikolai was not that petty.

In fact, not one word of Marlon's description matched the man who had shared his Russian peasant food with her.

"No," she said. "I don't believe it."

The other two ignored her.

"Enough to haul Nikolai in for questioning, you think?" Betsy asked.

"Uh, probably not alone," Marlon admitted, "but Nikolai's under suspicion anyway. The FBI, the CIA, and a host of other agencies drop in on him all the time."

Marlon shifted his gaze to Cassandra. "That's what he told you, right?"

"Yes, but...."

Betsy was shaking her head. "This'll all take too long, Marlon. We have until Monday, remember? That's when the Court's decision goes public."

Betsy stopped abruptly and stared down at her computer screen, her unspoken words obvious to them all. In less than forty-eight hours, the blackmailer would know. Wells refused to give in. The blackmailer would exact his revenge.

"We needed to find a smoking gun in those cases," Betsy continued. "Something to light a fire under the police. This yacht isn't it."

"Light a fire under somebody," Marlon replied, rubbing his chin. "Nikolai worries about being deported. We suggest somebody pay Nikolai a call. Question Nikolai about the yacht and a dead Court clerk. Raise the threat of deportation. Maybe Nikolai would back down."

This was all wrong.

"You people have heard of a lynch mob, haven't you?" Cassandra managed through gritted teeth.

That got their attention.

"You're talking about siccing the cops on a person based on zero evidence. After all, Sonya is a common name, particularly in Russia. And may I remind you why Nikolai worries about being deported? He doesn't want to be here. He stays only to keep an eye on his daughter and grandson."

Marlon looked confused. "Oh," he said, "maybe you've got a point. I had forgotten. Nikolai's not on the sanctioned list."

Cassandra wondered how Marlon knew that much about the list, but she was in no mood to ask him to explain himself.

"I think we're spinning our wheels, anyway," Cassandra continued, "and why? Because of a foolish old man whose stubbornness is going to get him...."

Betsy jumped to her feet. "Enough!" she yelled. "You think I'm stupid? But what am I supposed to do? What proof do we have?

Robert could deny everything. We all look like fools, and at what cost? I abuse his trust."

Betsy stopped abruptly and collapsed back into her chair like a rag doll.

"He'd hate me," she moaned. "I'd rather lose Robert than have that happen. He's the only family I have, you know."

"I'm sorry, sugar," Cassandra whispered, regretting having been so insensitive to Betsy's gut-wrenching dilemma.

"Heh, guys," Miranda called.

Cassandra swiveled around to see Miranda, face flushed, strutting through the door to the conference room, Chad in tow.

"We found the leak," Miranda pronounced.

"The what?" Marlon asked, echoing Cassandra's own thought.

"At Robert's," Miranda replied excitedly. "Wait'll you...."

"At his house?" Betsy asked. "When were you there?"

Cassandra glanced at Betsy, whose expression showed surprise and confusion.

"Uh," Miranda checked her watch, "we left fifteen minutes ago."

Marlon scrunched up his face. "You and Chad?"

"Yeah, shortly after you left, according to Wells. What's wrong with that, Marlon?"

"Now Chad knows, too?" Marlon barked. "Why'd you go there, anyway, Miranda?"

"Uh, well, Chad already knew, actually," Miranda replied, "because I told him."

Betsy, groaning, laid her face in her hands.

"Miranda, you'd better have a good explanation for this," Marlon said, smacking his palm on the table."

"Oh, I do," Miranda pulled up a chair, sat down, and propped her elbows on the conference table. "Chad helped me figure it out. Justice Wells was hacked. There's your leak. And we have a good idea who did it."

Marlon, frowning, shook his head. "No, he wasn't. After he received the first threat, Wells asked that the Court's network and equipment be checked for unauthorized access. Everything was fine."

"Well," Chad replied nonchalantly, "it's not."

Marlon, face flaming, jumped to his feet. "Then why's Gabe dead, smart ass?"

CHAPTER 29

Saturday, Sept. 9, 9:45 a.m., The Office

"Gabe?" Miranda asked, glancing around the room at the unhappy faces of her colleagues. She looked at Chad who shrugged, looking as confused as Miranda felt.

"Hi," Jim called, walking into the conference room.

He deposited a bulging white paper bag on the table.

"You're being the ass, Marlon," Jim said. "At least," he glanced around the room, "you've done a good job pissing everybody off."

Marlon flipped Jim the bird. Then, he exhaled heavily. "Sorry, guys. I'm losing it here."

"I haven't exactly been helpful either," Cassandra mumbled.

"You all just need to chill and have something to eat." Jim reached into the bag and extracted a bagel. "Who wants sesame?"

Miranda held up her hand and caught the bagel Jim tossed in her direction.

"Thank god," she said. "I'm starved. Cream cheese?"

While they all took seats and Jim doled out the food, Marlon explained to Miranda and Chad what had happened since the two of them left the gala.

Miranda set down her bagel. She had lost her appetite.

"I don't understand," she managed, "what Gabe has to do with this." She glanced at Chad sitting beside her. "Could we be wrong?"

Chad shrugged. "The facts are the facts," he replied.

"Okay, people," Miranda wiped crumbs from her hands. "Listen up. We've got news about Wells, too. Last night, on the way home from the gala, my car brakes failed. On purpose, because my car was hacked. With the fob."

"Are you sure?" Cassandra asked.

"What does that have to do with Robert?" Betsy asked at the same time.

"Yes, and I'll get to Wells. It must have been the parking attendant at the embassy who did it. I didn't recognize him at the time because he was wearing a hat, and he'd done something with his face. Maybe a fake moustache. Anyway, I realized later who it was. That tech from the hospital."

Marlon looked like he was about to spit out his mouthful of bagel.

"What tech from the hospital?" Betsy asked. "And why would he tamper with your car?"

"Oh, that's right, you were in court all day yesterday," Miranda replied. "Brenda's investigating what might be a serial hacker. She thinks the hacker got into the hospital system and manipulated the MRI data. The point was to trap Brenda in the MRI machine, without the hospital knowing about it. To frighten Brenda, so she'd back off."

"These reporters," said Jim, wagging the bagel clutched in his hand, "have dangerous jobs. First Ronnie, then Brenda."

"I went to the hospital yesterday to talk to the radiology tech," Miranda barreled on, "because I realized he had to be complicit in what happened to Brenda. He brushed me off. Then, apparently, he told his boss I was snooping around. The boss sent the tech to booby trap my car."

"Warning you away, too," Betsy replied, nodding.

Chad's shoulder brushed Miranda's as he leaned into the table, glaring at Betsy.

"She could have been killed," Chad said flatly.

"Sorry," Betsy said, flushing. "I didn't mean ... I mean, you must have been scared to death, Miranda."

In truth, she had not been that scared last night. Shaken, yes, and angry at what had been done to her car. By not giving in to fear, she had been able to keep her wits about her.

She had not dwelt on the thought of being the victim of attempted murder. But now that she knew Gabe was dead....

Miranda's skin crawled. Her brain felt frozen, as if she had been dumped headfirst into a barrel of ice water.

Chad reached over and put his arm around her.

"Miranda," Marlon said, "I may sometimes be an ass, but I'll always have your back." He paused to glance around the table. "All your backs."

Miranda took a deep breath and carried on.

"We left my car," Miranda continued, "and took an Uber to Chad's. Then we drove to Brenda's place. I told her about the tech and my car, and said she had to come clean. I knew too much, but not enough to know when to duck. 'Duck when you see Jeremy Ross,' Brenda said."

"Jeremy's the tech guy?" Jim asked.

Miranda shook her head. "No, no, Jeremy's the boss. The tech guy's his employee."

"Wait a minute," Marlon said. "You're saying Jeremy Ross, the CEO of a big, reputable company, is responsible for hacking your car?"

Miranda nodded. "The hospital, too."

"What next?" Marlon scoffed. "Murdering Jimmy Hoffa?"

Miranda had expected skepticism, but at least Marlon was still listening.

"As Chad said," Miranda responded, "the facts are the facts. Jeremy has the means and motive. Jeremy's company, Cerberus, provides data security at the radiology center."

"Se-cur-i-ty," Marlon drawled, "does not spell hacking."

"He had his fingers in the proverbial pie," Miranda retorted. "And guess which company is at the center of the story Brenda's working on?"

"Cerberus," Marlon grunted.

"Yep. She's identified a dozen companies, all having Cerberus as their data security provider. Big companies, international conglomerates, most of them. Transactions that look like insider trading, but the company's sure somebody outside the company, maybe a hacker, has access to confidential business information. Cerberus runs a system check and says everything's fine."

"So maybe the Cerberus system is defective?" Marlon proposed.

"Not likely," Chad replied. "I know the product. A successful penetration here or there? Maybe. But a dozen? In a year or so? That doesn't sound right."

"Those suspicious transactions," Miranda continued, "involve shell corporations, owned indirectly by one or more Russian oligarchs. Brenda thinks Jeremy's stealing information and selling it to the Russians."

"Jeremy and the Russians again," Marlon snipped. "Brenda's got a one-track mind, that's for sure."

Miranda pushed aside her flash of pique. "That's one of the reasons she's a world-class investigative journalist, Marlon."

"That's fair," Marlon grumbled, "but I met Jeremy last night. He seemed like a perfectly nice man, not a...."

"I met him at the gala, too," Jim interrupted. "I didn't like him."

Marlon stared at Jim. "His lawyer doesn't, either. Joe also said something about Jeremy making money on the side. Consulting, Joe called it. Maybe it's something worse. A lot worse."

"Can we please get back to Robert?" Betsy asked.

"Okay, well," Chad chimed in, "Cerberus provides data security at the Supreme Court, too. Wells said his blackmailer had access to confidential information. So it occurred to me to check Justice Wells's home computer, which he uses for work. Wells agreed. As I said a few minutes ago, it's been hacked. Which means the entire Court network is compromised."

"You're sure?" Marlon asked Chad.

"Quite sure. The evidence," Chad wagged his index finger, "is unmistakable."

"Why's somebody hacking the Court?" Jim chimed in. "All that stuff's public information, anyway, isn't it?"

"Eventually," Cassandra replied. "The published decisions, that is, anyone can read. But to know in advance how the Court's going to decide? You could place your bet in advance. That would be worth a lot, to the right people."

Marlon, frowning, was shaking his head. "If Jeremy is a data thief, and I think that's a big 'if,' how do we get to blackmail? That's on a totally different level. And why do it?"

Cassandra narrowed her eyes. "Something went wrong. Jeremy placed his bet on the outcome of a case, but he read the cards wrong. Now he's got to change Wells's mind. Or he loses the game."

"Back to the facts," Chad proposed. "Cerberus guards the Court's data. Valuable data. Wells suspects unauthorized access. He reports it. Cerberus checks the system and says all is well. It's not."

"Where does Gabe fit in this?" Miranda asked. She shivered. "Gabe's murder, that is."

"Jeremy pals around with the Chief Justice," Betsy replied. "The Chief knows Gabe and Robert are close. Jeremy probably sniffed that out and had Gabe killed. Another warning to Robert. Jeremy's serious."

"Enough talking," Miranda said. "It's time to act. We can do it without mentioning blackmail because I convinced Brenda to give me a copy of her files."

"Really?" Marlon replied. "I'm amazed. No reporter's going to give away their source material for what could be a blockbuster story. Unless you...." His eyes narrowed. "Please don't tell me you blabbed about Robert."

Miranda held up both hands, palms out. "Nope. All I said was that I'm on Jeremy's trail, too. That was enough."

"Wow," Marlon said, leaning back in his chair. "I can't believe Brenda, of all people, would do that."

"Surprising you, but not me," Miranda replied. She resisted the urge to stick her tongue out at Marlon. "Brenda said this investigation was not about her career, but about justice."

"To conclude," Chad said, "in addition to Brenda's stuff, we've got Wells's laptop with evidence of hacking. You go to the police. They'll have to investigate, at least."

"An investigation that will take forever," Marlon replied. "We have until Monday. We need something more to light that fire."

CHAPTER 30

Saturday, Sept. 9, 1:00 p.m., The National Mall
Miranda stood at the base of the Memorial facing east, as did Lincoln, across the reflecting pool, the Washington Monument, and the Mall to the Capitol. A chilly wind blew out of the northeast. Shivering, Miranda turned up the collar of her jacket.

Movement to her right caught Miranda's eye. Sully rounded the south end of the Monument. Miranda waved as Sully strode toward her.

Miranda had gotten lucky. Sully was available to meet, even on such short notice. He was close to her office, anyway, on the Mall, watching his daughter play volleyball.

"Hi," Miranda reached up to kiss Sully's cheek. "Sorry to interrupt the game."

"You didn't," he smiled. "We're between matches."

Miranda gestured, and they sat on the steps of the Memorial, Miranda slinging off her bag and setting it on the step beside her.

"Uh, I think you're going to miss the next match," she responded. "At least, I hope so."

Sully cocked a doubtful-looking eyebrow.

"Remember at lunch Thursday, I asked you about the DNC break-in? Back in 2016?"

Sully nodded.

"That independent player you were talking about? The theory that it wasn't the Russians, after all?"

Sully turned to look at her. "Yeah."

"We think we've found him." She reached into her bag, pulled out the thumb drive on which she had copied Brenda's files, and waved it at Sully. "Exhibit A."

"Huh," Sully muttered after Miranda explained what Brenda had uncovered. "The most plausible explanation is that the Russian oligarch bribes an insider for confidential information. The company just hasn't found its snitch."

"It's not a snitch. It's a hacker."

"But you said Cerberus checked and found no evidence of hacking. Are you saying Cerberus missed it?"

"No, I'm saying it was a cover up. Cerberus hacked its own software."

"You wanna explain that?"

"Yeah, here."

Miranda handed Sully the second thumb drive.

"Exhibit B," she said.

"What's on it?"

"Segments of the Cerberus software found on five of the companies in Brenda's files. I don't know the technical terms, but the security code has holes in it, like it's been hacked. Except, the interface with the underlying code is too smooth. Meaning, Cerberus hacked itself."

Sully's eyebrows flew up.

"Cerberus is spying on its own clients?" he said.

"Yep. Most of Cerberus's clients are happy campers. But for selected companies, the Cerberus software is contaminated with a hacker's footprints before it's installed."

Sully frowned, shaking his head. "Cerberus is a reputable company. This doesn't sound plausible." He held up the thumb drive. "Where'd you get this?"

"Uh, an anonymous source."

Sully looked her in the eye, asking for an explanation.

There was not much more she could tell him.

Ronnie had been handed Exhibit B in exchange for a promise to keep the source to himself. Ronnie had exacted the same promise from the lawyers to whom he passed the thumb drive on, as instructed.

Exhibit B turned up with Ronnie when he waltzed into the conference room a couple of hours ago. He had a smile on his face and a gleam in his eye, looking fully recovered from his rocky evening at the gala. Brushing aside their questions about why he passed out at the embassy, Ronnie said his memory was still foggy.

About the events of the morning, though, Ronnie was crystal clear.

"I got a call out of the blue. That's not unusual in my line of work, but what followed was new to me. He gave me no name, only instructions to meet in an underground parking lot downtown."

"Did he say what he wanted to talk about?" Marlon asked.

"Nope. Anyway, guy shows up, classic Deep Throat. He's in dark glasses, a trench coat, and wearing an obvious wig. Talked quietly out of the side of his mouth, then disappeared before I could ask questions."

"Dangerous," Marlon tutted. *"He could have pulled out a gun and shot you."*

"Well, he didn't," Ronnie replied. *"He said he's a whistleblower. He works for a reputable American tech company and has clear evidence of the company's criminal side gig."*

Ronnie held up a thumb drive.

"He said he can't risk going to the FBI. A reporter he could trust. Deep Throat would remain an 'unidentified source.'"

"Why'd he pick you out of all the reporters in D.C.?" Marlon asked.

"I think he came to me because of Sergey. Sergey's the guy I met at Dulles before I was attacked, remember? Anyway, Sergey and Deep Throat work for the same company."

Deep Throat had instructed Ronnie to get the thumb drive to his lawyer friends. Why, Ronnie had no idea.

After scanning the thumb drive, Chad, who was familiar with the Cerberus product, confirmed that Deep Throat's story was plausible. It would also explain the special contractors Jeremy flew in from time to time, the guys who did not interact with the regular employees.

"Miranda?" Sully prompted, bringing Miranda back to the present.

"Um, the source is legit," she replied. "He had authorized access to the code. It wasn't stolen."

"Wow," Sully said. He waggled the thumb drive between his fingers. "If the data confirms what you're saying, this is a sophisticated scam that had to be directed from the top of the food chain. I can't remember the CEO's name."

"Jeremy Ross."

Sully stroked his chin. "I remember Jeremy now that you remind me. Before he founded Cerberus, Jeremy was on the Agency's radar. He worked closely with the Russians, selling them high-end communication technology, software, too. All aboveboard, as far as I know, but we kept an eye on him."

"Makes sense, then," Miranda replied, "that he's still selling stuff to the Russians. Different stuff, and way below the water line, but still."

"Hmm."

Miranda could tell by his voice that she had Sully's full attention. She felt the same rush of adrenaline as she did toward the end of a good closing argument.

"Another thing," she said. "The hacker's footprints within the Cerberus software? Our unidentified source claims they're identical to the footprints found in the DNC files. Voilà. Your independent operator. Still out there hacking, cleverly camouflaged as a data security company."

"Or it's still the Russians," Sully said absently, "and your source is mistaken."

"Not the Russians."

Marlon had come up with the idea for crossing that "t." Nikolai, the spy, or ex-spy, whatever he was, would know where the Kremlin was snooping around.

"What," Cassandra protested, "I just turn up and ask Nikolai to spill Russian state secrets? Why would he? Besides, even if Nikolai said anything, Sully wouldn't believe it."

"It wouldn't hurt to try," Marlon answered. "Don't tell him exactly why you want to know. Just say you need the truth to protect an institution Nikolai holds in high esteem and leave it at that."

Cassandra came back from the Ritz looking as pleased as Ronnie had when he pranced in earlier.

Nikolai had been cagey about the DNC break-in, but regarding the recent footprints? It was so simple. Did the Americans think the Kremlin was that stupid?

"Assume the original break-in really was the Kremlin," Miranda instructed Sully, "spying on the DNC. Would they keep leaving the same footprints when the CIA and everybody else in the world knows whose they are? Not likely. For an independent operator, though, the tracks are great camouflage."

Sully grinned. "You're right. Jeremy came up with a beautiful scheme, really. Plausible deniability. You code your bugs into Cerberus software. Anybody reports a hack, Cerberus checks the system and claims it's a false alarm. Still, if the company calls somebody else in to check, they find Russians."

She had produced enough evidence for Sully to start the ball rolling. But he had not leaped into action.

Miranda had one more card to play, one she had had in her pocket since law school. Sully trusted her.

She put her hand on Sully's shoulder and looked him in the eye.

"You've got to move fast on this."

"Well, I'll make some calls, sure. Get these Exhibits, as you call them, to the right people. But I don't see why I can't watch the final match first."

"Jeremy upped the ante. I can't tell you how I know, but his beautiful scheme has turned ugly. As in deadly."

Sully stared at her, unmoving.

Miranda held her breath. If this did not work, should she say more?

She had almost decided the answer had to be "yes" when Sully finally spoke.

"The last match will go on without me."

CHAPTER 31

Saturday, Sept. 9, 5:00 p.m., The Office

Marlon flipped to the last page of the document in his hand. He glanced around the table at his colleagues. Even Jim visibly sagged.

Maybe it had been a mistake to go ahead with the scheduled case review. But after Miranda returned from the Mall, nobody wanted to go home, either. Tired, edgy, hoping for good news from Sully, even though they knew it could not be this soon.

"He's got to get freight trains rolling," Miranda had said. "Even for Sully, that'll take some time."

"But once they do...." Cassandra gave Betsy a thumb's up, getting a smile from Betsy in response.

Marlon had proposed that they get to work. The case review, although necessary, was mindless. Nobody was at the top of their game, but nobody needed to be. They all agreed.

But it had been a slog.

"One more case on the list," Marlon announced with as much enthusiasm as he could muster.

Miranda groaned.

"And then the Bomb."

The Bombay Club, their usual after-work watering hole, beckoned from only a block away.

"My treat."

Everybody's face brightened at that. The drinks at the Bomb were not cheap, and Marlon suspected they would each have more than one.

"'Scott v. Washington Hospital Center,'" Marlon announced the name of the last case on the list. "Isn't that yours, Miranda?"

"Yeah. Let me pull it up." She clicked keys on her laptop. "Okay, here are next month's calendar items."

As Miranda began to recite, Jim twisted around and grabbed the TV remote sitting on a side table behind him. "Let's get the local news," he said. "I'll mute it."

The monitor on the far wall clicked on.

Marlon idly watched as an attractive young brunette spoke silently into a microphone. Her bright red blouse contrasted sharply with the image behind her, a mountain of smoking rubble and the half-buried brick front of what once was a two-story house.

A firetruck and two police cars were parked haphazardly on the street. Uniformed police milled around the property. One officer stood on the sidewalk, strewn with charred debris, in conversation with a tall, blonde woman, her back to the camera, wearing black sweats.

"Turn that up," Cassandra commanded.

Miranda stopped talking.

"… an explosive device, although the investigation is still ongoing," the reporter, incongruously, chirped.

As the blonde turned her head to gaze at the ruined home, her profile came into view.

"Sonya," Cassandra gasped.

Marlon peered at the monitor, squinting. "Are you sure?"

"Explosive device, as in bomb?" Jim said at the same time.

Cassandra bolted upright and put her hand on her chest. "Her son?"

"Luckily, no injuries were reported," the reporter seemed to answer her.

Cassandra exhaled deeply.

"Never a dull moment around here," Jim quipped.

"It's not funny," Cassandra protested.

"No," Jim agreed, "but unusual. Or maybe not. Maybe it's normal for an oligarch's daughter to find her house blown up."

"Something like that, I guess," Cassandra said quietly.

She told them about the shooting the night before.

"The bombing may have been another reminder," she concluded. "They keep watch. Nikolai's supposed to be toeing the line."

"Who's 'they'?" Betsy asked.

Cassandra shrugged. "Nikolai didn't say. Not specifically. But I think he meant the Kremlin. Rivals, too, as in other oligarchs. Russians."

Marlon considered what Cassandra had said. "You should stay away from Nikolai," he glanced up at the television monitor, "and I'm guessing that won't be an issue anymore. The Bolkonskys have too much else on their plate right now. They'll want to drop the lawsuit."

Cassandra stared at him, a troubled look on her face.

"Don't worry about it," Marlon soothed. "They didn't need the money, anyway."

"That's not what's bothering me," Cassandra responded. "I wonder … why now? And twice?" She shrugged. "Coincidence, I guess."

Cassandra looked like she needed a very dry martini. Marlon could use one, too.

"We're done here," he said. "Pack up. Let's get going."

"I've gotta run home first and give my puppy her meds," Betsy said. "I'll be back before you've finished your first drink."

Fifteen minutes later, the tuxedoed maître d' waved the four of them to their usual spot in the bar lounge of the quietly elegant Bombay Club. A waiter appeared to take their orders as soon as they had settled into the lounge's black leather, overstuffed chairs.

The owner of the Club, himself a South Asian, had created a British colonial environment in the restaurant, a Washington institution. At least, the Club resembled what an Indian thought Washingtonians imagined when they pictured English ex-pats at the height of the Empire.

After their drinks were served, Jim started a convoluted tale about his disastrous blind date the previous weekend. Marlon listened with half an ear, but it must have been quite a story. Cassandra and Miranda were hooting and hollering in no time.

Marlon waved down the waiter and ordered another martini. Cassandra and Miranda switched to cabernet.

Miranda must have called Chad because he wondered in, joined their group, and ordered a coke. Party pooper.

Their second round and Chad's coke had just been deposited on the side tables at each of their elbows when Miranda's phone beeped. She fished her phone out of her bag and stared at the screen.

"Is it Sully?" Cassandra asked.

Miranda looked up and nodded. "And it's good news, I think."

She did not sound at all sure.

"Well?" Marlon prompted.

"Jeremy's dead."

"Good riddance to bad rubbish," Chad said dryly.

"Wha … they, they killed him?" Jim croaked.

"Who did?" Marlon managed, knowing it was the wrong question but finding it hard to focus.

"The CIA?" Jim asked, his voice pitched high.

"No, no," Miranda waved him away. "They never even got a chance to talk to him."

"What happened, Miranda?" Cassandra demanded.

"An agent showed up at the hotel in Tyson's Corner where Jeremy was staying. Jeremy wasn't in his suite. Instead, he was found splashed all over the sidewalk twenty floors below his room's balcony."

"Suicide," Jim intoned. "Huh. Seems to be a rash of it these days." His forehead creased. "But Gabe's wasn't.…"

"Jeremy didn't seem the suicide type to me either," Miranda interrupted.

"Suicide's possible," Marlon protested. "Suppose Jeremy got wind that he was being investigated?"

"Marlon, the so-called fall off the balcony?" Miranda replied. "Doesn't that scream Russians?"

Marlon ignored the niggle of his own doubts.

"I say we look on the bright side," he proposed. "All the evidence pointed to Jeremy as the blackmailer. He's dead. Problem solved. Betsy will be so relieved. Speaking of Betsy, where is she, anyway?"

"Stuck in traffic, probably," Miranda responded. She cocked her head. "Somebody's phone's ringing."

Marlon had not heard it. The noise in the bar had risen considerably since they arrived.

He plastered the phone to one ear and stuck his finger in the other.

Hello?

Marlon. Where are you, and who's with you?

Marlon frowned. His caller was Justice Wells, without a doubt. Still, the Justice's tenor voice was pitched an octave too low. He sounded phlegmy, too, as if he had a bad cold.

Uh, the Bomb. Bombay Club. With Cassandra and Miranda. Chad's here, too, and Jim.

Bring everybody here. Justice Wells cleared his throat. *We'll play bridge tonight. I can't make our usual time, and you know I hate to miss a week.*

Justice Wells regularly skipped their weekly bridge games because of the heavy demands of his work.

"*You need to come now,*" Wells barked savagely.

Marlon almost dropped the phone.

The image he had seen early that morning floated into Marlon's brain. The severed Matisse nude in Justice Wells's painting and the very long knife used for the dissection.

Justice Wells was still alive. Everything else about that conversation was very wrong.

CHAPTER 32

Saturday, Sept. 9, 6:30 p.m., Spring Valley Neighborhood
Marlon pulled up to the curb and turned off the car. The hinge had not yet been repaired. Otherwise, Justice Wells's house looked secure.

Marlon had been fooled that morning, too.

Marlon twisted around in the driver's seat to talk to his passengers, Cassandra and Miranda in the back seat, Chad riding shotgun. Jim had stayed at the Bombay Club to pay the bill and wait for Betsy.

"Who knows what we'll find in there," Marlon said. "We've got to be careful. We can't just barge in."

"We can't just sit here either," Cassandra replied. She grabbed the door handle. "We bang on the front door and make a lot of noise. If it's another hoodlum, at least he'll know somebody's here."

"What if he comes out shooting?" Marlon hated that his voice quavered.

Chad opened his door. Without a word, he stepped out onto the sidewalk.

"Get real, Marlon," Cassandra scolded as she pushed her door open, too. "That'd be a stupid move. Everyone on the street would call the police. They'd be swarming in a second."

"But...."

Marlon's protest died when the front door opened. Justice Wells stepped out. Alone.

Relief. At least he was not a hostage.

"Let's go around back," Justice Wells called, motioning for them to join him, "to the patio. It's too nice a day to...." The Justice glanced up at the foreboding gray sky. "I could use some fresh air," his smile was a grimace.

"This could be some kind of a ploy," Miranda muttered behind him.

She got out of the car, though. So did Marlon. He did not see that he had much of a choice.

Justice Wells led them around the corner of the house to a flagstone patio adorned with an assortment of empty flowerpots. Four dark wicker chairs surrounded a matching table on which sat two decks of cards.

"Deal the cards, would you, Marlon," Justice Wells said.

Marlon opened his mouth to speak. The Justice shook his head emphatically.

Marlon exchanged glances with his colleagues, but they all obeyed. He, Cassandra, and Miranda took their places at the table.

Justice Wells crooked his index finger at Chad. The two of them stepped to the rear of the patio and engaged in an inaudible conversation.

Marlon fought a bizarre urge to laugh. Outspoken, opinionated, occasionally boisterous, the three lawyers sat quietly with their heads down like kindergarteners chastised by their teacher.

A glance over at Chad and Justice Wells reminded him that this was no laughing matter.

Chad was not a big man, but compared to him, Justice Wells looked like a wraith.

"He looks awful," Marlon whispered.

"I know," Cassandra mumbled out of the side of her mouth. "Like he's lost ten pounds in a day."

The Justice pivoted and walked back to the table. He took his phone out of his pocket, pointed to it emphatically, then cupped his hand around his ear.

Miranda reared back. "It's bugged?" she asked, mouthing the words.

Justice Wells nodded, then muted his phone.

"I got a text," Wells muttered, his words barely audible, "twenty minutes ago. I read it. Then, the text disappeared. It was a warning. They've got eyes and ears everywhere. Pretend you heard nothing."

He unmuted his phone.

The steel in Justice Wells's voice brooked no dissent. Marlon froze.

Chad, meanwhile, had been strolling around the patio, hands stuck into his back pockets. Out of the corner of his eye, Marlon caught Chad casually peering into one of the pots. Chad strode across the hedge that bordered the back of the patio, seemingly admiring the vegetation.

Chad rejoined them. He put his hand on Miranda's shoulder and leaned in.

Justice Wells muted his phone.

"I didn't find anything yet," Chad muttered. "Audio would be bad out here, though." He glanced up at the bundle of wires crossing overhead from one corner of the house to the neighboring one. "So we could talk, quietly, except for your phone."

"I can't leave it inside, though," Justice Wells said, "with us talking out here. Too obvious."

"I really don't think…."

Justice Wells shushed Chad. Then, the Justice unmuted his phone.

"I'll be right back," the Justice said. "You haven't dealt the cards, Marlon."

Wells left the patio through the back door to the house. Chad returned to his perusal of the patio perimeter. A few minutes later, Wells returned holding two shiny red plastic boxes in each hand.

"We'll use the bid boxes today," Justice Wells announced, enunciating each word carefully.

Marlon preferred playing with the boxes, used to indicate a bid by selecting the appropriate cards from the box and laying them on the table. The boxes were always used in professional settings to prevent players from cheating by passing coded information to each other. Silent bidding, so no talking.

Miranda, on the other hand, always complained about the bridge boxes. Nazi bridge, she called it. Keep your mouth shut. No chit chat, no fun.

Marlon felt the corner of his mouth twitch.

All the Justice had to do now was mute his phone again. Whoever was out there would see the lawyers playing a game of bridge, silently, as the rules dictated.

If whoever it was knew anything about bridge.

"That means you, too, Miranda," the Justice shook a warning finger at her. "Bid with your box. Not a word until the game's finished."

With those words, Justice Wells cleverly clued his listeners in.

The Justice took his place at the table and muted his phone.

They all bent over their cards. Only a very close observer would be able to see their lips move.

"What's going on?" Marlon hissed.

"They're watching," the Justice whispered, "to make sure I obey. Before midnight. And tell nobody. I have no choice now. I had decided to tell the Chief. Too late. You be careful but find a wayaa...."

Robert's words stuttered to a stop. He licked his colorless lips. A pulse beat visibly in the vein on his temple and his forehead glistened with sweat. The corner of his mouth drooped.

"I haf to changlay," the last syllable came out in a throaty glob. "Ch … change my vote or they'll … thhh…." he lisped.

"Robert?" Marlon whispered, frightened.

"Too late," the Justice croaked. He leaned his head into both shaking hands. "Kkkill her…."

"Sir," Cassandra reached out to steady Robert's elbow.

"They have Betsy," Justice Wells gasped before falling face first onto the table.

CHAPTER 33

Saturday, Sept. 9, 6:45 p.m., Spring Valley Neighborhood
"A stroke," Miranda said. "I'll call 911."

She reached for her phone.

An image flashed through Cassandra's mind. Justice Wells, with an oxygen mask over his face, carried out of his house by the EMTs. With her next heartbeat, she realized what was wrong with that picture.

"No," Cassandra snapped.

"What are you talking about?" Marlon asked, incredulous. "He needs a doctor. Immediately."

"Whoever's watching can't see Wells leave in an ambulance. Unconscious."

"Why not?" Miranda asked, voice shaky.

"Justice Wells is expected to change his vote. Rewrite his opinion. If the blackmailer sees that he can't, what happens to Betsy?"

"Oh." Miranda blanched.

Cassandra fought against her own wave of panic.

Triage.

They had to deal with Wells first. Evade the "eyes and ears" he had warned them about.

"Help me get him up, Marlon," Cassandra commanded.

Cassandra stuck her right hand under Justice Wells's armpit. Marlon, imitating Cassandra, took Wells's other side. Gently, they lifted the Justice off the table. As they straightened him upright in his chair, Wells's head rolled clumsily back against his headrest but stayed upright on his neck.

"I've seen my share of strokes," Cassandra said. "Runs in the family, unfortunately. He's got some muscle control, which is a good sign. He'll survive. Got him, Marlon?"

Marlon, adjusting his grip on Wells, nodded.

Cassandra reached down into the bag sitting beside her feet, popped open the bottle, and fished out an aspirin. She leaned her shoulder into Justice Wells. Reaching around him, she popped the pill through Robert's lips.

Justice Wells grimaced, then swallowed convulsively. His hands, which had lain flat on the table, curled into loose fists.

"Cassandra," Miranda spluttered, "I understand what you're doing. But we're talking about a Supreme Court Justice who's extremely ill."

"Who risked his neck," Cassandra barked, "by choice."

"But they already saw Robert clunk over, anyway," Miranda continued. "It's too late to pretend now."

"Maybe not." Chad had reappeared at Miranda's shoulder. "Visual surveillance is probably limited. All I detected is a camera on that pole over there," he nodded with his chin. "The angle is bad, as is the lighting. The 'clunk' might look like any number of things."

"Fine, but what's the point?" Miranda asked. "Of pretending, that is, because Wells can't do what they're asking. He can't rewrite that damn opinion."

Cassandra blew out her cheeks. "We'll change it for him."

Miranda looked at her like she was crazy.

"Tamper with a Supreme Court opinion?" Miranda's voice faltered.

"We call the cops," Marlon countered. "Tell them everything. Wells would want us to, now. I think that's what he was trying to say."

"You do that," Cassandra said. "But what're the chances they figure out who's got Betsy and where she is before midnight? Wells said midnight was the deadline."

"It's the Russian oligarch," Miranda answered. "Has to be. Whoever's buying intel from Jeremy. Bought, that is, since Jeremy's dead."

"Yeah, but which oligarch?" Cassandra responded. "As Betsy said this morning, there are too many for the FBI to run them all down."

The other three stared at her. They still had their suspicions about Nikolai.

Cassandra felt her face get hot.

"Um," Chad spoke up again, "the camera. Isn't anybody going to bid?"

"Crap," Cassandra muttered. She reached for a bridge box, yanked out a clump of cards, and slapped a bid on the table.

"I'm starting to agree with Cassandra," Marlon said. "We get help for Robert, but Betsy is our priority right now."

"Which means," Cassandra said, "that we protect her as best we can by giving the blackmailer what he wants. We rewrite the opinion. In the process, maybe, we'll also find a clue who the blackmailer is. Bid, Miranda."

"But remember," Miranda replied, fingering the cards in her bid box, "we don't know which opinion he submitted. Plus, he may have submitted more than one."

She threw out a bid.

"Yeah, well, we'll just have to figure it out," Cassandra said.

Marlon nodded, squaring his jaw. "Let's get to work. But first, we arrange better camouflage. Robert can't stay sitting here doing nothing."

Marlon glanced around the patio, then turned to Chad.

"Are there cameras inside, do you suppose?"

"I doubt it," Chad answered. "Outside is easy, but inside would have required some advance planning."

"What about the break-in?" Marlon replied. "Couldn't the burglar have left bugs in the house?"

Chad wrinkled his nose.

"It'd be stupid to announce your presence by smashing things up, then install covert equipment," he said.

"We don't know if these people are stupid or smart," Marlon responded. "All we know is that they're murderers."

Marlon looked like he had more to say but kept his thoughts to himself. He placed his bid.

"As far as other surveillance," Chad continued, unperturbed, "they apparently hacked Wells's phone. The other electronics, like the television, too, probably."

"We'll talk about nothing inside the house except cards and, heh, how about a fake spate of indigestion?" Marlon proposed.

They all nodded.

Marlon grabbed Justice Wells's phone and unmuted it.

"Something you ate, I'm sure," Marlon said. He patted Justice Wells's shoulder. "You'll feel fine after you lie down for a few minutes."

Marlon and Chad got Justice Wells to his feet and half-walked, half-dragged him through the kitchen door. Cassandra and Miranda followed close behind, using their bodies to shield the men's movements from prying eyes.

They got Justice Wells settled on the settee tucked into a corner of the kitchen. Cassandra grabbed the throw folded over the back of the chair and tucked it over Justice Wells's still form.

"In a few minutes, the nausea will pass, sir," Marlon said, bending over Justice Wells, as though the Justice were really listening. "We'll let you rest and be back in a few."

Marlon set Justice Wells's phone on the kitchen counter. The others followed Marlon into the dining room.

"You know," Cassandra said, fanning herself, "it's stuffy in here. Let's wait outside."

They filed out, passing under the unblinking red eye of Justice Wells's security camera.

By unspoken consensus, they crossed the front lawn to where Marlon had parked the car. They propped themselves, side by side, against the hood.

"Call Kathy," Marlon motioned to Miranda. "Tell her to bring the crash cart. Stat."

Dr. Kathy Hammock, an old friend of the firm and a neurologist, owned a fully equipped, mobile hospital packed into her truck. She used it to provide medical care *pro bono* to the underserved population deep in the West Virginia mountains, where Kathy was born.

Miranda nodded. She straightened herself and walked back onto the lawn to make her call.

"Do you suppose there's any chance," Marlon proposed, "that the Betsy thing is a ruse?"

He did not sound optimistic. He was only covering his bases.

"She didn't show up at the Bomb, did she?" Cassandra responded. "Betsy would have texted if she couldn't make it for any, uh, good reason."

"I wonder where they have her?" Marlon's voice wavered.

Cassandra's chest tightened. She forced herself to think.

"I'm rethinking what I said about the police," she said. "We probably should call them. They do their thing while we rewrite the opinion."

"Yeah," Marlon responded. He frowned. "Not the police, though. It's too complicated. Besides, what do we have for them? An adult woman missing on a Saturday night for a couple of hours. Plus, a very sick justice who can't confirm anything we say and," Marlon paled, "who we haven't taken to the hospital."

Miranda rejoined them. "Kathy's on her way," she said. "What next?"

"Call Sully," Marlon replied. "Wait." He motioned toward Chad. "You said Justice Wells's phone was bugged. Any chance our phones have bugs, too?"

Chad shrugged. "Do any of you have an open Bluetooth connection?"

They all started scrolling through their phones.

"Well, yeah." Marlon muttered.

"Turn it off," Chad commanded.

"Are we safe now?" Cassandra asked after she had flipped the toggle in her settings.

"Probably," Chad answered, "but I don't know what level of expertise we're dealing with, here."

Marlon cleared his throat. "Do we take the risk?" he asked, voice husky.

No one had an answer.

Cassandra closed her eyes. She tried to imagine Betsy....

"Text Sully, Miranda," Cassandra blurted. "Ask for another meeting."

Marlon nodded, then looked at Miranda. "You'll have to be careful, though. Really careful. Make sure nobody follows you."

Miranda blinked. "I'll do my best," she whispered.

CHAPTER 34

Saturday, Sept. 9, 7:45 p.m., Bethesda, Maryland
Miranda stepped out of the Metro car, jostling with the other passengers exiting at the crowded Bethesda station. She followed closely behind a giggling young couple through the toll stile and onto the escalator to the street.

Emerging on Wisconsin Avenue, Miranda stopped to get her bearings.

"What the...." she yelled, stumbling forward as something bumped into her from behind.

Miranda whirled around, heart racing, to see a pimply teenager in a faded black T-shirt and jeans, eyes glued to his phone.

"Sorry," he mumbled, pulling a bud out of his ear. "Er, excuse me."

He ambled off.

Miranda closed her eyes. Get a grip. The chances were slim that she was being followed. Besides, she would never be able to detect a tail, even if she had one, so just get on with it.

Sully had invited her to come by his house. He and his wife had dinner guests, but if it was an emergency, as Miranda claimed, Sully could excuse himself for a few minutes.

Miranda declined the offer. She would not take the chance, remote though it seemed, of leading a bad guy to Sully's home.

Meeting near the Metro would be quicker, anyway. Miranda would take the subway to Bethesda, a speedier option than an Uber on a Saturday evening. Then, she could return on the train to Marlon's townhouse in Adams Morgan. In the meantime, the rest of them would get to work on the opinion.

Sully grumbled but agreed, giving her the address of a park near the Metro station.

Miranda headed north on Wisconsin, then turned right onto Avondale.

Halfway down the block, between a gap in the buildings, a brick walkway, twenty yards or so long, led to what Miranda could see was an urban park. Fairy lights on the trees shone on a scattering of benches perched on the sidewalk encircling the park and a child's playground with a swing set and jungle gym in the center.

The park looked serene and safe, if empty of people. Miranda took a seat on one of the benches, wondering if she should have hovered in the shadows at the edge of the park, instead.

Miranda glanced at her phone, then up, startled, as Sully glided onto the bench beside her.

"Wow," she marveled, grinning, feeling better already. "Looks like you're an old hand at covert meetings. I didn't know those were in your repertoire, too."

"Huh?" Sully asked as he settled back into his seat.

"I thought you mostly sat around in front of a computer all day. But you can do that spy thing, too. Appear out of thin air."

Sully smiled. "A man of many talents. Now, what's your big emergency?"

Miranda told him everything that had happened, not without glancing around first to make sure they were still alone.

By the time she was finished, Sully sat ramrod straight, hands on his knees, staring ahead.

"Justice Wells?" were the first words out of his mouth.

"In good hands."

Kathy had seemingly flown her truck from Kensington to arrive at Wells's house in Spring Valley, brakes squealing, fifteen minutes after Miranda called her.

"He should be in the hospital."

"He's as good as," Miranda argued, "and I explained why that couldn't happen. Besides, Kathy reported that Wells opened his eyes and seems to comprehend, although he can't speak yet. He's through the worst of it."

Sully did not look convinced, but he dropped it.

"You left Betsy at the office, correct? When you went to the Bombay Club?"

"Yeah. She was driving home to take care of her dog. Then she was supposed to join us."

Sully nodded. "We'll start with the security cameras in your office parking garage. I'd say there's a decent chance they nabbed her there."

He looked at Miranda and nodded, eyes softening.

"We'll find Betsy," he said, "and the goons who took her. Whether we'll ever figure out who's behind all this...." He shook his head.

"Russians, right?" Miranda proposed. "Whoever was buying info from Jeremy and using it for those suspicious transactions in Brenda's files. Then they killed Jeremy, so he wouldn't rat on them, I suppose."

"Yeah, we're working on it. Those oligarchs weave dense corporate webs around their business affairs, though. Untangling them is no easy task. We've got our eye on Nikolai Bolkonsky, but it's not a sure thing."

Oh lord. Nikolai. Miranda had seen him with Cassandra at the gala. Cassandra was smitten with Nikolai, it was obvious. Miranda hated to think how devastated Cassandra would be if it turned out to be Nikolai.

"I found out," Sully eyed her, "that you folks are representing Nikolai's daughter. Are you in touch with him? He seems to have disappeared."

"Oh," Miranda said, having forgotten all about the bombed house reported on the news. She told Sully about it. "I suppose he could have taken his daughter somewhere safe. I don't know."

"Well, if Nikolai turns up be sure and let me know."

"Will do. And while you're searching for the blackmailer, we'll figure out which case he's dying to win." Miranda shivered as the next thought struck her. "Killing to win, I should say. Chad's looking in Wells's laptop for the opinion he submitted."

Sully cocked his head. "I'm not sure that will tell you anything. If it's obvious who the decision will affect, and how? Sure. But I'm guessing it won't be that easy."

"Yeah, well, we'll see. We need the opinion, anyway, because we're going to rewrite and resubmit it, changing Wells's vote."

Sully turned to stare at her, frowning.

"I can't agree to that. We do not give in to the demands of blackmailers, kidnappers, or terrorists. I won't give you the full song and dance as to why, but, trust me, we've done our research."

"Screw you and your research," Miranda said, feeling her face flush hotly. "What that gets you is a video of a young man, clearly American. He's standing alone, shirtless, blindfolded, in the middle of a desert. A sword flashes. The man's head flies off in a gout of blood."

Sully sighed deeply.

"And his parents see their son's murder when the video goes viral," he mumbled. "I know."

Miranda's anger at Sully disappeared as quickly as it had come.

"Sorry," she said, putting her hand on his knee. "Look, it probably won't come to that. As you said, you people will find Betsy before midnight. But if you don't...."

"Tampering with a public document is a crime," Sully interrupted. "I can't approve of that."

"I'm not asking for your approval," Miranda said, jumping up from the bench. "Look, I probably shouldn't have told you, but it seemed the right thing to do. Don't let me down, Sully. I can't...."

Miranda felt her eyes welling.

"I'll never forgive myself if Betsy...."

Sully grabbed her wrist.

"I won't," he said. "I won't let you down. I'll figure something out."

Miranda managed a tight smile. "Thanks. And, you know, it won't really be a crime. After all, we'll only be doing what Justice Wells would do himself. If he could."

"Are you sure?"

No. Miranda was not sure of anything anymore.

CHAPTER 35

Saturday, Sept. 9, 8:00 p.m., Adams Morgan Neighborhood
"Done yet?" Marlon, standing at the foot of the staircase, yelled in the direction of his upstairs office.

"Shouldn't be long now," Chad's voice echoed from above.

Chad had parked himself at Marlon's desktop computer twenty minutes ago. Chad had imaged Justice Wells's laptop and was now scanning the disc.

Chad thought he could identify a judicial opinion from the data, but to be sure, Marlon told him to pull all correspondence between Wells and the Chief for the last few weeks. That should do it.

Staring into the shadowy stairwell, an unwelcome image came to Marlon's mind. Betsy, bound with duct tape to a chair, blindfolded, alone in a cold, dark warehouse. A man holding a gun stepped out from the gloom surrounding Betsy.

"How's this going to work, exactly?" Cassandra asked from behind him.

"Let me think," Marlon, turning, rubbed his aching forehead. "Um, we send the revised opinion from Wells's email account on his laptop. Chad will figure out how we can do that. That way whoever's bugged Wells's computer will see it's been done."

"How do we know it's still bugged? That they're still watching?"

"Chad left the laptop as he found it. Still bugged, in other words. He said he shouldn't tamper with the evidence."

"Okay. Who do we email it to?"

"The Chief, I guess, with an explanation. 'So sorry, John. I drafted two opinions. I mistakenly sent the wrong one. My apologies for any inconvenience.'"

"Then, they release Betsy."

Cassandra's expression when she said it reflected Marlon's own feelings. Unconvinced. Frightened.

"Or not," she muttered, a catch in her throat.

"Look," Marlon proposed, almost as doubtful as Cassandra, but hanging onto the thread of their plan, "it probably won't come to that. We're backup."

"Meaning?"

"An American woman is kidnapped in broad daylight on the streets of our nation's capital. The goddaughter of a Supreme Court Justice. If there's solid evidence that a Russian oligarch is involved, the State Department will rush to the Russian Embassy and threaten immediate and severe reprisal if she's not released immediately."

"And that evidence is going to come from?"

"Sully's people. They'll snap to it after Miranda tells Sully what's happened. Maybe we can help by finding a clue to the kidnapper's identity in the case."

Cassandra frowned. "We tried that before. And found nothing but a red herring."

"We try again. The search will be narrower, this time, at least."

Cassandra exhaled deeply. "Let's hope."

"I've got the data," Chad said as his legs appeared on the stairs, then his lanky torso. He held up a thumb drive.

Marlon reached out to Chad for the thumb drive. Chad tossed it to him.

"I'll leave you guys to your legal work," Chad said. "I can't help with it, anyway, and a client with an emergency called. A potentially compromised network that's, well, uh, important to national security. Tell Miranda to text me when she gets here, will you?"

With a wave, Chad turned and headed for the front door. Marlon trotted toward the kitchen where his laptop waited on the island, Cassandra behind him.

Marlon would not say it aloud, but he almost hoped, for Betsy's sake, that the opinion was in the yacht case. The Feds were already on Nikolai's tail. One more nail in that coffin.

Then, he remembered the bombing. Nikolai might be long gone.

Besides, he chided himself. What about Cassandra's feelings for Nikolai?

Marlon stopped his mind from skittering uselessly and focused on his laptop.

It took him only a few minutes to scan the documents on the thumb drive. From Wells's laptop, Chad had copied a handful of emails and three opinions authored by Justice Wells and submitted to the Chief.

Marlon looked up at Cassandra. "Three."

"Damn."

"All, thankfully, short, concurring opinions. Another justice wrote the opinion of the Court."

"That's good news, anyway. We have time for the rewrite, then. To change Wells's vote."

Marlon looked back down at the opinions. No yacht case. Nothing else that leaped out to say "oligarch," or even "bad guy."

Marlon stared blankly at his computer, feeling the knot of anxiety in his chest tighten another notch. He looked up at Cassandra.

"No clue which is the right one," he mumbled.

"We'll rewrite all of them, then," Cassandra said.

Marlon blinked, considering the ramifications of that option.

"Wells said we could maybe slip one by the Chief without raising eyebrows, but three? He won't accept that."

"The Chief can't simply ignore another justice. The worst thing he'll do is try to contact Robert. We'll deal with that later. For now, our only goal is to satisfy the blackmailer."

"Which won't happen if we submit three new opinions right before his midnight deadline. Come on! Even two would look suspicious. Our blackmailer would know something had gone wrong. What happens to Betsy then?"

Cassandra closed her eyes and scrubbed her cheeks with both hands. "So what now?"

Marlon glanced at the clock on his laptop. "Use our brains. Figure this out."

The doorbell rang. A second later, Marlon's phone beeped. Marlon hit the button.

"What're you, deaf?" Miranda's voice. "I rang the bell. Let me in!"

Marlon speed-walked through the living room with Cassandra close behind. Marlon opened the front door to the house. Miranda bustled in, plopped into a chair in the vestibule, and told them all about her meeting with Sully.

Marlon exhaled, nodding. "They'll find her. They'll find Betsy."

"By the way, have you heard from Nikolai?" Miranda asked Cassandra.

Cassandra shook her head, no. "It's not him, anyway," she mumbled.

"Sully won't like it, but we'll still have to rewrite the opinion," Miranda said, "just in case." She looked at Marlon. "Won't we?"

"Yeah, but it's not going to be easy...."

Marlon was interrupted when the doorbell rang again. He stared toward the front door, then stopped as the thought struck him.

"Is there any chance you were followed?" he whispered to Miranda.

Miranda shook her head. "I don't think so," she whispered back. "I was as careful as I knew how to be."

Marlon jumped when Cassandra put a hand on his shoulder. She nodded toward the peephole in the door.

Marlon forced himself up and peered out. Nobody. He flipped the lock and pushed open the door.

A Fed Ex package sat on his front stoop.

"I can't think what I ordered," Marlon muttered.

He retrieved the box, carried it inside, and set it on the side table next to Miranda. Cassandra sidled up to watch.

Marlon peeled back the tabs and propped open the Fed Ex package. He lifted the lid of the cardboard box inside.

An object lay nestled on a crumpled bed of newspapers. A waxy lump of clay, maybe, about three inches long, thicker than a pencil.

Marlon reached in and flipped it over.

With a manicured nail at the end.

Cassandra jumped back, knocking something to the floor with a crash.

Miranda, eyes riveted to the severed finger, shot out of her chair.

"My god," she croaked.

Miranda put her hands over her mouth before she toppled backward in a dead faint.

CHAPTER 36

Saturday, Sept. 9, 8:20 p.m., Adams Morgan Neighborhood
"Ow," Miranda raised her hand and rubbed her cheek.

"Wake up," she dimly heard Marlon's voice.

Miranda opened her eyes. Marlon, on his knees, loomed over her, hand poised for another slap.

"Wait, I'm...." Miranda pushed herself up to a seated position.

"You're lucky the floor's carpeted," Cassandra squatted beside them. "I don't think you did yourself much damage."

"Miranda," Marlon sank back from his knees onto his heels, "the finger is from a corpse. It's not Betsy's."

For a second, Miranda had no idea what he was talking about. Then, she saw the thing again in her mind's eye. This time, shocked horror did not immediately follow.

Miranda knew biology as well as Marlon did. The stiff, bloodless digit could not have been recently severed from a live person.

Still, somebody sawed that finger off a corpse, put it in a box, walked up to Marlon's front door, and set the box down no more than ten feet from where Miranda was sitting.

She felt light-headed again and flopped back onto the floor.

"Sully's right," she croaked. "We're way out of our league, here. We need to leave this to the cops."

They ignored her, talking over her head.

"Miranda was followed," Marlon proclaimed.

"Seems like it," Cassandra answered. "Miranda's not exactly trained to avoid a tail, after all."

"Or maybe they followed us here from Robert's house, suspecting we know something."

"Or our phones are bugged, and they know everything."

"Guys," Miranda protested. "Help me up."

Marlon reached down and grabbed Miranda's hands. He hauled her upright, ignoring her groan. Cassandra stood, too.

"We've got a lot of work to do," Marlon said, "and not much time."

"What work? The opinion? What good's that going to do now? They know we're on to them. Why else send that ghastly warning?"

Marlon shrugged. "Ghastly, but clever, maybe. They're telling us Betsy's unharmed. Plus, you're not dead."

"Jeez, Marlon, what's that supposed to mean?"

"That tells me they don't care what we know so long as Wells's vote is changed."

Miranda shivered. "But after that?" She tried but failed to keep her voice from shaking. "What then?"

"I'm … scared too, Miranda," Cassandra said.

"Me, too," Marlon echoed.

They were all frightened, which made Miranda feel better. Somewhat. She had not craved a cigarette in years, but she did now.

Get a grip, she told herself. Better than that, take one for the team.

"I'll do it," she forced herself to say. "Once we rewrite the opinion, I'll do the dirty deed myself and send it to the Chief."

Only if Sully and his people did not find Betsy first, Miranda promised herself.

"Thanks, Miranda," Marlon said, "but we've got to figure out which of three to rewrite first."

Marlon explained the situation.

"Boy, we just can't get a break here," Miranda spluttered. "How do we choose?"

"I've got a couple of ideas," Marlon answered, "but we don't have time to try both. Tell me which you think is more likely to work."

Miranda, intrigued, perked up a bit. Any plan was good. Cassandra looked like she felt better, too.

"Okay, first," Marlon began, "Wells inadvertently gave us a clue when he told us why he wouldn't recuse. It's the case in which the other justices are evenly split, 4-4, and Wells voted to overturn the lower court's decision."

Cassandra nodded. "You're right. Sounds easy enough."

"I wish, but," Marlon held up a warning finger, "in all three of these cases, Wells voted to overturn. So, we can identify the case only by finding the one in which the other justices are split."

"Crap," Cassandra muttered.

"Yeah, crap," Marlon agreed. "Not easy."

"The blackmailer figured it out," Miranda proposed, trying to be optimistic.

"No, he *knew*," Marlon replied. "Through Jeremy, the blackmailer had access to the entire Court network. The Court's ruling on this case comes out Monday. All the justices probably submitted their votes days ago."

Miranda sighed. "Okay, we do it the old-fashioned way. We research prior decisions of the Court and predict the votes, but...."

"It would be tough, time-consuming, and iffy," Marlon concluded for her. "Some of the justices are notoriously hard to predict, you know. So, thumbs down on that one?"

Thumbs down all around.

"Okay, here's the other idea," Marlon proposed. "The timing of all this keeps bugging me. Why did our bad guy wait so long to put the screws on Wells? He could have threatened Wells months ago. Right after oral argument on the case, let's say."

Cassandra eyed him. "Yeah, like I said this morning. Something went wrong. Jeremy misread the cards."

Marlon nodded. "Jeremy's spying on Robert's private notes, correspondence, and maybe draft opinions. Based on what he sees, Jeremy believes he knows how Wells will vote. But Jeremy got it wrong."

"Or," Miranda piped up, "Wells simply changed his mind at the last minute."

"Either way," Marlon continued, "Jeremy had already tipped off his partner, the oligarch, who bought or sold something based on Jeremy's prediction. Wells files his opinion, which Jeremy sees with his spyware. Oops! Guessed wrong! Jeremy decides the better of two bad options is to inform his client."

"And the Russian freaks," Miranda crowed. "That works. Our opinion is the one in which Wells changed course from what you'd expect."

Cassandra frowned. "We don't have access to the confidential stuff Jeremy saw."

"No," Marlon admitted, "but we can look at everything publicly available that Wells wrote about the issues in these cases. He must have given some indication of his position. We compare that with the opinions he submitted and find our flip-flop."

"It's still a ton of research," Miranda added, "but it's doable. Just. Let's get to it.

Marlon pinched his forehead. "It'll take all three of us, but I've only got two computers."

"I need food, too," Cassandra grumped. "I'm so hungry I can't think."

"I'll call out for pizza," Marlon replied.

"It's Saturday night! It'll take forever. I'll run home, get my laptop, and bring food. I've got tons of leftovers from Aunt Kitty's party. I'll take your car, Marlon."

Marlon motioned for them to follow, and they trooped into the kitchen.

Marlon was fumbling around for his car keys in an overflowing basket by the back door to the house when Miranda's phone rang. She pulled it out of her back pocket and checked the caller's number.

Only because of the insane events of the last few days did Miranda immediately fear this was not just a friendly Saturday evening call.

Brenda, hi, what's wrong?

Uh, nothing. I'm fine. I'm following up from last night. Did you get a chance to look through my files? Or have you been goofing around all day."

Brenda chuckled. Miranda grimaced.

I'm a little busy right....

I've found another one of Jeremy's victims, Brenda interrupted. *It's this company called TR Ventures. Cerberus provides its security. Anyway, TR owns a patented technology, used to detect oil, gas, and scarce minerals in the seabed.*

Brenda, can we talk about this....

TR sued another company for infringing its patent. The alleged infringer claims the patent is not valid.

Sued? As in a court? Miranda's mind snapped to attention. She put her phone on speaker.

In public, TR says it's confident it'll win. Behind closed doors, management was trying to figure out the best way to sell the division that owns the patent and produces the technology. They think they're going to lose the case. The asset will plummet in value.

Um, hang on a sec, Brenda.

Miranda muted the phone.

"Is one of those three a patent case?" Miranda pointed toward the laptop sitting on the kitchen counter and waggled her eyebrows.

Marlon nodded vigorously.

Miranda unmuted the phone.

Sorry. Go on, Brenda.

A bidder swoops in with a decent offer. Deal done on Tuesday. Guess who bought the division TR wants to unload? Even though nobody outside the company is supposed to know it's for sale? A company called Gazprom. Who owns Gazprom? Nikolai Bolkonsky.I think we've found our oligarch. Jeremy's partner in crime.

Uh, thanks, Brenda. I'll call you later.

Miranda disconnected, mind buzzing.

"It's just like you said, Cassandra," she proposed. "A deal gone wrong."

Marlon, eyes gleaming, nodded. "Jeremy predicts Wells will vote 'yes.' The patent is valid. Jeremy also knows about the division for sale because he's bugging TR."

"Jeremy gives Nikolai the nod," Miranda continued. "Nikolai buys the division from TR. When Wells submits his opinion, it's a 'no' vote. No patent protection. Nikolai is screwed unless he gets Wells to vote his way."

"That technology must be worth a lot of money," Marlon said, rubbing his chin.

"Only if," Miranda wagged a finger, "it's patented."

Marlon pumped his fist. "We've got the case and the culprit! Hats off to Brenda, I have to say!"

Cassandra cleared her throat. "The keys, Marlon," she croaked.

Oh, dear. Miranda had been so intent on figuring this out that she had almost forgotten whom she was pointing the finger at.

Cassandra's expression struggled between disbelief and despair.

Miranda took a step toward her, hand outstretched.

"Cassandra...."

"You guys rewrite the opinion," she said stonily. "I'll get the food."

CHAPTER 37

Saturday, Sept. 9, 8:40 p.m., Upper Northwest D.C.
Cassandra turned right off 16th Street. She muted Coltrane's sax, which had been blasting from the speakers since Cassandra pulled out of Marlon's driveway. Losing herself in the jazz had kept her from thinking about Nikolai, but the decibel level would disturb her quiet neighborhood.

She turned into her driveway, reached up, and hit the button on the garage door opener clamped to her visor. The door did not budge.

Damn, the battery must be dead again.

Cursing under her breath, Cassandra reached for her car door, then stopped. She had stupidly not thought to watch for a car following her from Marlon's.

She craned her head around and looked left, then right. No cars moving on the street. She squinted her eyes and peered into the darkness under the bushes lining the front of her house.

Seeing nothing, Cassandra clutched her keyring, leaving the keys jutting out for protection. She slid out of the car, pushed the door closed, and trotted across the lawn.

The security alarm beeped softly when Cassandra pushed open her front door. She disengaged it, relocked the door, and exhaled heavily.

She dumped her bag and coat on the table in the foyer, wishing she had left a few lights on in the house. Halfway across the living room, she froze. Her skin crawled.

She was not alone.

She spun back toward the front door. She stumbled as someone grabbed her shoulder from behind.

A meaty hand wrapped around her face, stifling Cassandra's scream. A black-coated arm snaked around her waist, holding her fast to a heavy male body.

She raised her knee and stomped, hoping she had broken his instep. A string of incomprehensible, guttural syllables told her she had hit something, anyway.

"Cassandra, stop," a deep voice commanded. The hand slipped from off her face.

Cassandra sank back, adrenaline ebbing as quickly as it had come.

"What the fuck are you doing?" she snapped.

"I … I came to say goodbye," Nikolai responded. "For now."

Cassandra pulled out of Nikolai's arms. She blew out her breath, turned around, and stared into his sky-blue eyes. She wanted nothing other than to fall back into Nikolai's embrace and kiss him.

She took a deep breath, considering this man in front of her. "Brenda must be wrong. You don't own Gazprom."

Nikolai's forehead crinkled.

"What are you talking about?"

"It's … a long story. And I can't say much. But did Gazprom, you, that is, buy part of, oh, what was the name of the company? TT? TR something? Did you?"

Nikolai's face cleared. "A division of TR Ventures. We did. Why do you ask?"

The anger hit so hard she could hardly breathe.

Cassandra reached up and slapped Nikolai across the face.

"You son of a bitch," she growled. "I'll kill you myself if anything bad happens to Betsy."

"Who's Betsy?" Nikolai asked, rubbing his reddening cheek.

"I can't believe you'd kidnap anyone's daughter!" Cassandra shouted.

Nikolai reached out and grabbed Cassandra's wrists. She fought him, but he pulled her close.

"Cassandra, look at me," Nikolai pleaded. "I didn't. I never would. You know that."

Cassandra blinked back tears. She almost believed him. What else did she need to know to be sure? She mentally put on her lawyer's hat. She would treat him like any other witness. She cleared her throat.

"Why did you buy a piece of TR?"

Nikolai tilted his head to the side, eyes narrowed. "Does this have anything to do with this Betsy person?"

Cassandra raised her hand, palm out. "Bear with me. Please."

Nikolai eyed her, clearly confused, but answered.

"That TR division produces state-of-the art seismic sensors. These are used on ships to explore the deep seabed for oil and natural gas reserves. Gazprom needs that technology."

"Which is only valuable because of the patent," Cassandra prompted.

Nikolai frowned. "I don't care about a patent. It's the sensors that are valuable to me. I need the equipment."

"How'd you know that division was for sale?"

"I didn't. I had my people approach TR with an offer. They accepted. That's all there was to it."

"You didn't get a tip from anybody? That TR wanted to sell?"

Nikolai shook his head.

He was almost in the clear.

"Uh, do you know Jeremy Ross? The guy who owns...."

"Cerberus, I know him. I used to do business with Jeremy, in Russia."

"What kind of business?"

"I bought software from him. Cassandra...."

"Do you still do business with Jeremy?"

"No."

Okay, but what if Nikolai knew the Russian who did?

Nikolai objected to being lumped into a category. Oligarch.

Labels aside, though, that was Nikolai's world. The oligarchs did business together, competed against each other, and no doubt spied on the competition whenever they could.

And if the rumors were correct, Nikolai would have been the most adept of them all at unearthing secrets.

The odds had to be decent that Nikolai knew which oligarch bought information from Jeremy. But would he tell her?

Only one way to find out.

"Nikolai, I know about Jeremy. Part of it, at least. I know he stole confidential information from Cerberus clients and sold it to, uh, a Russian. I've got to know who's buying."

Nikolai stared at her, expressionless. "You think it's me," he said flatly.

"I … I had good reason to suspect you," Cassandra stuttered, "but not anymore." She grabbed his arm. "You know who it is, don't you?"

Nikolai did not blink. She may have lost him.

"Look, we think this guy, Jeremy's partner, kidnapped Betsy. Betsy's my colleague, my friend, and the goddaughter of Supreme Court Justice Robert Wells."

"Kidnapped? Why?"

"Because of a deal gone wrong."

"Call your police."

"We did, but they're groping in the dark. And there's not enough time. The kidnapper set a deadline. Midnight."

"What's supposed to happen by midnight? What does this person want?"

"The deal to be fixed."

"Can that be done?"

"I'm not sure," she answered. "That's the problem. And even if it can be…."

Cassandra fought against the tears welling in her eyes. Of exhaustion as much as anything, she told herself.

Nikolai stared at her. Cassandra held her breath.

From the look on his face, she could tell he was still undecided.

"Betsy's the most important thing to me," Cassandra said quietly, "but it's bigger than that. This oligarch is messing with our highest court. In a way, he's kidnapped Lady Justice, too."

"If he doesn't get his way," Nikolai mumbled, "he'll kill both of them."

Cassandra winced.

Nikolai exhaled deeply. "I'll do what I can," he said. "Call in some debts."

Cassandra closed her eyes and breathed a silent prayer of thanks.

"But not until my daughter's flight departs."

Sonya. Her house. The bomb. It seemed so long ago.

"Oh, my god," Cassandra put her hand to her mouth as a dozen thoughts flew through her head. "Is she okay? Who did it? And why?"

"Cassandra," Nikolai reached out and gently laid a finger on her lips. "One thing at a time. Sonya's fine. For safety's sake she's leaving though, with her son. I was going with them, but...." He shrugged.

He glanced at the watch on his wrist. "She's scheduled to leave at 11:14."

"That's cutting it so close."

Nikolai held up a hand. "What you ask me to do is not without risk. I'll take that risk, for you, but I won't endanger my family. You understand. What if it were Mary and her kids?"

She had no comeback for that.

"How risky is it?" she asked. "I mean," she scrambled to sort out her emotions. If Nikolai really could save Betsy .... But what if Nikolai was shot, blown up, or worse, instead?

"Don't worry," Nikolai said, although his expression was grim. "I have an ace in the hole. I make money. Lots of it. I'm the best manager Gazprom has ever had. As long as I give my generous tithe to the Kremlin, I'll stay alive."

Given what Nikolai said last night about his enemies, Cassandra doubted that Nikolai was telling the complete truth. She decided to believe him, anyway, because it sure made life easier.

"Let's not think about the future right now," Nikolai added. He took her hand, raised it to his lips, and kissed her palm.

Cassandra felt herself flushing. "Speaking of risk," she chided lightly, "you might have missed your flight, anyway, coming to see me."

Nikolai smiled. "I might have."

"Will you be staying now?"

"No. I must leave when this is over. I'll be back. I promise. And I'm all yours until Sonya flies out of here."

He moved to embrace her.

She was so tempted.

"I can't," she said firmly, putting a warning hand on his chest. "I can't stay. I must get back ... oh, crap, they're wasting their time on the wrong case. Where'd I put...."

She trotted to the bag she had dropped in the foyer and retrieved her phone. She texted Marlon.

It's not Nikolai.

Marlon texted back immediately.

We figured that out. We're looking at the other options. We need food.

Cassandra glanced back at Nikolai.

The police were looking for Betsy. Cassandra could not help there. Her very smart friends were hard at work, analyzing the cases.

Cassandra decided that she deserved the kiss she denied herself earlier. She wrapped her arms around Nikolai's waist, reached up, and pressed her lips to his.

His response was all she could have hoped for.

"We have ten minutes," she mumbled into Nikolai's neck.

"An appetizer," he huffed. Then he grinned and pulled her close again. "But I'll take it."

CHAPTER 38

Saturday, Sept. 9, 9:25 p.m., Adams Morgan Neighborhood
Marlon's stomach growled audibly. Thankfully, he also heard a car pull up behind his house.

"She's back," he yelled.

"Okay," Miranda's voice sounded from upstairs.

Marlon walked out the open kitchen door onto the patio and unlocked the back gate. Cassandra clambered out of the car, one arm around a bulging brown paper bag and the other clutching a laptop. Marlon scurried out to help her.

Cassandra handed him the bag, redolent with the mouth-watering smell of barbecued pork. Marlon inhaled deeply.

"Took you long enough," he grumbled.

He took a good look at Cassandra. She sported the sunny smile he had not seen on her in days.

"What're you so happy about?" he asked as he turned and started back into the house. "I could've rewritten that patent case in no time. Now, we're back to the beginning."

"On the opinions, yes," Cassandra replied, huffing up the back stairs behind him, "but not on finding out who has Betsy."

"What?" Marlon dropped the bag on the counter and spun around.

Cassandra told Marlon and Miranda, who had joined them in the kitchen, about her rendezvous with Nikolai.

"Wow," Miranda breathed. "Do you really think Nikolai can do anything? Will he?"

"He can and he will," Cassandra said without a moment's hesitation.

Cassandra's smile was gone, but she sounded so certain. Marlon was inclined to trust her judgment. He wanted to, anyway.

"What's going to happen exactly?" Miranda rattled on. "Sonya's plane takes off, Nikolai does what?"

"I don't know," Cassandra answered. "Call in some debts, he said."

Uncertainty had replaced Cassandra's confident tone. Marlon came back to earth. "Let's get back to work. We have more research to do."

"How'd you figure it out, anyway?" Cassandra asked. "That it wasn't the patent case."

"Well, we can't exclude the case," Marlon answered, "but we know it wasn't Nikolai."

"Took us only a minute to figure it out after you left," Miranda said as she hauled paper plates loaded with food out of the bag. "Wells voted 'yes,' or that the patent is valid. Since Nikolai owns the patent now, he sure wouldn't want that vote changed to invalid."

"That's true even if, as he told you," Marlon added, "Nikolai cared more about the actual technology than the patent. The technology would be even more valuable with patent protection."

"In other words, Nikolai's the winner," Miranda continued, "and, obviously, our culprit must be the loser. He wouldn't be murdering and kidnapping to get the decision changed if he'd won."

"And who's the loser?" Cassandra helpfully supplied.

"A Norwegian company."

Cassandra laughed out loud. "Not exactly a good candidate for kidnapping and murder."

Miranda was smiling. Marlon realized he was, too, a welcome relief which he knew would be brief.

"Nah," he added, "it would politely pay the penalty for using TR's sensors on its ships."

"Who are the other losers?" Cassandra asked. "In the other two cases, that is?"

"One's a financial institution," Miranda answered, "in a case involving a tax treaty. The other's a German construction company in a customs case. Import, export law. No good candidates."

Marlon sighed heavily. "In other words, our blackmailer is not a party to these cases. It's somebody else invested in the outcome."

"Which could be almost anybody in the damn world," Cassandra retorted. "Patents? Taxes? Trade? Come on, who isn't interested?"

"I know," Marlon said. "I realized that from the very beginning. I keep looking for a silver bullet, though, something specific in these opinions, because...."

Because the alternative sucked.

Marlon would not say it aloud. He did not want to discourage his team, although his colleagues surely saw the writing on the wall. They had less than four hours. The chances that their research would pay off, they could confidently choose one case, and still have time to rewrite the opinion were slim.

His feelings must have shown on his face.

"We're doing the best we can, Marlon," Miranda soothed. "The three of us. We need help. I don't know...."

Marlon tuned her out. Through the course of the evening, he had gone from pleasantly tipsy back at the Bombay Club, to terrified, to headache-y, to exhausted and was finding it hard to concentrate. Gin is what he wanted. Coffee is what he needed. He got up to put on a pot.

Not a party to the case. TR had looked so promising, though. Not because the company itself looked suspicious, but because it was one of Jeremy's victims.

"Wow," Marlon whirled around, almost dropping the pot. "That could be it, but how would we....? Oh, Brenda's files."

"Huh?" Miranda responded.

"We keep looking for the blackmailer but forgetting Jeremy. He's the connection with the Court and the cases. Like the patent case. Jeremy was spying on TR."

"Yeah," Cassandra said, looking puzzled, "but Brenda got the TR thing wrong."

"Maybe another party is also one of Jeremy's victims." He motioned to Miranda. "The files?"

Miranda held up her index finger. "Back in a sec. My bag's in the foyer."

While Miranda retrieved the thumb drive, Marlon scrolled through the files opened on his laptop, scribbling down the names of the financial institution and the manufacturing company.

In a few minutes, they had their answer.

"No overlap," Miranda mumbled.

"Crap," Cassandra said.

"As I said before," Miranda pronounced, "we need help."

"Yeah, like who?" Marlon responded. "A superhero flying in out of nowhere? In a mask and cloak and answers to everything?"

Something about that image rang a bell. He pulled out his phone and started to punch in Ronnie's number.

Then, he remembered. Their phones could be bugged.

Nor did he want Ronnie in the house. Since that finger had been left on his front stoop, his home felt contaminated. No need to infect Ronnie, who was damage-prone, anyway.

Marlon thought for a minute. He made the call.

"What's up?" Ronnie asked. "You caught me at a bad time, buddy. I'm busy."

Marlon cleared his throat.

"Where are you? Can you come by, like immediately? I'm starved and there's nothing to eat here."

Silence.

"The dragons are circling," Marlon added.

Their old code. Save me.

My father won't stop screaming at me. Mom does nothing but cry. Nobody else at this party is gay, and they are all looking at me like I'm a freak.

"Give me ten," Ronnie said.

"I'll be waiting on the stoop."

"Why Ronnie?" Cassandra asked after Marlon disconnected.

"That Deep Throat guy," Marlon answered. "The guy in the lousy costume. He knows all about Jeremy's victims."

Marlon reached out, snagged the legal pad, and tore off the sheet with the parties' names.

"Ronnie can ask Deep Throat about these guys."

"What makes you think Ronnie can find Deep Throat?" Miranda asked.

Marlon shrugged. "Maybe he won't. But he met the guy. It's possible Ronnie can track him down. It's worth a shot."

"Are you really going for food?" Miranda asked.

She was not usually so obtuse. Miranda was as tired as he was.

"No. We'll drive around the block. You two drink coffee and work on the research."

Ronnie pulled up at 10:00 p.m. sharp. Standing on the front stoop, Marlon took a quick glance up and down the street before he trotted down the steps and hopped into Ronnie's car.

"I don't have time for food," Ronnie, curt, looked straight ahead.

"I don't need food," Marlon responded. "Just drive around the block."

Ronnie engaged the gears and pulled into the street.

"Ronnie, Betsy's been kidnapped."

Ronnie spun the wheel and nose-dived off the street into a too-small parking space on the curb. Marlon, rocking and rolling, straight-armed onto the dashboard for balance.

"What?" Ronnie panted.

"Keep driving," Marlon responded.

Ronnie pulled back into the street. While Ronnie circled the block, Marlon filled him in on what had happened since that morning. Back at the house, Marlon jumped out of the car.

"Deep Throat can identify Jeremy's victims," Marlon concluded, leaning into Ronnie's opened car window. Marlon held out the piece of paper he had been clutching in his hand. "Here are the names. Think you can find Deep Throat? And I mean in the next couple of hours?"

Ronnie ran a hand through his tousled red curls.

"I'll try," he responded. "I was on my way to meet Petrov when you called. Petrov can connect me with Deep Throat, and I think he will, once I tell him what I know."

"What's the connection between those two?"

"I told you I thought Petrov was CIA, remember? Deep Throat is, too, I think. I also think Deep Throat is the CIA mole I've been tailing, the agent planted in Russia to spy on the Kremlin's cyber espionage campaign leading up to our 2016 election."

Marlon, frustrated, could not keep the sarcasm from his voice.

"And you 'think,'" air-quoting the word, "that Petrov's going to come right out and admit all this? Plus introduce you to Deep Throat?"

Ronnie, unfazed, waved him off. "Keep the faith, baby. I'll get Petrov to talk."

"Sure." Marlon turned from Ronnie's car window to go back into the house, but then stopped. He did believe in his friend.

"Why would Petrov get you to Deep Throat?"

"Because I'm on to them," Ronnie smirked. "Look, it couldn't have been a coincidence that Deep Throat showed up with that thumb drive when he did. It's because of something I told Petrov."

"Huh?"

"At the gala. I've got a vague memory now. I was talking to Petrov, drinking a coke. Next thing I remember, Jim was lugging me to his car. I think Petrov drugged me. When I was out of it, I said something to Petrov that spooked him."

"What did you say?"

"That, I don't remember."

"What's this have to do with….?

"Petrov passed whatever I said on to Deep Throat, prompting Deep Throat to give me the thumb drive."

"You must have told Petrov something about Jeremy's hacking scheme, then. Deep Throat showed up with the thumb drive to prove you were on the right track."

Ronnie shook his head. "That can't be it. I knew nothing about Jeremy until you told me just now. But Deep Throat obviously did." He pumped a fist. "That'll be my first question. How? Then I keep digging."

"Uh," Marlon stammered, taking all that in, "Deep Throat's a good guy, then, right? Because he ratted on the bad guy? So he'd want to help us?"

"I'm not sure about that." Ronnie grinned. "But I'll leave him no choice. Well," he flicked a mock salute, "off to the lion's den. Wish me luck, old buddy."

"Be careful," Marlon called as Ronnie sped off.

CHAPTER 39

Saturday, Sept. 9, 11:00 p.m., Adams Morgan Neighborhood
Miranda sighed. She closed her eyes and rubbed the lids with her palms. She stood up from Marlon's desk and stretched. Then, she went downstairs to compare notes with Marlon and Cassandra.

"How's it going?" Miranda asked, walking into the kitchen. "Anything unexpected from Wells?"

Marlon looked up from his laptop. "His votes are always hard to predict. Which unfortunately means you could call them all 'unexpected.'"

He looked as discouraged as Miranda felt.

"That being said," Marlon continued, "I don't think it's the patent case. From prior decisions, I'd guess Wells would vote 'yes' on this one, and that's how he voted."

"Same with the customs case," Cassandra said. "His 'no' vote wasn't a complete surprise, at least."

"Both of which are reasonably informed guesses, at best," Marlon said. "What've you got on the tax treaty, Miranda?"

"Zip, zero. The key issue hasn't been reached by the courts in years. Decades. I can't find anything Wells ever wrote about it."

Marlon frowned. "So do we put our money on that one? It would be a shot in the dark, but...."

"Or change all three," Cassandra muttered.

Off and on over the last couple of hours one of them had raised that alternative.

Which was less risky? Change all three and the blackmailer would know the gig was up. Somebody other than Wells knew about the blackmail. What happened to Betsy then?

On the other hand, if they guessed wrong and did not choose the right case, the blackmailer did not get what he wanted. And then?

Miranda shuddered. The problem was, neither option worked.

"I agree with Cassandra," Marlon intoned hollowly. "The best bet is to change all three. Unless somebody has a better idea that I haven't thought of yet."

Miranda poured herself another cup of coffee. She took a sip. The caffeine cleared her brain fog.

"Heh, I do," she mused. "Have another idea, that is. We need to find something, anything, Wells wrote about this tax treaty. Right?"

Marlon nodded. "It sure would help. Otherwise, we have no idea if the opinion he submitted is a sudden about-face."

"Well," Miranda continued, "this tax treaty was signed thirty years ago. Wells was working as an attorney at the State Department. Maybe he wrote something reflecting his opinion on its interpretation when he was there."

"How many lawyers worked at State back then?" Marlon asked. "Fifty or so? Each handling dozens of international legal issues at any one time? Of all those, what're the chances Wells was assigned to this one treaty?"

"Does it hurt to try?" Miranda retorted.

"No, but how?" Cassandra asked.

"Like this." Miranda picked up her phone.

"Don't say anything more on the phone than you have to," Marlon warned. "Just in case."

Miranda dialed her friend Kay.

"Put her on speaker," Marlon said as they waited for an answer.

"No," Miranda replied. "She might be … grumpy."

Heh you."

Over Kay's greeting, Miranda dimly heard a television in the background.

It's late. I'm busy. Something wrong?

Miranda fought the insane urge to spill it all out. Say no more than I must, she reminded herself.

I need you to do me a big favor. Can you drive down to Marlon's and get me? Take me home?

Now? Why me? Call an Uber if Marlon's too drunk to take you.

Think, think.

I'm not feeling too well.

If you're sick call an ambulance, dummy.

It's ... not that bad. But I need some TLC.

Miranda could imagine Kay, curled up in her robe in the overstuffed chair in front of the TV. A glass of Malbec sat on the end table beside her.

Miranda dropped the pretense and the casual banter. For a moment, she allowed the chaotic and conflicting emotions of the last couple of days to take over.

I need help, now.

Kay paused.

You'll owe me. Big time.

She had done it. Miranda, breathing a sigh of relief, gave her colleagues a thumbs-up.

"You guys better rewrite all three opinions while I'm gone," Miranda said, "in case I don't find anything."

Marlon nodded. "Be careful," he called, as Miranda grabbed her bag and headed for the front door and the street.

CHAPTER 40

Saturday, Sept. 9, 11:10 p.m., Adams Morgan Neighborhood
Standing on the stoop, tugging at the collar of her coat, Miranda waited for Kay's black Mustang. When it slid to the curb, Miranda trotted around the hood to the passenger side and slid in.

Kay shot her a look from under the brim of a Nat's cap pulled low over her brow.

"Chad dump 'ya? I can't think of any other reason for this insanity."

Miranda almost laughed.

"It is insane, but it's not about Chad. I can't tell you why, but I need your help. Take us to the State Department. We need to find the negotiation files on an old tax treaty. We have less than an hour to get it done."

Kay stared at her. "Are you outa your mind?"

Miranda stared back. "It is, literally, a matter of life and death."

Kay's gloved hands on the wheel tightened. "Are you serious?" she whispered.

"Dead. Drive."

Kay peeled off.

During their brief ride to Foggy Bottom, Miranda told Kay the bare bones of what they needed. Anything written by a young State Department lawyer, now Justice Wells, about a tax treaty with the Cayman Islands negotiated decades ago.

"Not State then," Kay said. "That long ago, the documents would be warehoused off-site."

"Not anymore. I don't think. There's a case pending before the Supreme Court, an issue on the treaty's interpretation. The original documents would have been pulled out of storage when the case was first filed, right?"

Kay grunted. "Yeah, that's right. Litigation files are brought in-house."

"There can't be that many documents to read," Miranda proposed. "It's a treaty with the Cayman Islands, for god's sake. We're not talking about a nuclear arms agreement with Russia."

Kay glanced her way. "You don't have clearance, you know. You could get into trouble for this. Me, too."

Miranda ground her teeth. "Believe me, that's the least of my worries right now."

Kay shrugged one shoulder and drove on.

Kay parked in her designated spot in the underground parking lot. Using the fob on her key ring, Kay led Miranda into the building. They descended to the ground floor and then through a warren of corridors, stopping at a windowless steel door.

"Should be in here," Kay said, waving her fob across the security panel.

Inside, directly in front of them, sat a nondescript wooden table with two straight-backed chairs. Behind the table, rows of metal shelves laden with bankers' boxes marched up and down the room.

Miranda flashed back to her days as a young lawyer, assigned to document review. Her task was to find every piece of paper remotely related to the case. She spent days hunched over a bench, extracting one file folder after another, poring through page after page of dusty letters and memos in a gloomy, damp, mold-ridden warehouse.

"I'd wear my old cowboy boots," she murmured, "because of the snakes and rats."

"What are you talking about?" Kay asked.

Miranda glanced around the room again. A bubble of despair rose in her throat. "This'll take too long," she groaned.

"Nah," Kay said. "The staff around here is top-notch. Look," she said, pointing, "those placards on the end of each row of shelves should be an index to what's on them."

Miranda nodded. She moved right, Kay to the left. Beginning with the shelf adjacent to the wall, Miranda started scanning placards.

"Here," Kay called, beckoning for Miranda.

Miranda scurried over.

"Section B, 13-14," Kay said, finger on the placard.

"I hope that means two boxes," Miranda said.

She side-stepped down the aisle between the shelves, scanning the labels on the boxes. At shoulder height sat their target. Miranda grabbed one, Kay the other, and, in a minute, they had the boxes sitting side by side on the table.

Miranda lifted the lid off Box 13. She blinked.

"That's top-notch?" was all Miranda could think of saying.

This was not the neat row of files Miranda had expected. It looked like somebody had taken everything out of the box, rifled through it, and stuffed the contents back in, willy-nilly.

"Somebody's been here before us," Kay mumbled under her breath, "and I don't mean our staff." Her eyes narrowed. "Not the FBI or CIA rummaging around for some reason, either. Neither agency would want us to know they'd been snooping around."

Miranda shivered. Who else had eyes and ears everywhere?

She had not noticed it before, but in the silence that had fallen, Miranda heard it. A clock hanging on the wall, next to the door, ticking.

"C'mon, Kay," Miranda dug both hands into the jumble of documents. "Help me out here."

It was not as hard as Miranda had feared. After sorting out and discarding the bulky folders, not that many documents remained. Miranda leafed through the seven-inch pile she had retrieved from her box.

Miranda's heart skipped. She held it in her hand. A single-page cover sheet announced the document's contents as a memorandum from Robert C. Wells, Esq. The long "in re" line of diplomatic legalese included the words Cayman and treaty.

The memo itself was gone.

CHAPTER 41

Saturday, Sept. 9, 11:35 p.m., Adams Morgan Neighborhood
It had not taken long for Marlon to revise Wells's one-page opinion on the tax treaty and turn to the patent case. As he scrolled through his draft of the rewrite, the pesky acronym kept catching his eye.

EEZ. Where had he seen it before, and not long ago?

"Have you read anything recently about the EEZ?"

Cassandra, who was changing Wells's vote in the customs case on her computer, looked up at him.

"I don't think I've ever read anything about it. What's the EEZ? Something about your patent case, I take it?"

"Yeah. The central issue in the case is whether patent protection extends into the EEZ."

"What's the EEZ?"

"The exclusive economic zone. This is from international maritime law, about which I know almost nothing, so don't quote me on this. But the EEZ extends out from a country's coastline, up to two-hundred nautical miles."

"And?"

"This EEZ is sort of half fish, half fowl."

Cassandra's lips quirked. "Cute."

Marlon smiled. "Meaning, within a country's EEZ, the government has some sovereign rights, but not others. Nobody from another country can mine or fish in the EEZ, for example. On the other hand, ships bearing any flag can freely sail through the EEZ."

"I'm with you so far."

"Okay, remember our Norwegian company? The defendant in this case? Its ships in our EEZ off the coast of Alaska were using TR's seismic sensors for undersea exploration. Guess what the Norwegians' defense to the infringement claim is."

"Hmm, it's arguing that there's no infringement because the TR patent isn't valid in the EEZ?"

"Correct," Marlon replied.

"Well, interesting enough, and a nice diversion, Marlon, but I'm about done thinking about the intricacies of the law for tonight."

Cassandra managed to smile, but her weariness was evident in her drawn face.

"Wait, this may be important," Marlon persisted. "I'm just sure we're missing something in these cases. Some clue that will tell us which one to rewrite. The image of those Norwegian ships trolling around in the EEZ nags at me. I can't quite put my finger on it, though."

"It's not the Norwegians."

"I know, but…."

The beep from Marlon's phone interrupted him. He stared at the text from Miranda.

"Is it Miranda?" Cassandra demanded. "Did she find anything?"

"Yes and no. There was a memo from Wells. But it was lost, stolen, misplaced. Take your pick. It's disappeared."

Marlon scrubbed his face with his palms.

"Kay thinks it must have been stolen," he continued. "Was the thief our blackmailer? But why? This has all been about stolen data, not old paper memos. And how did he get into the bowels of the State Department?"

"Makes no sense," Cassandra agreed, "and Kay could be wrong. I still think we go with all three."

Marlon stared at her, trying to think. At the end of the day, his colleagues would look to him to make the decision.

Sully and the Feds had boots on the ground and ears on all available wiretaps. Ronnie searched for a mystery man whose tracks had thrice before led Ronnie into harm's way. Nikolai, if Cassandra's faith in him proved warranted, was risking his life and his fortune.

The lawyers had one small part to play. Use their brains to figure out which of three votes to change.

Marlon knew Miranda's trip to the files in the State Department was a long shot. Still, in his gut Marlon believed Miranda would solve the puzzle.

He hated to fail.

He had this time.

"Fuck."

Go big or go home, his father always said. He texted Miranda.

Have Kay take you to Robert's house. I'll email you the three rewrites. Send them to the Chief on Wells's laptop.

He thought a minute, then added another line. Miranda was exhausted when she left. She would be even more addled by now.

BEFORE MIDNIGHT!

Marlon stared glumly at his laptop.

"Here's my rewrite," Cassandra said.

Marlon downloaded the document Cassandra had just emailed him, then sent it, along with the other two opinions, to Miranda.

"Don't feel too bad," Cassandra reached over and patted his hand. "The opinion was always only insurance. I'm sure the Feds have Betsy. They've only been too busy to let us know."

Marlon shrugged, numb.

He started closing the tabs on his laptop's scroll bar, links to all the Supreme Court opinions he had perused since that morning. The title of one caught his eye.

"United States v. Michael's Maritime, Montevideo, S.A.," he mumbled. He snapped his fingers as he remembered. "That's it!"

"Huh?"

"It's in this case, too. The EEZ."

Marlon opened the document and scanned it. The weight on his chest lifted. Maybe they had figured it out.

"What if the penalty was having your boat taken away?"

"The penalty for what?"

"For infringing a patent."

Cassandra shook her head, eyeing him with suspicion. "Don't tell me we're back to yachts. Isn't that what the Michael case is about?"

"Yeah, a yacht confiscated in the EEZ," Marlon replied, "from an oligarch under sanctions by the U.S. government. The oligarch argues that the power to sanction does not extend into the EEZ unless the yacht was doing something illegal."

Cassandra's eyes rounded. "Like infringing a patent. Is that what the Michael's yacht was doing?"

"No, that's not an issue in this case. But if another oligarch *is* sailing around in the EEZ with a boatload of bootleg technology, he's at risk of losing his boat, or his whole fleet of boats, if the TR decision comes out the wrong way."

She stared at him with doubt written all over her face. "You're thinking we submit our revised opinion for just this one, right? Look, Marlon, it's a good theory. But it's just a theory."

Cassandra was right. Still, Marlon had a feeling this was it.

He was not thinking like a lawyer, though. Where was his evidence?

Marlon had already made his decision. Submit all three. His father always told Marlon not to second-guess himself when taking multiple choice exams. The first answer was usually the correct one.

He must have lost his mind. Since when had his father ever given him good advice?

Who did Marlon trust?

Marlon's phone rang. He grabbed it and put it on speaker.

Ronnie? Did you find….

Submit the patent case.

Are you sure?

Hundred percent. Gotta go.

In his haste, Marlon's fingers stumbled on his text to Miranda. *pwent confrm*

"Crap." *patent case confirmed submit only that one*

Miranda's thumbs-up emoji popped up immediately.

Cassandra jumped up from her barstool, hooted, and held up a palm. Marlon vigorously slapped the high five.

"We did it, we did it," Marlon chanted.

"Wait, what's that?" Cassandra held up a warning finger.

Marlon heard a crack, followed by a series of muffled pops.

"Where's that coming from?" Cassandra asked, face screwed up.

Marlon snatched his phone off the counter. He had not disconnected from Ronnie when he texted Miranda. Marlon tapped on the icon to put Ronnie's call back on speaker.

A hail of gunshots. Ronnie screamed. The connection died.

Marlon jumped off his barstool, sending it crashing to the floor. He snagged his keys and flung open the back door.

"C'mon," he called to Cassandra.

"Where're we going?" she panted as they pounded down the back steps.

"The Russian American Forum."

"What's that?"

Marlon jammed his key into the back gate and swung it open. He and Cassandra hustled out.

"That guy Petrov's group. He's got an office, I hope. You'll look up the address on the way."

"An office? It's Saturday, and the middle of the night!"

"I've gotta find Ronnie. He was meeting Petrov, maybe at the guy's office. Anyway, Petrov is the only one who might know where Ronnie is. Get in!"

They jumped into the car and roared off.

CHAPTER 42

Saturday, Sept. 9, 11:53 p.m., Spring Valley Neighborhood
Miranda stared at the clock on the computer screen, willing Betsy to walk through the door. For the rescue party to arrive. For someone to call it all off.

Instead, the house stayed quiet as a tomb.

11:53 p.m. ticked to 11:54 p.m.

Miranda shivered. Her teeth chattered, even though the radiator in the overheated study hissed steadily. Her shoulders and back burned from overstressed muscles. Her head felt peculiarly light, as if it were trying to float off her neck. She rubbed her tired eyes.

She glanced at her phone on the desk beside the computer. The corner of her brain still functioning noted that she was almost out of charge.

Kathy had let her into Justice Wells's house five minutes ago.

"How's Robert?" Miranda asked as she walked into the foyer.

"Awake, responsive, sitting upright in the lounger in his bedroom," Kathy responded. "I'd be happier if we took him to the hospital, though."

They had told Kathy little except that Wells could not go to the hospital that night unless his life was in imminent danger. Instead, Wells had to stay at home and appear as normal as possible.

"You look like shit, by the way," Kathy added. She pulled Miranda in for a hug. "Can I help?"

"You already are," Miranda said.

Miranda exhaled. She pushed gently out of the comforting embrace before she fell asleep on Kathy's broad shoulder.

"I'll come in and see Robert," Miranda nodded toward Wells's first floor bedroom, "in a few minutes. I have an, uh, errand to do for him first."

Kathy, nodding, disappeared down the hallway. Miranda took the stairs.

Miranda sat at Wells's desk. She dialed Marlon. No answer. Cassandra, nothing.

Miranda opened the laptop sitting on the desk. She accessed Wells's secure email account as Chad had instructed. She typed the message they had agreed on. She clicked on the icon and attached the revised patent opinion she had uploaded. And waited.

11:59 p.m.

She had cycled through adrenaline, nausea, fear, and despair. All she felt now was a suffocating numbness.

Maybe she should say a prayer. For Betsy's deliverance. For herself. She had never in her life imagined that she could commit a felony. Miranda had not prayed in years, but now seemed like as good a time as any to give it another go.

The clock ticked past the final minute. Miranda hit "send."

Legs shaking, heart pounding, Miranda stood. She had the presence of mind to text Marlon a thumbs-up emoji, then started back downstairs.

Miranda stumbled on her way out of the room, just managing to pivot on her back leg and plant her bottom on one of the wing-back chairs. She tilted her head back onto the headrest. She would rest for just a second.

A noise from downstairs woke her. Miranda's eyes flew open. She clutched her throat.

She heard it again. Voices. Female voices. That couldn't be bad, could it?

Miranda pulled herself to her feet. How long had she been asleep? It was still night, anyway, because past the penumbra of light from the office lay darkness. Miranda tiptoed down the stairs in her stocking feet.

She heard them again. Kathy said something. The response came from ... could it be?

Miranda rushed down the hallway. Betsy sat on her heels beside Robert's chair, holding his hand.

"Betsy!" Miranda cried, lunging forward.

"Sshhh," Betsy warned, nodding toward her godfather.

Kathy held up a warning hand.

Miranda stopped in her tracks, chiding herself. Wells was in a fragile mental state from his stroke. He did not need to hear Miranda shouting or watch her jump all over Betsy.

Still, Miranda could not resist pumping a fist, and she could do nothing about the crazy grin she felt on her face.

Betsy murmured something to Wells, patted his hand, and rose. She looked at Miranda and motioned with her head. Miranda followed Betsy out of the bedroom, down the hallway, and into the living room.

Miranda grabbed both of Betsy's hands.

"Thank god," Miranda burbled. "Thank god you're safe. Are you hurt? What happened?"

Betsy forcefully disengaged her hands. "Why isn't Robert in the hospital?" she hissed. "Kathy said his stroke was hours ago."

Miranda rocked back, nonplussed. Betsy should be effusive in her thanks. Why was she angry? Did that mean....

"Did the cops find you? We should have stayed out of it, like Sully said?"

Betsy's face wrinkled in confusion. "Cops? I saw no cops. They just let me go."

"Then it was us," Miranda pumped her fist again.

"I ... I gotta sit down," Betsy sank onto the sofa. "What's happened, Miranda?"

"Your kidnappers texted Robert," Miranda began, "telling him he had until midnight to change his vote. To rewrite the opinion he'd already submitted. Robert contacted us. I'm guessing he already knew he was ill. Anyway, shortly after we got here, he had his stroke. He couldn't revise his opinion to change his vote, so we did."

Betsy's eyes rounded. "I see," she said. "So you had to pretend...."

"That Robert was fine," Miranda interrupted. "Kathy's as good as a hospital, anyway. Well, almost. Your turn. What happened to you?"

"Well," she exhaled heavily, "I left you guys and went to the garage. As I was unlocking my car, a man stopped me. A big man. When he spoke, I knew he was Russian. Anyway, he didn't pull a gun, or otherwise threaten violence. I knew I had no choice, though."

"You must have been terrified," Miranda whispered.

"Not at first. I was furious. I knew it was about Robert. The sons of bitches had doubled down. I knew what Robert would have to do. Change his vote for my release." Betsy clenched her fists. "I hated that it would be because of me."

"You thought earlier that he should change the opinion to save himself," Miranda said quietly.

"This was different," Betsy said. "I never wanted to cause Robert problems. Well, anyway, the man put me in a car. Another guy drove. Not a dark paneled van, and they didn't blindfold me. I was doing okay."

Miranda tried to imagine herself doing okay in those circumstances and failed.

"They drove me to the Washington Hilton, into the underground parking garage. They took me up to a room. That was about it. The two of them sat around fiddling with their phones. They'd taken mine, of course. I didn't have anything to do."

She grinned sheepishly.

"I found the Gideon Bible in the top drawer of the dresser. I read that."

Miranda giggled.

"As time passed, I got more scared. I couldn't decide what was going to happen. I mean, I was sure Robert would rewrite his opinion, but I had moments of doubt. He loves me, but he loves the law, too. And he's got this steely core, you know."

Betsy cleared her throat.

"And then I thought why wouldn't they just let me go? Whether Robert did what they asked or not? Why make it worse by ... hurting me? But on the other hand...."

She swallowed hard.

"I figured there'd be a deadline. For Robert to change the opinion, that is. But I didn't know when it would be. And we just sat there, while I pictured all kinds of things."

Betsy wrung her hands.

"I didn't have my phone, but there was a digital clock on a table by the bed. I could see it was ten past midnight when one of my captors got a call. After he disconnected, he mumbled something to the other guy. I speak some Russian, you know, but I didn't catch it. I had no idea what was coming. I kept my shit together, but just barely."

She shuddered.

"They took me back down to the garage. Once outside, they told me to get out, and gave me my phone. It was dead, of course. I didn't know what else to do, so I decided to come here. The concierge in the hotel called a ride for me."

Betsy, closing her eyes, leaned her head back against the sofa. "I'm fine. Robert will be okay. All worth you guys' perverting justice, I suppose."

Poor girl. Betsy was putting on a brave face, but she had been through a horrible ordeal. Even worse, she was almost blaming herself.

"Don't worry," Miranda leaned over and put her hand on Betsy's arm. Betsy opened her eyes. "The old girl will survive. Lady Justice has survived worse."

Betsy grinned.

"Get up," Miranda continued. "Let's charge our phones. We've gotta let the others know you're safe."

A string of text messages popped up on the recharged phone. Miranda opened the most recent one, sent at 1:00 a.m. from Marlon.

Ronnie's in surgery. Anything on Betsy?

Miranda frowned. Could be anything, she supposed. Appendicitis, maybe?

Betsy's fine. She's here, at Wells. Why surgery?

He's been shot.

Miranda gasped.

How bad is it? Where are you?

Metro. Don't know yet.

There was nothing Miranda could do, but she would not be able to sleep, anyway.

On the way.

CHAPTER 43

Sunday, Sept. 10, 1:20 a.m., Metropolitan Hospital
Cassandra returned to the waiting room clutching two Styrofoam cups of black coffee. She took a sip out of one as she scanned the rows of men, women, and children in various states of disarray and distress, anxious for news from the surgical suites surrounding them.

Cassandra wended her way down an aisle. She paused to smile at a wide-eyed child swimming in a T-shirt too big for her, clutching a doll in one hand and her sleeping mother's knee with the other.

Marlon sat in the far corner, pale, head laid back against the wall. He was anxious and frustrated. They knew so little.

After they flew out of Marlon's house a couple of hours ago, Cassandra found an address for Petrov's foundation on its website. When they arrived at their destination, a fashionable, downtown, multi-floor office building, the facility was locked up tight. The reception desk in the lobby was deserted.

The only other contact information provided was an email address, to which Cassandra had sent a string of unreturned messages.

Parked in front of the office building, she and Marlon started calling area hospitals, checking for the admission of a Ronnie Sloan.

Cassandra's phone had pinged. A response to one of her emails to Petrov. Ronnie had been shot and taken to Metropolitan Hospital. He was alive.

She and Marlon knew their way to the surgical wing of the hospital.

The nurse at the desk was tight-lipped. They had no proof of kinship with the patient. All she would say was that Ronnie had a gunshot wound to the shoulder. He was in surgery. They should wait.

The good news from Miranda about Betsy cheered them up a bit. After that, though, Marlon withdrew into a jittery silence.

Cassandra sat next to Marlon and nudged his shoulder. "Here," she said, handing him a cup, "although I'm not sure it's safe to drink. You might end up in surgery, too, getting your stomach pumped."

She got a wan smile.

"He's going to be fine," she soothed. "The nurse said 'shoulder.' Not the heart. Not the head."

Marlon sat up, grunting. "Better the head," he muttered. "It's hard as a rock." He sipped his coffee. "I wonder what in the hell happened?"

"Excuse me," a man's voice said. Cassandra looked up and almost laughed out loud.

Short, dumpy, with a large, square head, bald, a bulbous nose, and deep-set eyes squinting out of a round, doughy face, the man was the spitting image of the cartoon character from her childhood, Mr. Magoo. He even held what looked like a porkpie hat in his hand, the topper complementing his dark suit and narrow black tie.

"May I introduce myself?" the man asked in a tenor voice carrying the slightest hint of an unidentifiable accent. He held out his hand. "Tony Blunt."

Cassandra automatically shook hands. Tony's sharp, dark gaze startled her. She felt like he was scanning her brain, extracting secrets. Tony's grip was muscular, and his fingers callused. The Mr. Magoo image vanished.

Tony turned slightly and reached out for Marlon. Marlon ignored Tony's hand.

"The inexplicable appearance of a mystery man," Marlon's voice rasped. "Again. I'm guessing you must be Deep Throat."

Tony nodded.

"And the CIA mole Ronnie was chasing. What are you doing here?" Marlon demanded.

"Waiting for you. In case," Tony tipped his head toward the front of the room, "Ronnie came out of surgery before you arrived."

"How bad is it?" Marlon asked.

"It was a through-and-through. He'll live."

Marlon, red-faced, jumped up and grabbed Tony around the neck. Cassandra, startled, dropped her cup, spilling coffee over her shoes.

"It's your fault," Marlon yelled. "Who was it? Cerberus? The CIA? You're on their shit list too, I've heard. Who missed you and shot Ronnie instead?"

Tony reached up with his left hand and touched Marlon on the neck. Given the angle, Cassandra could not see exactly what Tony had done, but Marlon's arms dropped as if the nerves had been severed.

"Ow," Marlon rubbed his neck.

"Sorry," Tony said, "but you're wrong. It wasn't my fault. I warned Ronnie to stay clear of me. Twice, in fact."

Marlon blanched. "I sent him to you anyway."

"It's not your fault either, Marlon," Cassandra protested.

"You're wrong about the shooter, too," Tony continued. "It wasn't Cerberus or the CIA. Russian. A sniper. Caught us in the alley. But you're right about one thing. Ronnie got in the way. They wanted me."

"You've got a lot of enemies," Cassandra observed.

Tony grinned with no humor in it.

"Some I chose, some not."

"Why a Russian?" Cassandra asked.

"They've been after my head since the Agency got me out of Russia in 2016. Whether for past sins or because they think I'm still in the business, I don't know."

Marlon's gaze shifted abruptly to his left. In the same moment, Cassandra realized the noise level around them had increased. She cranked her head around to see Sully in phalanx with two other men in suits marching toward them.

"How'd Sully know we'd be here?" Marlon mumbled beside her.

"I don't think he came for us."

The men in tow with Sully hustled up to Tony and grabbed him, pinning Tony's arms. Tony twisted. One of his handlers stuck his arm under Tony's and crammed Tony's head under a half-Nelson.

"Let him go," Sully barked.

His sidekicks obeyed.

"Agent Blunt deserves some respect," Sully continued in a milder tone. "He reported for a debrief voluntarily. He told us where he'd be. He's not your prisoner." Sully tipped his chin. "You three go on. I'll meet you at Langley."

The suits stepped away from Tony, who straightened his lapels, then addressed Marlon.

"Ronnie's a good man," Tony said. "Like me, he sinks his teeth into the truth and worries it like a dog with a bone."

Tony turned and walked away.

"There aren't many like Tony anymore," Sully mused, his eyes on the departing agents. "Too many toe the company line. It takes real balls to cross it."

"What'll happen to him?" Cassandra asked. She hoped nothing bad. She had taken a liking to the enigmatic Tony Blunt, the spy who had come in from the cold.

"Depends," Sully replied curtly, "on the debrief. Tony was right about Jeremy. That's a good start."

Cassandra blew out her breath, fluttering her lips. "All we need is Ronnie out of surgery, and all's well. Where'd you find Betsy, by the way?"

Sully's eyebrows rose. "We didn't. Her captors let her go. You didn't know?"

"She was?" Marlon blurted, as Cassandra shook her head, no.

"Miranda only texted that Betsy was fine," Cassandra said. "What did happen, then?"

"Why don't you tell me?" Sully said sharply. "Nobody else will."

"Huh?" Marlon muttered.

"We had Feds posted at Wells's house. They saw Betsy arrive in a cab, called in for orders, then went in. Miranda and Betsy aren't talking. Neither will that doctor."

Cassandra and Marlon exchanged glances. In silent agreement, they decided what to do.

"We'll consult with counsel first," Cassandra said.

Sully sucked his teeth. "C'mon, don't lawyer up on me. I know exactly what you did. Miranda told me your plan. Still, we need all your cards on the table. Then we can sort this out."

Sully narrowed his eyes.

"Or maybe I don't know what you did. I can't believe they let Betsy go just because you gave them what they wanted."

"We haven't confirmed we did," Marlon said.

Sully ignored him. "The kidnappers would surely have, uh, disposed of Betsy if they didn't get that damn opinion changed. But we figured Betsy was a goner, either way. Unless we found her first. Is there something else you aren't telling me?"

Sully looked pointedly at Cassandra.

Marlon flicked Cassandra a questioning look. She knew what he was asking. They had talked about it. Should Cassandra tell Sully about Nikolai?

Nikolai had to have played a role in Betsy's release. Who or what Nikolai had threatened or promised, Cassandra had no idea. But he had kept his word to her, she was sure.

Marlon had suggested to Cassandra that Nikolai would stand in very good stead with the authorities if Cassandra disclosed Nikolai's role. No more Feds showing up with endless questions, no longer a fear of deportation.

Cassandra had pointed out to Marlon that Nikolai had probably already left the country, anyway. Who knew when he would return? Besides, there was a bigger problem with telling. After Nikolai got his gold star from the Americans, he would get a knife in the back from whichever Russian he had strong-armed.

She made her decision.

"Uh, you lost me there, Sully," Cassandra said after donning an innocent smile.

Sully's phone squawked. He pulled it out of his pocket and squinted at the screen.

"Gotta run," he said. "You people," he wagged his index finger, "get your heads screwed back on. We'll be in touch."

CHAPTER 44

Friday, Sept. 15, 6:00 p.m., The Bombay Club

Marlon pulled the door to the restaurant open with one hand and cupped Ronnie's free elbow in the other. Ronnie's other elbow was snugly encased in the sling around his neck.

"I'm fine, Marlon. Quit fussing like a hen with her chicks."

Marlon ignored him, hovering closely behind Ronnie as they entered the club and turned into the bar lounge.

"All hail our returning warrior," Jim cried, standing to raise his martini glass. "A toast to Ronnie!"

"Heh, what about me?" Betsy teased, but she joined in the toast, as did Miranda and Brenda.

"Here, come, sit beside me, Ronnie," Cassandra said as she patted the chair beside her.

Marlon ordered his drink and a coke for Ronnie from a passing waiter as the others chatted companionably.

"Where's Chad?" Ronnie asked.

Miranda wrinkled her nose. "Saving some client from a data meltdown. If Chad wasn't so, uh, clever, I'd consider finding another guy."

"Clever my foot," Cassandra jeered. "That's not the attraction. You two moon all over each other like teenagers."

"Do not!" Miranda cried, flushing.

"Okay, okay," Marlon said, "enough chit-chat. Let's get down to business."

Their boss had announced his return to the office the following Monday. Marlon, relieved, pleased, was also mildly terrified. It would be Marlon's job to explain what the firm had been occupied with in Aaron's absence.

The girls had suggested they just not tell him, but Marlon could never deceive Aaron like that. Besides, Marlon trusted Aaron.

But only so far. It would be best not to push it. Aaron's first instinct, like most people's, was self-preservation.

A practice run is what Marlon needed, which is what the firm did with a mock jury before a trial. Use a friendly audience to mold the story to its best advantage.

So here they were.

"Make it simple," Jim suggested.

"It's not," Marlon replied.

"It can be," Jim insisted. "You know what the old guys say to the young lawyers. Explain it to the jury like you're talking to fourth graders."

"Well, Jim," Marlon grinned, "you can tell me if I'm doing it right."

Jim flipped him the bird. The others hooted.

"Maybe I'll start at the end," Marlon proposed. "My crowning achievement. I rewrote a Supreme Court opinion completely, reversing the outcome. When the Chief got it, he had no idea it wasn't written by a justice. What'd the Chief's email say again, Miranda?"

"He thanked Robert for the minor changes that only strengthened the argument."

Marlon stood up and bowed.

Catcalls. Jim frowned.

"That was way over the head of a fourth grader," he said. "Worse than that, Aaron would go ballistic when he heard 'rewrote a Supreme Court opinion.' You're already toast."

Marlon sighed.

"Okay," Marlon started again, "but this next version starts out in left field. 'You'll remember the hacking of the DNC in 2016, right, Aaron?'"

"You've already lost his attention," Cassandra called.

"Try this," Jim suggested. "This CIA agent named Tony knows about a big scam. An American software bigwig, Jeremy Ross, is spying on his clients, selling confidential info to a Russian oligarch. Problem is, Tony doesn't know which oligarch it is."

"You should note that Tony's on the outs with the CIA," Miranda said. "He's working mostly on his own, although he's still got a few old friends at the Agency on his side."

Jim tutted. "No more sidebars, please. Anyway, Tony sets a trap to uncover the oligarch. He gets a job at Jeremy's company. A plum job, coding Jeremy's spyware. This job gives Tony access to the Supreme Court because the Court's one of Jeremy's victims. Tony plants a fake document in Justice Wells's work files."

"Not bad, Jim," Marlon admitted. "Go on."

"The document is an opinion Justice Wells supposedly wrote. Wells didn't detect the fake. He had already submitted his real opinion and never looked back at his files. Um, where was I?"

"Tony's trap," Ronnie prompted.

"Oh, yeah, thanks. Tony's plan is that Jeremy will leak the fake opinion to the oligarch. The oligarch will act on it and, bingo, Tony's got his man. An oligarch jumped, but it wasn't the right oligarch."

"Don't you need to explain that in more detail?" Marlon asked.

"No," Jim said firmly. "The right oligarch, I mean the bad oligarch buying stuff from Jeremy, gets the fake opinion from Jeremy. The oligarch thinks Wells changed his vote. The oligarch doesn't like the change. He kidnaps Betsy to force Wells to rewrite the opinion."

"Wait, you're out of order," Brenda protested. "What about Jeremy?"

"Oh, yeah," Jim nodded. "With Brenda and Tony's help, the authorities nail Jeremy."

"Help?" Brenda protested. "I practically had Jeremy nailed all on my own."

"Don't we get any credit?" Miranda grumbled.

"And what about me?" Ronnie asked. "We got the thumb drive from Tony because of me. If I hadn't been...."

Jim shushed him. "Put it in your book, Ronnie."

Ronnie smirked.

Marlon grinned. He was delighted for his friend. Tony told Ronnie that once the dust settled, he wanted Ronnie to write Tony's memoir. It would be a hell of a book.

"And the rest of you shut up and let me finish," Jim added. "Wells can't do what the oligarch wants because he has a stroke. Our fearless lawyers rewrite the opinion. Betsy's saved."

Jim stood and bowed. Everybody clapped.

"Anything important I missed?" Jim asked.

"I'll say," Marlon protested. "You forgot the ending. Because of my superb analytical skills, the Agency caught the bad oligarch."

"Not exactly," Jim grumbled.

No, not exactly. Still, the Agency was pleased with what they did catch.

Marlon had surmised that the culprit must be an oligarch, presumably one on the sanctioned list. The oligarch knew, through Jeremy, how Wells voted on the patent case. He had voted "no," or that patent protection did not extend to the EEZ.

With that knowledge in hand, the oligarch planned on sailing freely through America's EEZ without risking the seizure of his ships due to a patent violation.

Then, the fake patent opinion showed up. Wells had apparently changed his mind and voted "yes." The oligarch's plan was kaput unless he forced Wells to go back to a "no."

The CIA and the Feds went to work on Marlon's theory.

They discovered the imminent sale of a fleet of ships from a Chinese manufacturer, a deal worth over $25 billion. The ships were reportedly equipped with the latest in AI-assisted underwater sensor arrays and other communications technologies pirated from the U.S. patented versions.

With those technologies, ships sailing close enough to Alaska could detect a sneeze from onshore. Trolling in the EEZ, in other words, quietly spying for the Kremlin.

The prospective buyer of those ships? Anatoly Guschev, the smart, supposedly cultured Russian who was overly friendly with female opera singers. One of the good oligarchs, everybody thought. Now the Americans knew better. Forewarned was forearmed. Anatoly would be on the radar screen.

Flexing some muscle here, offering concessions there, the Agency stopped the sale of the ships.

"Heh, Marlon," Betsy's voice interrupted his thoughts, "after you mention the stroke, you should follow up. Tell Aaron that Robert's expected to make a full recovery."

"Mental note taken," Marlon replied.

"You should include the part Nikolai played," Cassandra added. "Sort of an important point, don't you think?"

Marlon nodded but said nothing. The problem was, they didn't really know what Nikolai did. Oh, they all agreed something happened, behind the scenes, between Nikolai and Anatoly. But Marlon suspected whatever it was would benefit Nikolai somehow, down the line.

Marlon had a hard time believing in such a thing as a truly good oligarch.

Cassandra, as if reading his mind, glared at him. "He'll be back. I'll get him to tell me what happened, in broad strokes, anyway. You'll see."

Marlon did hope, for Cassandra's sake, that she was right.

"Marlon, pay attention," Miranda snapped her fingers. "Another thing you've got to include is the fact that we didn't change the law. We reversed the fake, moving the pieces back to square one. A 'no' vote."

"Wasn't that clear from what I said?" Jim demanded.

"Uh, sort of," Miranda pretended to concede, "but it's worth emphasizing. Oh, and another thing Aaron needs to know. Nobody's going to be prosecuted."

"He'll be more worried about his reputation than our going to jail," Cassandra added.

That got a rueful laugh all around.

"Well, it's true," Cassandra continued. "So be sure and tell Aaron that nobody aside from a select few will ever know anything about any of this."

"Not a word from the CIA, for sure," Marlon said. "They want all this closed tightly in a black box. There'd be hell to pay if it came out that an agent was fiddling around inside the Court. The CIA will put a lid on the Feds, too."

"Show Aaron that nondisclosure agreement the Agency made us all sign," Jim suggested. "What was it, twenty pages long?"

"I don't know if Robert signed it," Betsy said. "Don't tell Aaron, though," she quickly added, "unless he asks. Robert feels guilty about not 'fessing' up to the Chief. With a promise of strict secrecy, I think Robert will tell him."

"Wells will figure out some way to do the right thing without getting any of us in trouble," Marlon said. "He's a smart guy, after all."

"Best bridge player in Washington," Betsy said, smiling, "and he'll be back at it soon."

The reference to bridge triggered a memory. That odd conversation with Justice Wells at the gala. Wells compared a discussion among the justices to a bridge game, noting that Wells had responded to the Chief's opening bid with a Michael's cue.

"It's a useful bid to remember," Wells had said.

Marlon understood, now. Wells had given Marlon a clue to what his blackmailer wanted in case everything went south.

"Heh, guys," Marlon started to tell them about the cue bid, but nobody was listening.

They had reverted to party mode. Ronnie and Jim, huddled over Jim's phone, giggled at something on the screen, probably a beefcake screenshot. Brenda tilted her head back and laughed at something Cassandra said. Miranda blushed. Girl sex talk, most likely.

Marlon raised his empty glass. "I'll get the next round."

Jim stuck out his lower lip, miming offended petulance. "Next round?"

"We're only here because of you," Miranda protested.

"Okay, okay," Marlon conceded. "Drink up. Tab's on me," which had, of course, been his plan all along.

Marlon turned toward the bar, scanning the crowd for their waiter.

"Oh!"

He swung back around at Cassandra's exclamation. Staring at her phone, she was cuddling it in both hands as though the device were a precious jewel. Smiling broadly, Cassandra looked smugly triumphant.

The smile abruptly disappeared. Cassandra dropped the phone in her lap and put her face in her hands.

"What's going on?" Marlon asked.

Cassandra glanced up at him. Her lips trembled. Her round eyes welled.

Then, Cassandra closed her eyes.

"No," she whispered. "No," she repeated, fiercely. When she looked at Marlon again, her face was set and stern.

Cassandra picked up her phone and eyed it, head cocked. "After all," she said, "it's a common name."

She held out the phone so that Marlon could see the screen.

Marlon leaned forward to read the text.

Greetings, Counselor. We are well and trust that you are, too. Many thanks for all you did for us. Stay faithful to who you are and what you know to be true. Regards, SB.

With the text, Sonya had posted a picture of herself, with her son in her lap, and Nikolai, in colorful, casual clothes, lounging in canvas chairs on the deck of an enormous yacht cruising in an azure sea.

Stenciled in gold letters on the yacht's stern, clearly visible below Nikolai and to his left, was the boat's name.

Sonya.

About the Author

Marian K. Riedy is an attorney, professor emeritus, swimming instructor, and the author of two previous legal thrillers, *Fatal Accusation* and *Surprise Witness*. Her collaborator, Kim Sperduto, is a litigator with decades of experience representing Washington, D.C.'s usual denizens. The two have worked together in the legal arena for over twenty years. Both are avid golfers with Marian also pursuing Tai Chi, Tae Kwon Do, swimming, and jogging. She has run the Boston Marathon, hiked in the Himalayas, swum in Lake Geneva, and has master's points in bridge. Kim loves baseball, bourbon, the blues, and fly-fishing. Both authors were born in Kansas but lived most of their lives elsewhere.

Other Stein & Associates Thrillers

Note from Marian K. Riedy

Word-of-mouth is crucial for any author to succeed. If you enjoyed *The Tenth Vote*, please leave a review online—anywhere you are able. Even if it's just a sentence or two. It would make all the difference and would be very much appreciated.

Thanks!
Marian K. Riedy

We hope you enjoyed reading this title from:

BLACK ROSE
writing™

www.blackrosewriting.com

Subscribe to our mailing list – *The Rosevine* – and receive **FREE** books, daily deals, and stay current with news about upcoming releases and our hottest authors.
Scan the QR code below to sign up.

Already a subscriber? Please accept a sincere thank you for being a fan of Black Rose Writing authors.

View other Black Rose Writing titles at
www.blackrosewriting.com/books and use promo code
PRINT to receive a **20% discount** when purchasing.